## "END OF TH[E]
### TY ANNOUNCED

"What do you mean?" Alison whispered.

Delicately he outlined her mouth with his fingertips. "I mean your story smells like a skunk. I'd say some of it's true, some of it's false, but I'm damned if I know which is which." He traced her lips again, clockwise this time.

"If you're so sure I'm lying, why did you hire me?"

"I didn't. I wouldn't have. You're Mother's idea, not mine." His finger pressed gently between her lips.

She nipped harder than she'd meant to, then grinned in spite of herself. "Then maybe you should mind your own business, Ty!"

His dark brows slanted with amusement. "I find that...*difficult*, where you're concerned." His hand curled softly around the back of her neck.

"Don't!"

"Why?"

"Because I don't *want* you to! Will that do?"

"There you go, lying again."

## ABOUT THE AUTHOR

Peggy Nicholson spent her horse-crazy childhood in Houston, Texas. But she ventured north to Rhode Island for college and has been freezing with the Yankees ever since. Besides writing, her great love has been sailing. *Soft Lies, Summer Light* was written aboard various sailing vessels near Newport harbor.

## Books by Peggy Nicholson

HARLEQUIN SUPERROMANCE
193—SOFT LIES, SUMMER LIGHT

HARLEQUIN PRESENTS
732—THE DARLING JADE
741—RUN SO FAR
764—DOLPHINS FOR LUCK

These books may be available at your local bookseller.

Don't miss any of our special offers. Write to us at the following address for information on our newest releases.

Harlequin Reader Service
P.O. Box 52040, Phoenix, AZ 85072-2040
Canadian address: P.O. Box 2800, Postal Station A,
5170 Yonge St., Willowdale, Ont. M2N 6J3

# Peggy Nicholson

# SOFT LIES, SUMMER LIGHT

## Harlequin Books

TORONTO • NEW YORK • LONDON
AMSTERDAM • PARIS • SYDNEY • HAMBURG
STOCKHOLM • ATHENS • TOKYO • MILAN

To Antoinette and to Amy,
for all your listening, and all your words

Published December 1985

First printing October 1985
Second printing January 1986

ISBN 0-373-70193-4

# CHAPTER ONE

HARDLY WIDER THAN A DRIVEWAY, the turnoff plunged into the scrub oak and disappeared uphill into sun-flecked shadows. "I can't do it, Forrest, I just can't!" And anyway, she was glued in place, her bare legs heat-fused to the seat of the parked car. The moist vinyl squeaked as she swiveled to face her driver.

She knew him well enough to guess that the expression on his over-the-hill cherub's face was meant to convey patience, knew him well enough to know it did not, and gave him an *E* for effort. But Professor Forrest Osgood was entertaining no such charitable impulse. "We've been through this already, three times or more, Alison, and the inevitable, irrefutable, irrevocable conclusion is that you can, so let's just get on with it, shall we? These are just last-minute-performance whim-whams." The upward jerk of his lips was shorthand for an encouraging, but altogether implacable, smile.

"Forrest, lying to little old ladies isn't my strong suit. *Lying* isn't...isn't my strong suit." Her tone of heartfelt conviction wavered as he fingered his bow tie. The wisdom around the Brown University Art Department was that their illustrious chairman's head would come off with that tie, that he showered and slept in it. It would almost be worth this trauma to see him...

As he caught the direction of her fascinated gaze, Forrest's fingers froze, then lifted casually to fan his face. "Lying? What we propose to establish here is the truth, my dear—a highly significant, even historical truth. If circumstances—"

"Ah-choo!" And a cold coming on, in the bargain! Hadn't she troubles enough?

"Gesundheit." Seasoned lecturer that he was, the professor didn't miss a beat. "If regrettable, perhaps even deplorable, circumstances necessitate our stretching the truth a trifle, well, the truth has a certain resiliency." From beneath eyebrows the color and texture of Brillo pads he surveyed her, daring his class of one to dispute that premise. "The truth is remarkably elastic. And I thought we'd already decided that in this case the ends justify the means."

"You decided. I didn't." Moving much too fast for the winding, two-lane back road, a truck thundered past them on its way into Stonington, leaving the professor's ancient Volvo shuddering on its springs. A diesel-fume breeze chased after the truck, sucking the last bit of air from the Volvo's interior even as it cooled in passing. Perhaps she'd be sick.

"Well, I am the boss, after all, am I not?"

Bluntly put—even crudely so for a man who prided himself on his verbal delicacy. But then, in New England, civilization breaks down somewhere above eighty-five degrees Fahrenheit. It was closer to ninety-five in the car, and Forrest must have been melting in that white ice-cream suit. He wasn't a man who approved of sweating. She would have to go. Alison sighed and groped behind her for the door handle.

The professor's face relaxed into a smile. "The name of the house is Shady Breeze, Alison, if that be any consolation. I regret that I can't deliver you to the doorway."

But thinking of the coming interview, Alison ignored this olive branch. "When will you pick me up, Forrest?"

"Let us see...ten minutes to the top of the hill, if that, ten minutes down again, an hour to charm your way into their hearts—"

"Ah-chooo!"

"We shall rendezvous here at two-thirty."

"And if for some reason I'm delayed?" Expect the worst and you won't be surprised, after all.

"Then I shall return at three-thirty, at four-thirty and at five-thirty," he promised, generous in victory as always.

"And at six-thirty, I expect you to send in the Marines!" She didn't quite slam the door after her, then bent down to lean in the window. "He did throw you off the porch, didn't he?" It wasn't a question she'd have asked from inside the car.

"He...most certainly...most emphatically did not!" The professor's hot-pink face turned a fine shade of magenta. "As I believe I explained, I tripped over a dog."

Who also tore your shirt collar? But she didn't dare ask that, and wasn't supposed to even know that lurid detail she'd gleaned from the department secretary who'd seen Forrest limp back from his interview at this house four months ago.

"You don't suppose I'd send you on this mission, if I conceived of a possibility of violence, do you, Alison?"

"Forrest, if it bought you a glimpse of this painting, I expect you'd deliver me to the lions, piece by gift-wrapped piece...tenderized."

Too hot to look indignant, he settled for wounded dignity instead. "There are no lions up there, Alison. Perhaps a cur or two, but no lions. And it is Mrs. O'Malley you will be dealing with, not the son. Now please go."

But she wouldn't be dismissed quite so easily. "What if I don't get the job, Forrest?"

The car was rolling slowly. "Get it."

Sure, just like that, get it! She glared after him as he pulled out onto the blacktop.

"And try not to..." he called back over his shoulder as the car gathered speed.

"Try not to what?"

"Sneeze!" it sounded like. The Volvo disappeared around the bend toward Stonington, and no doubt toward the air-conditioned comfort of its finest seaside restaurant and the crispest, coldest glass of white wine that money could buy. The professor didn't believe in flying second class.

In the meantime, the sunlight was hammering down onto the blacktop. Despite the heat, a cold sweat emerged between her breasts and a headache pounded between her narrowed eyes. It had no right to be this hot in June! "Shady Breeze," Alison muttered faintly. Looking both ways, she crossed the road and started up the turnoff and into the trees.

TEN MINUTES to the top of the hill, Forrest had promised, and perhaps it was as the crow flies, but not as that road meandered. Each beckoning rise, once mounted, revealed yet another gentle, woodsy slope to be climbed; she'd have never dreamed the Connecticut coast boasted hills so high, though perhaps it was just the dips and turns and the dizziness from her oncoming cold that made it seem so.

Beneath the trees the air seemed to drone with a distant, lazy vibration, more sensed than actually heard, eerie and yet hauntingly familiar. Alison stopped to listen and catch her breath at the third fork in the road she came to. An airplane, perhaps? "Ah...hh-choo!" More likely this cold buzzing in her ears. Really, Forrest was mad to think that anyone would hire her in this condition. But then, he'd gone dotty over this entire matter, and there'd just been no stopping him once she'd discovered that help-wanted ad in the *Westerly Sun* last week; it was the chance he'd been praying for, and he was terrified that someone else would snatch it.

He had applied for the job—in her name—that very day, but hadn't bothered to tell her so until all arrangements had been made for the interview. He'd spent all of yesterday browbeating her into accepting his mission, and had appeared on her doorstep this morning to ransack her closet for his idea of the proper attire for a lady's companion. She'd chased him and the dowdy wool blazer he liked out of the bedroom, and had chosen instead a white gauze blouse with a bit of blue embroidery at the neckline, a plain short skirt and low-heeled sandals.

But if she'd taken that battle, Forrest had won the war. In spite of all her protests that his scheme was not only dishonest but downright immoral, there she stood, a very long way from her cozy little apartment on the east side of Providence, Rhode Island. Sighing, Alison stopped to blow one tawny curl out of her eyes, then took a moment to ruffle her damp hair back into something resembling her usual cap of soft, loose curls. That done, she turned back to the road and started again.

From a lilac bush alongside the upper fork, civilization confronted her in the form of a mailbox. Shady Breeze, it announced in quiet, block-lettered satisfaction. Patrick and Harriet O'Malley.

Patrick...but he was the husband who had died late last year, surely? If Forrest had gotten his facts straight. Perhaps in his wishfulness, in his willfulness, the professor had gotten his entire story garbled. Quite likely they were chasing after a red herring, some unicorn of Forrest's midlife crisis, rather than a near-mythical painting.

Climbing this last slope, Alison recognized the lazy, summery mutter for what it was: someone cutting grass in the near distance. Above her head, taller trees arched and interlaced to form a tunnel, while beyond the rhododendrons' dark leaves, glimpses of sun-brightened grass and patches of blue sky gave a sense of impending climax. She was climbing up to a view, and her heart quickened with anticipation. But turning the final bend in that lane, Alison found, framed in that last, near-perfect gothic arch of the elms, not the house she'd expected to see but a truck—a red pickup. Atop its cab, a sign crowed in Day-Glo purple, Henry's Landscaping and Lawn Service.

"Eyesore!" she snapped, stepping around its fender. But if Henry had spoiled the drama of that first view, he could do nothing to spoil its beauty. Alison stopped short. Backing up a step, she encountered the truck again and leaned against its hood.

"Wow!" she whispered huskily.

Beneath randomly spaced trees, a path of sun-spattered, grassy shade led the eye up that final slope to the house that crowned the hill. Three massive wind-sculpted pines leaned above the house's wide front porch, casting more darkness there, but beyond that, all was blue sky and sunlight. The house looked out on a wide-open slope of new-mown grass, a soul-satisfying, sunstruck sweep of green that was closer to meadow than lawn, by the size of it.

"Ah...ahh-choo!" As if that had been a signal, the mower started up again somewhere behind the house. She hadn't even noticed its stopping. Its grumbling reminded her of people and the hateful, ridiculous interview awaiting her.

Yet somehow, as Alison looked at Shady Breeze, Forrest's premise didn't seem quite so farfetched. The people who lived here lived with—owned—beauty. The whole sun-drenched hilltop was an Impressionist's dream, nature depicted as a dazzling frolic of light and color. Minot and his friends would have been very much at home painting and romping on this hillside. Somehow it seemed possible, just possible, that a painting by that raffish genius could have come to rest here.

As her path curved out from under the trees, the sunlight pounced on her like a tiger and Alison stopped, blinking up at the house in dizzy, dazzled approval.

A three-story Victorian summer cottage, with graceful, airy porches and open windows, smiled back at her from between the pines. Shingled in weathered-gray cedar, with its fanciful angles and bay windows jutting hither and yon, the house had the look of a playful, once-beautiful lady who had aged very well indeed. This house welcomed children and dogs and promised picnics in summer, cozy, fire-lit nights in winter and laughter always.

"Ah...hh-chooo!" So much for fevered flights of fancy. It was time to stop dreaming—or stalling, really—time to play her part in the farce the professor had scripted, then bow out before she ran out of tissues...or nerve. Squaring her shoulders, Alison marched up the steps down which Forrest had either tumbled or been tossed. Whichever way, he'd limped for weeks—elegantly, with an ivory-headed cane—and now she could understand why. There were quite a few of them up to the porch.

From the varnished front door, a dolphin door knocker grinned back at her, daring her to reach for it, and suddenly Alison could not. "I must be mad," she whispered, and for once in her life, she wasn't thinking of her shyness at meeting strangers. She who'd been raised in strict and straightforward honesty by the sternest of Swedish fathers, she who'd learned her own bitter reasons for detesting lies and deceptions as an adult, she was supposed to knock on this door and then lie her head off? It wasn't just detestable, it was impractical: she was a rotten liar. "I must be mad!"

The dolphin's brassy smile seemed to suggest that many a lunatic had knocked and been welcomed through this doorway. What was one more?

"Ahh—" wheeling away from the door, Alison muffled her sneeze in a swirl of tissue "—chhhhoo!" Her nose was getting sore and probably pink by now, as well. Tickling today, it would be torrential by tomorrow; the worst was yet to come, if she knew her colds. On the other hand, perhaps this cold was a blessing in disguise. No one, but no one, would hire a plague-carrying, pink-nosed snuffling stranger to be a lady's companion. She would not be hired, and Forrest would have to find some other way to weasel into this house.

On that happy thought, Alison looked up and gave a yip of purest, startled delight. The sea—she'd never dreamed it was so close! The height of the porch allowed her to stare down across the meadow, down over the tops of the dark ring of trees that enclosed it, down and away over an undulating carpet of treetops out to a glittering, white-flecked band of cobalt stretching from northeast to southwest.

"Oh, my good heavens!"

Whirling toward that exclamation, Alison would have gone backward down the steps herself, had not one flailing hand caught the balustrade.

"I had no idea anyone was out here! Oh, dear Lord, you scared me!"

*Well, that makes two of us!* Alison steadied herself and managed a shaky smile for the older woman in the doorway, while that lady switched the broom she'd been gripping to her left hand, the better to fan herself with her right. "I'm sorry. I was about to knock, but I couldn't help stopping to admire your view."

"Oh, dear, don't apologize!" Stepping stiffly down onto the porch, the woman pulled the door shut behind her. "It's entirely my fault. I was trying to make up my mind between the stew or the baked ham for supper, and all of a sudden there you were among the potatoes and carrots! Scared me out of a year's growth—not that that wouldn't be a favor," she confided, beaming. Behind the wire-rimmed bifocals, a pair of faded blue eyes examined her frankly, and Alison, given the chance to remember her shyness, promptly did so and became tongue-tied.

Mrs. O'Malley was a bit younger than she'd expected, perhaps forty-five or so. Built like a little fireplug, she stood several inches shorter than Alison's medium height and quite a few inches wider, that width being further emphasized by her dirndl-style apron, whose front pockets bulged with a bottle of window cleaner and a roll of paper towels. She looked utterly homey, utterly friendly and utterly different from Alison's admittedly Victorian conception of the kind of lady to require a lady's companion.

"You look like you skipped your breakfast this morning, and maybe your lunch, as well," her observer remarked all too shrewdly, "though heaven knows, I haven't gotten Mrs. O'Malley to eat her lunch yet, either, not that she ever eats much nowadays." She leaned the broom against the railing beside Alison. "But then, she's still interviewing that Miss Gloom and Doom who blew in around noontime, and I sure hope she doesn't hire *her*, because we've had enough gloom and doom around here to last us awhile.... Why that one started telling me about the state of her kidneys before she even got in the front door!''

Alison glanced at the open windows behind the woman, whoever she was, and mustered a nervous smile. Miss Gloom and Doom must be an intrepid complainer indeed to have launched her kidneys against this conversational floodtide!

''Now are you Alison what's-her-name who was due at one-thirty, or Mary whozit who's due at four-thirty?''

''Ah...I'm...ahhh-choo!—excuse me—Alison Eriksen.''

''Bless you, but that's what you'll get for eating like a bird, you know—colds and worse things! Now suppose you come with me, Alison. I'm June Hurley, by the way, the housekeeper, of course, and we'll tuck you away on the back patio till Miss G and D takes her kidneys and goes.'' So saying, Mrs. Hurley stumped away along the porch, which must have encircled the house, and Alison hurried after her.

She should have guessed that June Hurley would not be the owner of such a house! Just because she, herself, came from a background where one did one's own housework or it didn't get done, it didn't follow that the rest of the world swept their own front porches, as well. Idiot. But then her mind always seemed to stop for a moment when she met someone new. After that first inwardly quailing second, she would steel herself to the encounter, step forward and say her piece, but usually by then she'd lost the just-introduced person's name and his first three comments.

At least no one ever guessed she was shy. No doubt people found her a little stiff, perhaps even a little cold at first meeting, but no one ever guessed that she simply suffered from tongue-hobbling, heart-stopping shyness. And that was the way she preferred it.

The left side of the house offered a continuation of the front porch's stupendous view. Snatching glances southward along the coast, Alison dodged a wicker armchair pulled up to the railing and tried to give half an ear to the ongoing monologue beside her. "She's not usually so picky at all. In fact she's a darling to work for, but this time you'd think she was looking to *marry* one of 'em, rather than just hire a companion...though of course she's not *that* kind, if you know what I mean, but I swear she's been through twenty or so this last week. It just—"

Turning the corner to the back of the house, Alison bit back another cry of delight. It was a different world! The front of the house had been relatively austere. No landscaping could have competed with that expanse of ocean and sky, and none had been permitted to try. But at the back, the porch widened to become an open wooden deck walled in by climbing roses. The wide sweep of the world narrowed to an intimate, flower-bound, jewel box of a patio, a place to retreat.

"Now you sit right here out of the sun. Can you believe it's this hot in June?" The housekeeper indicated a chair by a glass-topped iron table. Curling above the table, a wave of roses looked ready to topple over and break across its surface in pink confusion. Alison sat warily. "Now I'll just get you some lemonade and then it's back to the kitchen for me. I guess we'll have ham..." Mrs. Hurley disappeared, still talking, behind the screen door leading into the back of the house, leaving Alison to savor the undemanding buzz of the mower, still munching grass somewhere downhill, and the tinier echoing murmur of the bees in the roses above her. Heaven.... Reaching up, she caught a branch and pulled an especially elegant blossom down to her nose. Nothing. Those velvety, curling petals might as well have been plastic for all she could smell.

"Well, I'm afraid she's still talking—some people just don't know when to quit—so I hope you're not in a hurry. No? Well, that's good." Setting a tall glass on the table, Mrs. Hurley bustled away as abruptly as she'd come, and Alison heaved a sigh of relief.

Lifting the ice-filled glass, she rubbed it slowly across one cheek, across her dry lips, across the other burning cheek. Ahh... Finally, she drank. The lemonade was deliciously, blessedly icy—and nearly tasteless. This was going to be a whopper of a cold....

A whirring, metallic sound ending in a hiss brought Alison's head around. Beyond the roses, the sound repeated itself and then continued, creating a rhythmic, audible pattern of machinery and human effort—whir...hiss, whir...grunt—that somehow brought back sweet-sad memories of childhood summers.

By sliding her chair back a few feet, Alison found she could peer through a gap in the roses. Before her the hill dropped gently away in wide, terraced steps, each level edged by beds of flowers and bushes, with rough stone stairs leading down to the next level.

Whir...hiss... A machine and a man lunged into view, and Alison smiled in sudden recognition. Of course—someone cutting grass with a hand mower! Old Mr. Haggerty across the street had used one when they'd lived in Newton. She hadn't heard those sounds since her mother had died and her father had moved them back into Boston.

Whir...grunt... He was cutting a neat swath away from her and she watched with fascinated, childish pleasure, feeling like a kid spying on the adults from her rose-decked hideout.

It was hot going out there in the sunlight and the man's naked back was slippery with sweat. Beneath that golden-brown hide, muscles clenched and then lengthened, creating elegant patterns of dark and sweat-glittering light as he forced the mower through the grass—heave, grunt, whir...heave. Alison found herself remembering the time last year when the guard at the Rhode Island School of Design museum had left the room for a moment. She'd seized that chance to run her open hand slowly, blindly up the spine of a marble torso—Roman, second century. The back before her now had that same exquisite play of hollows and bunching muscles, but it would feel different, hot and quivering with the blood rushing beneath the skin, rather than stone cold and unyielding...She shivered, a spasm that shook her all the way through to the backbone, left her thighs rough with goose bumps and her breasts straining against the damp tightness of her brassiere. Fever...she must be getting a chill. It was suddenly too cold in the shadows. Standing, she collected her lemonade and strolled slowly along the wall of roses.

From the sounds below, Alison guessed the mower must have been paralleling her course. She caught glimpses through the leaves of muscular forearms ending in large hands clenched on the handles of the mower, saw his profile once for a second—an intense frown below a shock of brown, sweat-darkened hair. He jerked his head, tossing the hair out of his eyes, and plunged away again. From his sounds, the man was mowing as if his life depended on it, as if he were training for the Olympics of mowing. She grinned as a particularly fervent grunt carried across the hedge. Henry took his lawn service seriously, it seemed.

But the purr of the power mower farther down the hillside reminded Alison that there were two men at work. So her man wouldn't even be Henry then, but just some assistant. The boss would no doubt claim the easier job of power mowing.

Looking for gaps in the roses, Alison nearly stepped on a dog. "Why, hello, you!"

Sprawled on his side in the shadows beneath the hedge, a golden retriever lifted his head at her murmur, then collapsed again with a sigh. The lazy thump of a feathery tail assured her that she would have been given a proper welcome, if it weren't such a dog of a day.

"Poor thing! Just too hot to budge, aren't you?" Crooning her sympathy, Alison crouched on her heels beside the beast and ventured an ear tickle. His groan of dreamy contentment was all the invitation she needed. Laughing to herself, Alison buried her fingers in that red-golden pelt and gave him a proper ruffling, glorying in the feel of silken fur sliding over muscle and bone. God, when had she last touched something live?

Still stroking the dog, Alison suddenly became aware of the silence, and a turn of her head told her why. From beneath the branches she had an excellent view of the terrace. The lawn mower stood alone in the midst of smooth-clipped grass; he had finished. Oddly disappointed, she turned back to the dog.

But the man was back again in a moment, striding into view from around the side of the house, dragging a green garden hose behind him. Facing away from her, he stopped to rinse the bits of grass off his legs.

And they were nice legs at that. Long and well muscled beneath his cut-off ragged jeans, they were nicer than Don's had ever been. At the thought, her hands clenched in the dog's fur and he squirmed in protest. Apologizing with her fingertips, Alison scowled at the man before her, as if he were to blame somehow.

But oblivious to her irritation, he was drinking from the hose, and she got another look at his profile. A straight nose ending in the slightest of upward tilts should have given him a girlish look, but did not—perhaps because the uncompromising lines of jaw and eyebrow more than compensated. Tough with a romantic streak, she decided, and her lip curled in sudden distaste. That did sound like a description of Don, didn't it? Especially the romantic—but what was making her think of him today?

Her thoughts stopped as the man before her raised the hose above his head. Eyes closed, he stood straight but at ease beneath the fall of water, his face turned up to meet it, his chest expanding with an obvious sigh of delight. In the sunlight, the water silvered his skin and, with his seal-brown hair dripping into his darker eyebrows and his lips curled up into something that was not quite a smile, he looked, not happy, but utterly at peace, utterly at one with his world. Perhaps she should give up art history and take up lawn mowing instead.

As if he had heard that sardonic thought, he gave a sudden, water-slinging shake of his head and moved out of her sight, still dragging his hose, leaving her staring at the spot where he'd been.

"Milo!"

Beneath her hands, the dog stirred. Turning toward the sound of his voice, a brisk and pleasant baritone, Alison noticed the gap in the hedge some ten feet beyond her. Good grief, he wasn't coming up...

*"Milo!"*

As if he'd been hoarding his energy for just that moment, the retriever erupted to his feet. One golden shoulder bumped into her knees, and Alison found herself suddenly sitting. "Hey!"

But her friend was a gentleman, albeit a bumbling one. The wet kiss planted full on her mouth was obviously meant to be an apology.

"Yuk! Ahh-chooo!"

Her sneeze was taken for approval, and the dog gave her a second enthusiastic kiss. "Yuk! Stop!" Laughing, Alison caught at his ruff to fend him off. On his feet, he was much larger than she'd realized!

*"Milo!"* The retriever reared and then swung away from her as someone lifted him aside, and Alison

found herself laughing up into the face of the man she'd been ogling a moment ago.

Her laughter caught in her throat.

"Are you all right?" He didn't seem to know whether to frown or laugh down at her, but a smile seemed to be winning the struggle.

He looked oddly Homeric, with that wet, muscular body and his dog prancing on his hind legs beside him like some golden fleece he'd just captured. Perhaps it was the blue-gray eyes dancing beneath those dark eyebrows; she'd always thought of the ancient Greeks as being light eyed.

"Are you all right?" he repeated, dropping the dog onto all fours and holding out his hand.

"Yes, I'm fine, thanks." Ignoring his offer, Alison scrubbed the back of a hand across her lips. "I was just petting him."

"And he returned the compliment? That almost restores my faith in Milo's good taste."

She looked up indignantly, then dropped her eyes before his laughing attention. But his hand still hovered patiently before her; quite obviously it wasn't going anywhere until she used it. Cornered... Face tight with shyness, Alison sighed and gave him her hand. His fingers were shockingly, vitally, warm against her chilled skin. He lifted her up into the sunlight with the same effortless strength he'd used on the dog and then steadied her for an instant as she wobbled. "A black-eyed Susan among the roses," he murmured, releasing her at last.

That was obviously a reference to her coloring. Dark brown eyes and black eyebrows look strange with light hair; she didn't need to be told that. Still it was a poetic metaphor, and an appropriate one, coming from a gardener. And it left her absolutely nothing to say in reply. Smiling a thank-you, Alison tried to find something to look at besides the sharply defined pectorals at her eye level. The chest before her now, with those damp curls just beginning to spring away from the drying skin, was all too alive...and much too close. Perhaps it would be easier to look him in the eye, after all.

"You don't smell very well, do you?"

*That* brought her eyes up, widening with outrage. It was a stunningly rude non sequitur as well as an ungrammatical one—and a damned silly observation for a sweaty man to make! "I *beg* your pardon?"

But he laughed outright, a flashing white laugh, as she met those light eyes. "I don't mean that. I mean your nose can't be quite up to snuff," he assured her, still grinning, "though I'm afraid the second applies as well by now." He jerked a thumb downward. "Milo, here, was off making love to a skunk last night."

Making love to a... At her feet, Milo gave her a tongue-lolling smile of joyful agreement. "A skunk," she managed faintly.

"'Fraid so." Reaching down, he caught her wrists and lifted them toward his nose. His hands encircled her bones completely, giving Alison a sudden, panicky feeling of being handcuffed. Her fingers strained away from his face, trying not to touch him. But he was flinching, as well, his nose wrinkling even as he grinned down at her. "*Whew!* You can't smell *that*?"

"No!" She snatched her hands away, uncomfortably aware of the fact that, had he chosen, he could have kept them. "I have a cold." She made a wiping gesture toward the sides of her skirt, then stopped herself as he exclaimed.

"Don't!" Catching her shoulder with the easy familiarity of a born toucher, he turned her toward the gap in the roses, where wooden steps led down to the lawn. "I was about to give Milo his third bath of the day. We'll wash you, too."

"No, really, thanks, but—"

His fingers spread across her shoulder blade as she stopped, starting her forward again. "No trouble at all," he assured her pleasantly. "Just step this way."

With her hands dangling before her like useless, broken toys, Alison felt absurdly helpless, and it wasn't a good feeling; she'd worked too hard to earn her independence these past two years. But the man striding along at her shoulder had a momentum that made him hard to resist. For now it was easier to go along, submissive but resentful. He stopped her at the top step. "Wait here."

He was back in a moment with the hose and a bottle of shampoo. "Present arms."

Biting back a sigh, she held out her hands.

Her skin felt hot, though only minutes before she'd been cold, and the water was lovely. Liquid ice. His face below her held an odd, absent intensity as he wet down her hands and forearms, as if he were elsewhere, listening to music.

The shampoo was measured into her cupped palms with that same half-dreaming deliberation. "See if that does the trick," he murmured at last, backing down another step to watch. He was back in the present with a snap, his attention as suddenly palpable as sunlight pouring through a wide-swung door.

With those blue-gray eyes following her every move, Alison made a business of working up a lather, her own eyes fixed stubbornly on her hands. An audience she didn't need.

"So you've had a cold, hmm?" he commented finally.

"Yes." *Keep it short and to the point.* The sooner he tired of this sport, the sooner he'd go back to his chores and leave her in peace. Teasing women was obviously more interesting than mowing grass.

"That's good," he allowed thoughtfully.

But that was too provoking to be ignored. "Oh? Why's that?" she snapped, soaping each finger in turn with ferocious care.

"I was afraid you might be a problem drinker, with that stoplight nose." He was waiting for her outraged look, and fielded it with an eye-crinkling grin that assured her he'd thought no such thing.

There was no dealing with such a man. She stuck out her arms in soapy resignation to let him rinse her with that same absent-minded thoroughness. Seen from above like this, the joker had lashes as dark and thick as her own; there was no justice in life.

He caught her right wrist to finish the job, turning her hand gently to wash the back of it, then tossed the hose away from them. Milo bounded down the steps after it. "So let's see how this smells."

But Alison had had enough. Too much. As he lifted it, her hand clenched into a fist, a purely instinctive gesture of rejection. His smile fading, her tormentor glanced up at her in thoughtful silence. After a moment his lips curved, but his smile was almost gentle. Raising her fist, he socked himself lightly in the jaw with it. "Pow! Take *that*, you brute!"

With the feel of his jaw imprinted on her knuckles, she smiled in spite of herself, and he lifted her hand again. This time he brushed the inside of her wrist in one long, searching sniff, his breath moving hot and slow across her damp skin.

For the effect his touch had on her, he might just as well have been using that nose to trace slowly down the length of her spine, but if he felt her trembling he gave no sign of it. "Summer skin with just a whiff of old skunk," he pronounced with his lurking almost-smile. "Beats musk any day. Bottle it, and we'll make a fortune."

There had to be some way to break this spell, break the connection between those ocean eyes and her own.

"I...didn't...know skunk was so strong...." She pulled her hand gently away from his face, but found that his hand came along with it.

His laugh had an oddly breathless quality to it, a huskiness she hadn't noticed before. "Oh, lady, this is a mild case! I guess ol' Milo didn't take a direct hit..." His words pattered aimlessly, as if the brain behind them were working fast and furiously on something else entirely. "He was just grazed, as the Lone Ranger used to say."

"Ah-*choo*!"

"Bless you," he murmured mechanically, then said it aloud again. "Bless you."

But her sneeze had broken the moment nicely. Alison reclaimed her hand and used it to rub her prickling nose—stop-light, indeed!—then made a show of sniffing her fingers.

"Not good enough? Well let's try this, then." Reaching up beside her, he caught a rose and decapitated it with one ruthless yank. It was unnerving, the way he moved, one moment so still and apparently relaxed, the next in muscle-taut motion. He pulled a second rose and a third with the blitheness of a man who has seen too many roses. "Hold out your hands."

Wondering, she obeyed. He stripped the petals away from their centers and showered them down upon her by the handful, a pink drifting cloud, feather light, almost too soft to feel. "Stop!" She found herself laughing, perhaps because he was. "Enough already!"

"So use 'em, then. Rub 'em around."

"They're too pretty."

"There's a few more where those came from."

True enough, but she crushed the petals with a guilty delight, a feeling of wicked, delicious luxuriance that startled her. It could only have been more heavenly if she could have smelled them. How had he known...? She looked up to find him holding one petal to his nose and watching her.

"So who are you, Dark Eyes?" he asked softly. "I've run through the entire list, every daughter of every friend of my mother's, and you don't fit anywhere.... A friend of a daughter? A strayed skydiver? An evicted angel?"

Petals scrunched between her fingers, Alison stared down at him in wide-eyed horror. Of course. How had she not known? Not the gardener, but the owner of these roses. The son...the man who'd tossed Forrest down the steps, who'd stood between Forrest and the painting like a stone wall these past seven months. The man she'd been sent to trick....

"Hmm?" Those blue-gray eyes roamed slowly across her face. "Cat got your tongue again?"

She'd had a teacher in high school who used to taunt her with that. Alison flicked the pink debris into the bushes. "Not at all," she said coolly. "I'm here to apply for a job—lady's companion to your mother."

*"You?"* He shook his head slowly, then again with quick decision, frowning now. "But you won't do at all!"

A stream of water arched across the steps and his feet. On the lawn below them, Milo was wrestling with the hose, his teeth clamped on the back of its neck in mock ferocity. Alison skipped backward as he reared and shook it again.

"Milo! Drop it!" O'Malley started down the steps, turned to scowl back at her, then disappeared around the corner of the hedge after the retreating dog and his prey.

*"You won't do at all."* And what had he meant by that? Frowning, Alison turned to stare up at the house.

Movement behind the darkness of the screen door caught her eye; then slowly, the door swung wide. A tall, thin woman stood in the doorway, her arms braced on the silver walker that framed her body from the waist down. Something in her pose suggested that she'd been standing there for quite some time. "You must be Alison," she said quietly.

# CHAPTER TWO

"YES...I..." As usual, speech had deserted her.

"Good!" Mrs. O'Malley smiled, a lovely, familiar smile—a softer version of her son's flashing grin. Then the smile faded as she glanced down at the single step leading to the porch level.

Navigating it would be difficult for an invalid, perhaps dangerous. "Could I—"

"No." The refusal was polite, but carved in granite. With a sudden jerk, she lifted the walker and set it down on the deck, leaning out above it at a precarious angle.

"Mother! For God's sake—" O'Malley sprang up the stairs to the patio two at a time.

"Be still, Ty!" That command slowed his charge for an instant, but didn't stop him. It was all the time Mrs. O'Malley needed. Her small feet touched the porch as he reached her.

Not needed, his open hands hovered around her for an instant; they closed at last on the front of her walker. Face-to-face they glared at each other across the support, so alike in their anger that Alison had to smile. The hard, clear lines of his face, those high cheekbones and the resolute chin were just bolder, masculine versions of his mother's fine-boned features. Light eyes clashed with eyes of the same luminous color, each pair large but deep-set beneath brows that lifted at the ends when they scowled.

"When did you learn to do that?" he asked at last, the muscles of his jaw beginning to relax.

"I've been doing it for nearly a week now." Tall enough to look him in the eye, she was only a couple of inches shorter than his six feet, but again gender made all the difference. Where she was willowy, he was oak, wide and solid to her slenderness.

"For a *week*? And you didn't tell me?" His jaw hardened again and her chin lifted in answer.

"I'm supposed to brag about stepping down onto my own back porch, Ty?" she snapped. She had that pale, clear skin that flushes easily and, with Mrs. O'Malley's cheeks in flames, Alison could suddenly picture her at twenty—tall, proud and very lovely indeed. She jerked the walker, and her son let go of it with obvious reluctance.

He fell back a step, his hands flexing tensely at his sides, ready if she should need them but trying to hide that readiness. "Why not crow a little?" He grinned crookedly. "I'd have brought champagne and kazoos...any excuse for a party."

She gave him that sudden, eye-crinkling, lovely smile and then turned. Pinned in her clear-eyed gaze, Alison found the eyes a shade lighter than her son's—gray without his blue. And once she must have had red hair; there were still a few fading streaks of copper within the white of her neat chignon. "In the meantime, I'm sure we're scaring Alison half to death," she said lightly. "She doesn't look as if she comes from a fighting family."

"Alison..." Turning, he tasted it slowly, almost caressing the last syllable. "So that's your name."

Unable to escape his eyes, Alison jerked out an answering smile that was more shrug than pleasure. *Yes, Alison—so what?* Why couldn't they stop staring at her? Her mind was a total blank. She should say something...anything...

"You haven't introduced yourselves yet?" Mrs. O'Malley came forward stiffly, the walker rocking before her.

"Not in the usual way." His eyes flicked down to Alison's hands, clenched so tightly that the nails were hurting her palms, and then up to her face again. "I was too shy."

Mrs. O'Malley laughed quickly at what she assumed was a joke. "In that case, Alison, I'd like you to meet my son, Tyler Channing O'Malley—Ty on those rare occasions when he's behaving. Ty, this is Alison Eriksen."

"Hello, Alison." Mercifully, he didn't offer to shake hands; something in the slant of his eyebrows said they were past the hand-shaking stage.

"And I'm Harriet O'Malley, of course." Mrs. O'Malley did offer her hand, giving Alison a fleeting impression of cool bird bones, surprising strength and eyes that searched as deeply as her son's.

"Oh, there you all are, and here's lunch!" Mrs. Hurley stepped onto the back porch, balancing a tray loaded with sandwiches and a pitcher atinkle with ice. "And I'm expecting everyone to eat three sandwiches, if not four," she announced, setting three places at the table in the shade. "Keeps the kidney stones away, I don't doubt."

"Kidney stones?" Ty pulled a chair out from the table and waited for his mother, his eyebrows lifting.

"We've been learning all we ever wanted to know about kidneys from a Miss Cornelius who just left." Mrs. O'Malley sank into the chair with a fleeting grimace that might have been pain but could have been merely distaste.

"All we wanted to know and then some!" June Hurley snorted, stumping back into the house.

"If you've got 'em, flaunt 'em, hmm?" He eased the chair forward a few inches, then adjusted it again an inch or so.

"Exactly, but not at lunchtime, please." Mrs. O'Malley glanced up at Alison and then tapped the table across from her in cheerful command. "And as for flaunting, I could say the same for bare chests, Tarzan. Not at the lunch table." She twisted to smile up at him. "What have you been up to?"

"Just cutting the grass." He said it casually, all his attention seemingly focused on Alison as he pulled out a second chair for her and waited. She sat reluctantly, all too aware of him looming just above her, his hands by her shoulders as he held the chair back.

"Cutting the— Oh, Ty..." Across the table, Mrs. O'Malley's eyes glittered suddenly. She squeezed them shut almost angrily, then groped for the blue linen napkin beside her plate. "You don't have to do that, just because... Henry can do that!"

Alison's chair creaked as Ty shifted above her. "I've been doing it all this spring—just the top two terraces," he explained easily. "And Dad was right. It is good exercise." One of his fingers brushed across Alison's shoulder blade, an idle, accidental touch that lifted the hairs at the back of her neck. Why couldn't he move? As if he'd caught that thought, Ty drifted away a step, his eyes still on his mother as she wiped her eyes. "I'll be back in a few minutes," he told her gently. "Save me a sandwich or three."

As the screen door closed behind Ty, Alison felt a twinge of pure panic. She'd wanted him gone, but now that he was, there was only herself to deal with this grieving woman. And she didn't know how. To offer comfort to a stranger would be presumptuous; to ignore those tears and reach for a sandwich would be unthinkable. At the thought, her stomach awoke with a snarl. Horrified, she looked up to find Mrs. O'Malley laughing at her through her tears. "Alison, don't look so worried! Please help yourself."

"Thank you." She found herself returning the laughter with a feeble grin as she chose a roast beef on rye. "It's just that sometimes I don't know what to say..."

"Nor should you!" Mrs. O'Malley dried her eyes again, then selected a sandwich herself. "People aren't supposed to cry in public; it's terribly rude. No one knows what to do." She took a small, fierce nip of bread and then set it down again hastily. "You'll just have to learn to ignore me, as Ty does. I lost my husband recently, in a driving accident, and I'm like a time bomb nowadays...the silliest things set me off..." Turning toward the roses and the lawn beyond, she let her words trail away to a murmur. "It's just that Pat always insisted on mowing the back terraces. He was so proud of his grass..."

*Had lost him recently.* But Forrest had said the car wreck had happened last December. Well, perhaps that would seem recent if your whole life had stopped that moment, as well.... And she wasn't supposed to know about that wreck already, was she? "I see," Alison murmured belatedly. "I'm sorry..." What condolence could be lamer? Or more despicably hypocritical? She put down her sandwich as a wave of nausea swept over her.

"Thank you." Suddenly brisk again, Mrs. O'Malley poured lemonade for them both, then filled the third glass. "Well, Alison, I suppose we should get on with this. I read your résumé, of course, but let's see if I have my facts straight."

*You mean your fictions,* Alison corrected her mentally. Forrest had written that résumé, had, in fact, first shown it to her only yesterday. It was an artful fabrication, an intricate patchwork of truth and falsehood stitched together with just two aims in mind: to make her seem an experienced, plausible candidate for this position—complete with a reference if need be; and to erase all connections with art history from her past, most especially the study of art history with a certain Forrest Osgood of Brown University. His story stuck in her throat now like a piece of dry bread crust.

"As I recall, you were born and raised in Boston and went to college there," Mrs. O'Malley recited gently.

"Yes." So far, that was the truth.

"You studied French and history?"

Well, that was half-true. Alison managed a shaky little smile and half a nod. French and *art* history, actually.

Those crystalline eyes studied her for a moment, dropped to her fingertips braced on the edge of the table at each side of her plate, then lifted again. "After college, you moved to Providence, where you took a position as live-in companion to a Mrs. Sandhurst, I believe."

Utterly, absolutely false, so why should she suddenly feel better? Alison's nod this time was almost cheerful. Old Mrs. Sandhurst had indeed existed, but her only companions had been Professor Sandhurst of the Brown History department—her son and Forrest's favorite chess partner—and seven surly, overfed cats. Reaching for her lemonade, Alison found the answer to her question. Of course. She liked that lie because, with a few typewritten lines, Forrest had wiped out the four most miserable years of her whole life. Those steely-eyed cats would have been heaven in comparison! She nodded again, almost fiercely this time. That lie she could embrace.

"Upon Mrs. Sandhurst's death you returned to academia, to Brown University this time, to study history again. For the past two years you've been a graduate assistant there, but now you've decided not to pursue your Ph.D."

Alison swallowed and nodded again mutely. Really, Forrest was clever in sending that résumé. It was so much easier to agree to a lie than to speak one. And this last part was half true, anyway. Two years ago Forrest had admitted her to the *art* history program at Brown, where she was now a graduate assistant. But she had every intention of completing her Ph.D.…and she couldn't do that without Forrest. Which brought her full circle to today and these miserable lies.

"And you're not married, Alison?"

"No!" Surprised from her reverie, she answered that question too harshly, then tried to soften the effect with a smile and a quick shake of her head. "No, I'm not." By now, she'd learned not to look down at her hand when she said that. It had been a silly reflex for the first six months or so, silly because that white band of skin had disappeared from her finger the day she'd walked out, leaving the ring on top of her note on the kitchen table. She'd burned the mark away, burned her skin red and clean out in the dunes of Plum Island all that long summer day; she'd shed her past in flakes and tatters for two weeks after that.

"I...see." Somehow those clear eyes across the table did seem to see. Too much. Alison looked down at her plate and found her sandwich still waiting. *Impolite not to eat it...* She picked it up reluctantly.

"Are you engaged?"

"No." She almost smiled at that question. "No, I'm not." One marriage had been quite enough, thank you. Feeling a sneeze coming on, she slapped the sandwich down again and whirled away from the table. "Tchoo! Excuse me."

"Certainly," Mrs. O'Malley agreed laughing, "and bless you." She waited while Alison found her tissues, then remarked, "That *is* a cold, isn't it?"

"I'm afraid so."

"Good. This is no place to live with hay fever."

That was an odd statement, surely. It seemed to imply that she would be living here, as if this interview were just a formality. But no, Mrs. O'Malley still had some questions, apparently. "Are you...committed to anyone, Alison?"

Alison did smile this time. She meant living with someone, of course. "No, Mrs. O'Malley, I'm not."

"Harriet, please, Alison."

"Harriet, then. No, I'm quite single." She almost smiled again, thinking of Forrest's sweating over the résumé. He hadn't given one thought to her sex life as a topic for this interview, and it did seem a bit strange, didn't it—the emphasis Harriet was placing on the subject? But then, everything seemed a little strange today: colors were brighter, the edges of objects seemed knife sharp, certain words, certain faces loomed out of the hot air with sudden, inexplicable force.

"I said to save me a sandwich, not the whole picnic!" Ty was suddenly beside her, helping himself to a couple of sandwiches. He glanced up, and Alison almost jumped as their eyes met. She would have to get used to that trick of his. Just when you thought he was elsewhere, safely preoccupied, he'd look up and bam!—there he was, right between your eyes, slipping inside your head before you could blink. Perhaps it was just the color of those eyes—that deep, clear-water-at-evening color that gave the effect, or maybe it was the way his upper lids formed a peak where they passed under his browbones, giving his eyes a triangular, piercing look, like a young hawk staring into the sunset. And now *she* was staring, Alison realized as his lips curled suddenly. She jerked her eyes away and down, found her sandwich, and took a bite of it.

But that was a mistake. She could feel his eyes on her lips as she chewed, on her throat as she forced the bite down. The question was whether he'd know the

Heimlich maneuver once he'd succeeded in making her choke.

"So what experience do you have, Alison, that makes you suitable for this job?" he asked cheerfully as soon as the bite was safely landed.

A very good question, as she might say to one of her brasher sophomores in French Impressionism 113, and the true answer was none. "I—"

"Just a moment, Alison." Glass clinked against glass as Harriet put down her drink and turned on her son. "Just *who* is in the market for a companion here, Ty, you or I?"

The corners of his mouth twitched in a fleeting smile, and his eyes swung back to Alison. They moved across her face from lips to tensed eyebrows like teasing, gentle fingertips—exploring, testing, rejecting and then gone as he turned away again. "You are, Mother," he told her gravely, "but you have another one coming at four-thirty, June tells me. I'm just trying to speed up the process."

The process of rejection, he meant. So she wouldn't do at all, not for his mother and quite patently not for himself. Not good enough. A small wave of acid washed across her empty stomach. She'd known those words before, many times in her life.

But Harriet was delivering a rejection of her own. "Thank you, Ty, but when I need your help, I'll ask for it."

"*That* would be a novelty!" he shot back, turning to frown at her. He'd showered and dressed in a white cotton knit shirt and khaki shorts. And he was older than she'd thought, Alison suddenly realized, closer to his mid-thirties than her own age, as she'd first believed; the hardness of his body was deceptive. With that covered, you had a chance to notice the little squint lines at the corners of his eyes, those first faint lines around the mouth, a small scar on his left cheekbone...

"Just knowing your help is there if I need it is generally all the help I need, darling." Harriet delivered that warning with a mixture of tenderness and temper that was altogether charming, and Ty's lips quirked upward in spite of his obvious irritation.

"Yes, but—"

"No buts about it!" The imperious swing of her head back to Alison dismissed him.

With a snort that might have been exasperation, laughter or both, Ty pushed his chair back from the table a foot or so, effectively removing himself from the interview. "All right."

But if Ty had failed to take over the interview, he had succeeded in changing its pace, and Harriet gave up all pretense of eating. "I suppose I should tell you something of what would be expected of you, Alison, should I decide to hire you."

As described, the position sounded rather pleasant, for someone who enjoyed the quiet life. She would not be expected to clean house or act as nurse or lady's maid, nor apparently was Harriet seeking an entertainer. She would merely be expected to be on hand, much as a live-in daughter might be, available to run errands up or down stairs as needed, to help with light meals and dishwashing on weekends and in the evenings after June Hurley had gone home to her own family. And she would be there at night, of course, on call in case of—those cool, gray eyes flicked past Alison toward her silent neighbor in an expressionless glance, then returned to her face just as quickly—in case of emergencies. "It would be just the two of us in the house at night, Alison. Ty has his own apartment in Mystic. That wouldn't...worry you?"

Smiling, Alison shook her head. The prospect of encountering Ty O'Malley each time she ventured forth from her bedroom to brush her teeth was far more unnerving than anything that might go bump in the night at Shady Breeze; it was a relief to hear he was not part of this package.

"Good," Harriet continued. "And, of course, I'd expect you to be my chauffeur, at least for—" Catching Alison's expression, she stopped.

Thank heavens, an out at last—and one for which Forrest couldn't blame her! It was hard to hide her delight, impossible to look disappointed as Alison shook her head quickly.

"Don't tell me, let me guess!" Ty was as pleased as she was, Alison realized as she turned to meet his blue-gray appraisal. "You don't drive."

"I'm afraid not." She packed all the polite regret she could muster into that disavowel, then turned quickly back toward Harriet as his eyes sharpened above that hint of a smile. "I'm afraid it never occurred to me that that would be one of the requirements for this position, Harriet. I'm sorry to have wasted your time like this."

But all Harriet's attention was focused on her son. That watchful, almost calculating expression softened as her eyes returned to Alison. "Would you be willing to learn?"

"Ahh..." How did you tactfully say no to such a direct question? The irony of it was that she'd been scrimping all spring, saving money to take the driving lessons this summer and had passed the written exam just last week. But learning to drive was a pleasure she'd gladly forego to escape this job.

Ty stirred beside her. "Mother, I don't think—"

"Everyone ought to be able to drive, Alison." Beneath the gently persuasive words something tougher seemed to be lurking. Harriet leaned toward her, those clear eyes compelling. "There's no way to be independent otherwise."

That she knew only too well. Was that why Don had never wanted her to learn? A vision of his red Corvette sliding down the street flickered across her mind, and his casual backward flip of the fingers as he waved goodbye without turning. "I suppose so, but—"

"Mother, for God's sake!" Ty cut across her hesitant words. "You're just now recovering from your last accident! D'you want to risk another with a beginner driver?"

Harriet met her son's irritation with wide-eyed, gentle detachment. "Who taught Patsy to drive, Ty?"

His dark brows jerked upward, then stilled. "Oh, no," he said softly, beginning to shake his head. "*No*. Don't you remember what I went through? It wasn't life and limb I was risking, it was sanity—bless you," he growled mechanically as Alison sneezed.

"Alison impresses me as a much more...rewarding pupil than your sister," Harriet murmured thoughtfully. "She's several years older than Patsy was when you taught her. She's highly motivated, quiet..."

"Is that what you are, Alison—quiet?" Ty mocked, swinging around to inspect her.

The best answer to that jab was silence, and that was all she gave him, her chin defiantly high.

His faint smile widened for a second then vanished as he turned away, shaking his head again. "I haven't the time for that."

"Ty..." Harriet hesitated, obviously weighing her words. "You said that I never ask for your help..." She paused again delicately.

Ty let out a low, exasperated sigh. Picking up his glass, he studied the sunlight shining through the lemonade, then took an abrupt swallow. "And you're asking for it now?" he said finally to no one in particular. "Even against my better judgment?"

Mischief glimmered in her eyes and her voice as she answered. "It's your help I may want, Ty. Not your judgment."

But he wasn't to be charmed out of his disapproval. "I take it that means Alison is hired?"

"Not exactly." Harriet shot her an apologetic glance. "I've three more interviews scheduled, but if I *should* decide..."

Shrugging away that unwelcome possibility, Ty pushed his chair back from the table. "Could we discuss this later?"

The subject was closed, Alison realized; she'd missed her chance. She should have backed Ty, and painted herself a mechanical moron and potential scourge of the highways. Instead, her silence would be taken for acquiescence in Harriet's rather quixotic scheme. Why *was* she bothering? Were presentable chauffeur-companions in such short supply that Harriet had to train her own? Alison looked up and blinked. Ty was watching her.

"In that case, if you can't drive, how did you get up here?" he wanted to know. "I thought you'd dropped out of the sky." His irritation appeared to be fading already, the straight line of his mouth relaxing slowly into its natural smile.

"I—" Thoughts of Forrest made her feel deceitful and shy all over again. "I...got a ride with a friend," she managed finally. "Then I walked up from the highway."

"In this heat?" Ty looked incredulous as she nodded. "And how are you going back?"

"The same way." Alison tried to look delighted at the prospect of trudging down that hill again, when all she really wanted to do was put her head down on the table and close her eyes. The sun had moved since they first sat down and was now reflecting off the pitcher before her, stabbing bright needles beneath her lowered lashes.

Ty stood up abruptly, towering above her. "In that case, I'll drive you down to the road, whenever you're ready."

"Oh, no!" That would be a disaster! Her head felt like an overstuffed pillow as she shook it. "No. I like to walk."

But Ty was not convinced. "Look, just be sensible and let me—"

*"No!"* No doubt there was a tactful way to refuse his offer, but with her head thrown back to meet his eyes, she was too dizzy to find it. The blunt word hung in the air between them, repeating itself in her ringing

ears. "No, thank you," she murmured belatedly, trying to soften it.

"All right." Standing there staring down at her, Ty looked less offended than puzzled. But with her guilty conscience, that was an unwelcome reaction. He seemed like a man who could find the answers once he had the questions.

"Ty?"

"Hi, Henry." Ty swung lightly around on the balls of his feet. "Are you done?"

"Yup." Stopping on the top step up from the lawn, the older man hitched the belt of his sweat-darkened trousers over an impressive paunch and nodded. "You got time to help me load the mower?"

"Sure." Starting forward, Ty stopped as his mother made a motion to rise; he eased her chair back from the table, still talking over his shoulder. "And I want you to take the hand mower in and sharpen it for me, Henry."

Shoving hands the size of rakes into his already gaping pockets, Henry shook his head mournfully. "You oughta junk that thing, Ty. Leave the mowin' to me." Beneath the weight of his fists, his trousers sagged slowly downward again and he hitched them up automatically.

"No." Ty stared down at the top of his mother's head, his eyes unfocused. "Not this year."

"As crazy as your dad," Henry pronounced in disgust. Both O'Malleys grinned at the same instant, and Harriet laughed softly under her breath, her eyes suddenly brilliant with tears. Henry seemed to notice her for the first time. "Oh, er...uh, Mrs. O'Malley, how are you?"

"Better every day, Henry!" She leaned out around Ty to smile at him. "How are you?"

"Uh...just fine." He backed down a step uncertainly.

"Go ahead, Henry. I'll be right with you." He turned back to his mother. "Can I help you inside?"

"No." Harriet smiled as she said it, but there was no doubting her determination. "But thank you."

He gave her a little lopsided grin, half rueful, half admiring, and turned to Alison. "Alison." He sketched half a nod and then strode away across the patio without so much as a pleased to meet you. But then it hadn't been exactly pleasant, had it?

The screen door opened and June Hurley stumped out. "Well, the next installment's in the living room, Harriet," she announced cheerfully, "and wait'll you see *this* one!"

"Oh, dear," Harriet murmured fervently, glancing up at Alison in comic, almost conspiratorial dismay. They both laughed.

# CHAPTER THREE

STOPPING WHERE HENRY'S TRUCK had been parked, Alison turned. Her last impression of Shady Breeze matched the first. The sun had moved behind the house and was shining back at her through the encircling porches, turning the delicate gingerbread into black lace arching against the heat-filled, glowing air. She sighed, suddenly sad and not sure why.

Too much pleasure for the eye to hold and none of it hers? Perhaps...but she should be used to that. The art historian's stock-in-trade was beauty, after all; that didn't mean that you took it home with you from the museums and galleries at the end of the day. She'd trained herself not to want, to look but not touch. Funny to be blindsided by a house, of all things.

She took a step backward, not able to look away yet. She'd seen more elegant houses in Boston, grander ones in Newport. Why this one?

She saw Harriet's lovely old face again, laughing through her tears at some memory of her husband. That was it. If some houses could be haunted by past evils, then couldn't others be haunted with happiness? Up there on her hill, Shady Breeze seemed to whisper of past joy, seemed to hold out the promise of joy to come.

But not for her. Alison turned on her heel, then stopped as the elms seemed to keep turning. She blinked. They swayed slowly back into position, waiting for her to the left and right, forming a green tunnel arching down the hill and into the heat. She stepped into the lane and the air closed around her like a wet, green blanket dropped over her head.

Rounding the last bend in the lane, Alison stopped short again. Below her Ty O'Malley stood with his hands in his pockets, his head tilted at a thoughtful angle as he studied the lilac bush before him. He glanced up at her with that almost-smile, then returned to the object of his contemplation.

Short of bushwhacking, there was no way around him, and as she stopped beside him, she realized what held his attention. It was the mailbox that nestled in the bush, or perhaps the names painted on the mailbox. Patrick and Harriet O'Malley. "Shouldn't you change that now?"

He shook his head slowly, still without turning. "Not till she asks me.... She's got to accept this. And I can't rush her, Alison."

Odd how nice her name sounded, spoken by that quiet voice. As if a warm, gentle hand had reached out to stroke her hair—that was how it felt. She kicked a weed at her feet. "More likely she's just forgotten about it."

"No, I've—" He turned to face her and the words faded away for a moment. "I've seen her face when we drive past," he finished absently. "She hasn't forgotten.... You don't forget that easily...." He turned downhill and started walking, glanced back at her with those dark brows lifting, then waited till she fell reluctantly into step.

Good grief, he didn't mean to stroll all the way down the hill with her, did he? One glimpse of Forrest and the game would be over. All those rotten lies invented just to conceal the connection between the professor and herself would have been for nothing. Worse yet, she would have to explain matters.

"You're not blond."

"I beg your pardon?"

"I've been wondering how to describe your coloring," he explained, as if this were the most sensible question in the world at the moment. "And you're not quite blond."

"Gee, no kidding?" She packed a day's worth of tension, self-loathing and sore feet into that retort, but it bounced right off him. The corner of his mouth nearest her seemed to deepen a trifle—that was all.

"No kidding," he confirmed easily "But it's not brown, either. Too light."

True. And there was no need to snarl at him like that, even if she was tired and worried. Rudeness implied a certain intimacy that didn't exist here. "My brother always says it's cocker-spaniel colored," she admitted grudgingly.

"Cocker colored?" Ty grinned and reached out to capture a curl.

This was too much. She'd been touched more today than she had in the whole previous two years, and she didn't like it. As she wheeled to face him, that message was clear in her narrowed eyes. But all Ty's attention was focused on the specimen he'd taken. "Perhaps..." he murmured judiciously, spreading the lock out between thumb and forefinger, "if you kept that spaniel on a strict diet of honey and butter..."

Really, he was impossible.

"No," he decided. As if of its own volition, his other hand came up. Feather light across her cheek, his fingers combed slowly into the hair above her ear, gathering the silkiness between them as they slowly closed.

Speechless, trapped between those gentle, impersonal hands, Alison stood perfectly still, watching the blue-gray eyes above her shift from one handful of her hair to the other with an almost scientific detachment. "Butterscotch," he pronounced finally, with an odd satisfaction.

"What?" It was hard to think, harder to breathe with those cool fingertips barely stirring against her aching head.

"It's the color of a hot butterscotch sundae," he told her gravely, meeting her eyes at last. Without releasing her hair, his thumb curved to rest on the end of her nose. "With the cherry on top." His eyes crinkled.

That did it! Her nose had taken enough abuse. "I *hope* you're aware," she announced in her iciest classroom diction, "that the common cold is transmitted through touch?"

"It is?" Undaunted, his thumb traced a small, insolent circle around the tip of that aching feature. "I thought you had to have something more...intimate, say...mouth-to-mouth contact." Those smiling, deepwater eyes moved down to her lips. Then slowly, gentle and sure, his thumb followed.

How could an action enrage at the same time it aroused? Lips parting, she stood transfixed, torn between two utterly incompatible emotions while his thumb followed the hot, dry curves of her mouth.

"You are going to get my cold," she managed weakly. For a curse, it didn't carry much conviction.

"Uh-uh. I never get colds." His voice was a husky, confiding murmur, laughter shimmering somewhere behind it.

"Well, you're going to get this one." And mumps, measles, and bubonic plague, if there were any justice at all in the world! She hadn't felt this way since her first year with Don. It was a rotten discovery, that she could still be so vulnerable to a man's touch. Damn her body, anyway. Did it never learn?

But it was the body that saved her. "Ahh... ahhh—" hands fell to her shoulders and spun her around, aiming her downhill "—choo!" The backlash sent her teetering against his chest.

He was laughing. She could feel it through her shoulder blades, feel it through his fingers as they curled around the tops of her shoulders, supporting her while she ducked her head and rummaged furiously in her bag for tissue. "Lord, Angel, who set you loose on the world? You ought to be home in bed!" His hands tightened suddenly on the last word, then let her go as she shrugged and twisted away.

"Thanks. That's just where I'm going." She started downhill again as if that bed were turned down and waiting for her just around the next bend.

Ty fell into step again. *Depart, desist and drop dead, can't you?*

But he didn't get the silent message. Those rather large and battered dock shoes continued to pace along beside her own marching heels. His arm brushed her shoulder once, and she could feel that blue-gray gaze tickling her right cheek, but she kept her hands jammed in her skirt pockets, her eyes fixed on those big blasted feet padding nearer and nearer to the professor. Blast him. Blast them both. They deserved each other. Probably he had thrown Forrest down the stairs. Next time she would help him.

"Why do you want this job, Alison?"

*I don't. I do not. I want the summer the way I'd planned it, in my own apartment, helping Forrest research for his book on Minot, working on my own dissertation, planning my lectures for next year's classes. The last thing I want is to spend the summer deceiving someone as nice as your mother. No, that's the second to last thing. The absolutely final last thing I want is to spend a summer in your vicinity, Tyler Channing O'Malley. What a name.*

"Hmm?" the owner of the name prodded gently. "Why would a college-educated, obviously intelligent young woman want a dead-end job like this, charming as my mother may be?"

Because Forrest had decided that she could best further his research—and his reputation—by taking that job, and Forrest was the boss, her thesis adviser and department chairman. The man who signed her paycheck. Without his approval, there'd be no dissertation, no graduation and ultimately, no jobs teaching art history for her. "Money," she muttered bitterly. "I want the job for the money." Wasn't that the first principle of lying? Keep it simple? "That's simple enough, surely?"

"Very simple." Ty wasn't smiling, but he wore that alert look that seemed to suggest a grin was waiting in ambush. "You're sure that's the reason—money?"

"Of course!" she snapped, guilt giving her lie an unexpected conviction. Did he suspect something? But how could he?

"All right." The smile spilled over his eyes, reaching the waiting mouth at last, but it was an oddly measuring kind of smile. "In that case, Alison, I'll offer you even more money *not* to take that job. You can work for me instead."

"Err..." Above that smile, his eyes gleamed with wicked amusement, and she shut her mouth again with a snap. Trapped. Neatly and efficiently. He'd opened the gate and she'd toddled inside like a myopic goose. She sneezed, more to fill time than from need, and tried to think. "Doing what?" she shot back at random. But that was a bad choice.

"I don't know. I'll think of something. What are you good at?"

Not at what he was obviously thinking about, that was sure; she'd not been so very good at that. Too shy and inexperienced at the start, and then later, too bitter. Frigid, Don had called her toward the end. But perhaps frozen would have been a better word.

Above her, Ty's eyebrows were drawing together, the eyes sharpening beneath them as another question formed. "Why don't you want me working for your mother, Ty? That's the point of all this, isn't it?" It was the first time she'd said his name aloud. It fit nicely on the tongue—brief, neither too soft nor too hard.

"Yes, that's the point." All the mischief had faded from his eyes, leaving the alertness and that searching look.

"Why?" Flinching away from his gaze, she started downhill again.

He fell into step once more. "Because you're not what my mother needs. And I've worked too hard selling her on this idea of a companion to want you spoiling it now."

So it had been his idea. Somehow she was not surprised. "Why am I so wrong for the job?"

After flicking her a partly friendly, partly puzzled look, he stared at the road. "It's this way, Alison.... My mother has just lost my father. In the same car wreck in which she was injured. I suppose she told you? Well...she lost a best friend as well as a husband. They were as close as any couple I've ever seen." His sigh was so low that perhaps she'd imagined it. "So now she needs someone to care for her. Someone to be there at night in case of...emergencies. Someone who could become a good friend, someone to travel and talk with, someone to grow old with. I was picturing another widow, maybe, a woman with no one of her own."

No one of her own. Alison fought back an ironic little grin. In that case, she was eminently qualified. "Well, so I'm not as old as perhaps you imagined...otherwise I'd say I'm very well qualified for the position. Why won't I do?" Anyone would think she *wanted* this job, from the way she was arguing!

"I told you." Ty glanced back at her impatiently, but slowed his pace. "I want someone permanent."

Permanent. And that was the one thing she would not be. Forrest had promised she could leave as soon as she'd seen the painting, if it proved to be an obvious fake; she could simply make some excuse and quit. She glanced up at him guiltily. But there was no way Ty could guess that, surely no way he could have drawn some connection between Forrest and herself, just because they both came from Brown? It was a large institution, after all, its graduates and employees scattered all along this coast. "What makes you think I wouldn't be permanent?"

"It's very simple. You wouldn't last more than a year or two. Sooner or later someone will marry you, take you away, and that would leave my mother lonely all over again."

A jab in the solar plexus would have left her as winded as that matter-of-fact statement did. It was so far from the truth that it was laughable. "What makes you think that?" she managed finally.

"Don't you ever look in the mirror, Dark Eyes?"

She did. And when she did, above the mad-dog foam of her toothpaste she saw a pair of angry eyes, eyes determined never to depend on another again, never again to leave her happiness resting in someone else's clumsy, careless hands.

Beneath her descending foot, a rock wobbled, then scraped downhill. "Uh!"

As she stumbled forward, Ty caught her arm, then her waist with his other hand. "Take it easy there!"

"Thanks!" Her face averted, she stood stock-still within his hold, trying not to shiver, and cursing herself. *Clumsy, moronic, cretinous…His hands were so large.* With his thumb and forefinger nipping her waist, the other fingers rested against the flat curve of her belly, and for one endless moment, those fingertips seemed to press into her, testing her softness. Then, just as slowly, they withdrew, leaving her hotter and even dizzier than before. Fever… Beneath the trees, the ground was spinning ever so slowly…. Her heart seemed to have slipped, seemed to be beating down there, somewhere near where his fingers had touched her.

"Are you all right?" Just above her elbow, his hand tightened. She could feel the blood throbbing there, as well. "Alison, are you—"

"Yes! I'm…fine, thanks. Just dizzy. Got a fever, I guess." She stared downhill, wide-eyed, focusing on one especially large tree, willing it to stand still. If she could control that one, she could stop the rest.

His other hand closed around her other arm, steadying her, giving her a sudden, sick sense of entrapment. "You're goose bumps all over." Too hot, too large, too gentle, his hands slid slowly up her bare arms and then down again.

"Yes, fever," she repeated absently, leaning forward against those hands, trying to put some space between herself and the radiant heat of his body looming just behind her.

"Damn it, I knew I should have driven you down to the road. Come sit down."

"No." She shook her head, still arching away from him. "I've got to go. Let me go, please, Ty."

"And watch you fall flat on your funny face? No, thank you." His hands tightened, swaying her back against him. Their bodies touched and seemed to fuse together in the dripping heat.

*Lord,* she would melt! A shudder racked her suddenly as his lips brushed the back of her neck, and that brought on a spasm of sneezing. "Ah-choo!"

"Bless you." His hands moved; an arm wrapped around her waist, holding her more securely and trapping her against the hard, warm length of him.

"Ah-shoo!"

"God bless."

"Ahh...ah-choo!" Each sneeze rattled them both as he held her; without those arms to contain her she would have exploded—sneezed herself into a thousand bits of oblivion. "Ah-choo!" Damn it, he was laughing again. She could feel it as she sagged back against his chest at last, gasping for breath, her head thrown back against his shoulder.

"Here!" His hand dipped into her purse, came up with a tissue and waved it under her nose.

"Thank you." She applied it vigorously, trying to ignore his silent laughter, which shook them both, trying to shut out the feel of that hard male body imprinting itself against her back and buttocks. In a minute, when she could stand by herself, she would step on his toes. That should free her.

She drew a shuddering breath, nerving herself for that separation, and felt him inhale, as well. "Angel?" His voice was a husky murmur, still shaky with laughter.

"Mmm?" Why in heaven's name was she answering to that?

"Who brings you chicken soup when you've got a cold? Who takes care of you?"

*Nobody*. Despite the arms around her, that answer filled her with sudden, self-pitying desolation. Well, the rolling stone travels fastest that travels alone. So you give up certain things when you opt for freedom...moss...chicken soup...pain..."I take care of myself!" She squirmed as his arms tightened suddenly.

Something—his lips? his face?—brushed back and forth through her hair. "Not very well, it would seem."

"Everybody—ahhh!...everybody—ah-shoo!— everybody gets colds." She twisted against his arms and felt them ease a little.

"I don't."

"What's your secret, hero? Clean living and orange juice?" That snarl gained her a few more inches of freedom; her back was suddenly cold as the air flowed between them.

"I'm afraid it's been just the opposite these past few years." His voice was cooling, as well, huskiness reverting to politeness.

The opposite of orange juice? Staring down at the muscles in the forearm wrapped around her ribs, Alison puzzled that one for a moment. Oh—the opposite of clean living! Well, yes, there was something very...practiced about the way he held her. A wave of depression washed over her. What was it about her that attracted men like that? "Do you think you could possibly let me go?" she asked tonelessly.

"Do you think you could stand?" The low voice behind her was equally correct. When she nodded, his arms slid away slowly, leaving her shivering and shaky, but upright. "There's a good sitting rock over here. Come along." He touched her elbow.

"No. Really. Thanks." She shook her head, and that set the trees to swinging majestically around her again. "I've got to meet my ride."

"Alison, it's a quarter of a mile down to the main road, and your face is the color of spring asparagus." Wrapping an arm around her shoulders, Ty nudged her off the road. "After we've talked, I'll go back and get the car and drive you down."

Oh, super! Just chauffeur her down to meet Forrest! She shook her head in alarm, but the rock loomed before them; turning her carefully, he lowered her onto its sun-warmed smoothness, then sat beside her.

"Put your head down." His command was reinforced by the hand that closed around the back of her neck.

Hissing with exasperation, she leaned forward and pillowed her forehead on her forearms thrown across her knees. She shut her eyes and immediately felt better.

At the back of her head, Ty's fingers moved slowly, ruffling her hair in the same sort of idle, unthinking caress she'd given his dog earlier. With her eyes shut, she could almost pretend, catlike, that she didn't notice this attention.

"Better?" he asked finally.

"Mmm." Though meant to be noncommittal, it sounded more like a purr.

His fingers worked slowly down her neck, massaging the tightness out of cramped muscles. "Now, about my job offer, Alison... You'll take it?"

"No," she murmured dreamily.

The fingers stopped, and then, after a long moment, moved again. "Why not? I'm offering more money."

"Ah-choo! 'Cause I'd rather work for your mother." She mumbled it against her forearms, half hypnotized by the heavy warmth of his hand on her head.

"Why?"

"No sexual harassment on the job." He'd practically handed her that excuse on a platter, but as she spoke it, she realized it was much more than an excuse; it was the reason. It would be crazy to be near this man. He was as sexually aggressive as Don had ever been, and she was not as immune as she'd thought. It would be too dangerous even to work for his mother.

"That's what you consider this?" he asked slowly, his low voice oddly intent. "Harassment?"

"Ahhh...yes...ahh-choo!"

"I see...." The weight of his hand lifted away. "Sorry. I thought... Sorry."

"Sure." Suddenly Alison was sorry as well, sorry and not sure why. "And, anyway, isn't this all a bit premature?"

"How's that?" Ty's voice came from a distance. He was standing above her now.

"She hasn't offered me the job yet, you know. And she's interviewed a lot of women, I hear."

His feet scuffed the dark earth beside her shoes. "Yes, but something tells me that it's you she'll be hiring." He decapitated a delicate mushroom with one vicious flick of his shoe.

"So tell her not to." That would solve both their problems nicely. Alison started to sit up, then changed her mind.

Above her, Ty laughed shortly. "I can suggest, but I cannot direct, Angel. She's as independent as you are." Reaching down, he lifted a curl and tucked it gently behind her ear. "So all I can do is ask, Alison, and I'm asking. Don't take the job if my mother offers it. If you need money, let me help."

It was hard to resist that kind of direct and open appeal, hard to dislike the man at all. He was doing what he thought was best and had no doubt been doing so when he thwarted Forrest. But she had no intention of accepting his help. She shook her head gently without lifting it. "No...but thanks, Ty."

Above her, he took a deep breath, then let it out slowly—between clenched teeth, by the sound of it. "All right." His toe found another mushroom near her feet and flipped its wig off. "All right. Will you sit still while I go get the car?"

Bracing her hands on her knees, Alison sat up carefully. At the perimeter of her vision the woods slowly dissolved into a red-tinged darkness. The circle narrowed as the darkness advanced, leaving her only a tanned face to look at, a face with eyes like bits of evening sky below ironic black brows. "I can walk."

There was a flash of white as he shook his head. "I'd end up carrying you." He set the back of his fingers against her damp forehead, and his eyebrows jerked slightly. "Not that it wouldn't be a pleasure, but I expect you'd consider it sexual harassment."

"I expect I would." His fingers felt icy cold against her face—lovely. Odd how easy it was to talk with him; she wasn't usually like this with strangers.

The cool, steady hand dropped away. "Okay, Alison. Sit tight and I'll be back in ten minutes. Promise?"

"I promise." It was so much easier to agree than disagree, and she was too tired to fight, anyway.

"Good." His forefinger touched her nose in a gentle, impudent salute and then he was gone.

But he would be back. Ten minutes, he'd said. Alison inspected her watch. Four-twenty. Ten minutes would make it— "Oop...!" In ten minutes Forrest would be waiting for her down below.... And she had promised...

Standing shakily, Alison waited for the trees to stop their slow dance again. Lies and broken promises; what an ugly day this had turned into! But Forrest would never, ever forgive her if she gave his game away. He'd make her pay for it. And what was one broken promise, after all the lies she'd told?

She floated all the way down the hill, her balloon-tight, throbbing head bobbing at treetop level while far below, her feet chose their own weaving path without sound or sensation. Only an occasional sneeze broke the dreamlike silence.

It was only when Alison wandered out from under the trees that time seemed to start up again. The sun in her face burned away green-drifting thoughts and the image of blue-gray, searching eyes. Lord, what time was it?

Four-thirty, with no professor in sight. And Ty would not be far behind her in his car. Alison stared over her shoulder, half-expecting him to burst from the trees like vengeance on wheels. But the woods above her loomed empty and silent.

*Forrest, where are you?* Heat shimmered up from the empty blacktop, turning the air over the road toward Stonington into clear shivering Jell-O. No one could move quickly through such sludge, least of all Forrest, who thought punctuality was for students, waiters and the delivery of his Sunday *New York Times*.

Ears straining, Alison glanced over her shoulder again. Perhaps she should hide? But a faint hum snapped her head around. In the distance, the Volvo swayed round the bend and crept toward her like some slow-motion, heat-stunned white beetle. "Move it, Forrest!" Gesturing frantically, she crossed the road to meet him.

Returning her wave with airy good humor, Forrest advanced at the same majestic glide.

Out on the open roadside she felt like a bug on a tabletop, exposed to all eyes from above. "Come *on*, Forrest!" She was almost dancing her impatience now.

Her head jerked up as, far up the hill, something bright caught her eye. Sunlight winking off chrome?

"Come on, come *on*, can't you?"

Before the car stopped moving, she had its door open. "Get going!"

"Good heavens, what's your hurry, Alison?" The professor inspected her with bemused indulgence. One glass of Chablis had turned into two or three, apparently.

"He's after us! Drive, can't you?" she snapped, shaking his shoulder.

"He? You mean—"

"Yes, your friend, Tyler O'Malley! Now let's—"

"Go!" Tires squealing, the Volvo lurched into motion, as if it had grasped the situation while the professor still gaped. Thrown back against the seat, Alison watched him convert his pedal-to-the-metal takeoff to a dignified but hasty retreat. Then, head low, she peeked over the headrest at the fast-diminishing turnoff.

A long, dark blue hood slid out from beneath the trees and stopped. At this distance, his face was just a golden-brown patch in the dimness of the open car window; the piercing, blue-gray gaze that pursued them was supplied by her memory, not her eyes. There was no way that Ty would have been able to see the top of her head from there, no way for him to be certain that this was the car that had collected her at all. The Volvo swayed around a curve and he was gone—gentle hands, cutting eyes, all gone.

Numbly she turned away and huddled into the corner between seat and door, ignoring Forrest's nonstop questions. It must have been hot inside; his cheeks and nose glistened in the westering light, but her teeth were chattering. A thought floated up above the professor's clucking and her own general misery. "Forrest?"

"I would just like to know what's going on. If you would be so kind as to—"

"Forrest?"

"Oh ho, so you *are* with us, after all! Yes?"

"Did he see your car, the time you met?"

Lips pursed, Forrest scowled at the road ahead of them, his stubby, exquisitely groomed fingers tapping their own nervous tango on the leather-covered steering wheel. "I...suppose he might have," he admitted reluctantly. "I refused to give him the satisfaction of my looking back, but I had the distinct impression that he was still standing on the porch when I gained the car."

"Then my cover has been blown." Relief mixed oddly with—what?—disappointment?—in that conclusion.

"No-oo. Not necessarily. Did he actually see you enter this car?"

"No, I don't think so, but—"

"And how many white Volvos do you suppose there must be in New England? Few, granted, in the exquisite state of preservation that Jessamyn enjoys." He gave the wheel cover a swift, possessive little pat. "But at a distance, a Volvo is a Volvo is a Volvo, Alison. There must be hundreds in this part of the world."

"But your Volvo coupled with our both coming from Brown—"

"Only someone with a guilty conscience would hazard such a connection."

"Why should he have a guilty conscience?"

"Why indeed?" Forrest murmured darkly. "I keep asking myself that. Why won't he show me that painting?"

She could think of half a dozen good reasons, starting with the fact that Forrest could be an insufferable twit with no effort at all. Perhaps he'd gotten Ty's back up, or perhaps... But with her head throbbing in time to Jessamyn's pampered engine, she was too tired to think about it, and it didn't concern her anymore. The whole miserable affair was over. Fini. She hugged herself as her teeth started again.

"Well, by the by, did you get the job?" The casualness of the professor's question in no way concealed the passion that propelled it.

"She hasn't decided. She said she'd let me know in a few days." Alison clenched her teeth over the next words, but they popped out, anyway. "But it doesn't matter. I'm not taking it if she offers, Forrest." She couldn't even tell herself that it was her outraged ethics taking a stand at last; it was something much more selfish and primitive...something closer to fear. She'd become a survivor these past two years and had learned to walk a straight and narrow tightrope of emotions toward her own kind of happiness. Nothing and no one was going to knock her off that high wire. No one...

"Alison..." The warning note quavered in his voice like a plucked guitar string, but she was past caring.

"Forrest, please! I feel so awful. Please let's not argue, please." Shoulders shoved back against the door, she stared at him wide-eyed, willing him not to push her into this corner, not to force it. Once it started, heaven knows where they'd stop. She owed him so much already and needed his goodwill for her future so desperately. *Please don't make me fight*.

But perhaps he had as much at stake as she did. Forrest shot her a doubtful glance, then turned back to the road, and his fingers crept up to soothe his bow tie. "Very well, then...we won't discuss it now." He swiveled the rearview mirror between them an eighth of an inch, then turned to inspect her again. "You are rather pale, my dear. You look quite exhausted."

Coming from Forrest, this was tantamount to apology. Thank goodness, then, no fight. Not today, anyway. Alison gave him a wan smile and wished he'd keep his eyes on the road.

But the professor had not finished placating her yet. He sniffed tentatively. ''That's quite an, ahhh... *arresting* perfume, my dear.'' He inhaled deeply, and his bird's nest eyebrows rose along with his chest. ''Can't think why I didn't notice it earlier. What d'you call it?''

''Milo's delight,'' she mumbled grimly, closing her eyes. Pretending to sleep, she focused on the drone of the Volvo's engine and made her body go limp. The mechanical song faded, rose and faded again, changing gradually to the effortless sigh of the sea breeze. She was standing on an open hilltop now, staring up into endless, blue-gray sky. Drifting slowly down around her, rose petals brushed her cheeks in soft benediction. One touched her lips...

# CHAPTER FOUR

"THAT HAS TO BE some kind of record, Forrest! Twenty-four hours to make it up the stairs!" Swinging her apartment door wide, Alison greeted her visitor with a wary smile. But it was good to see him. After four days of sneezing solitude, even Greeks bearing gifts were welcome.

The professor's face was almost blank as he paused in her doorway, small paper bag held carefully away from his pale linen trousers. "I beg your pardon?"

"Wasn't that you yesterday? I looked out my window just in time to see you—I thought it was you—coming up the front steps." She waved a hand at the pride of her apartment, the giant Palladian window that, seen from the outside, surmounted the front door of a once-graceful Benefit Street mansion now chopped into a dozen student apartments. Seen from the inside, the window started at her living room floor and completed its arch just inches below the twelve-foot ceiling. And that *had* been Forrest she'd spotted through its panes yesterday morning. "I hurried off to put on a pot of tea, and then I waited, and the water boiled..." Finally she had checked the stairs to see if he'd dropped along the wayside, but no Forrest. At least his apparition had motivated her to get dressed and go down to check her mailbox for the first time in three days, and she'd been on the mend ever since.

"Well, actually—" Forrest cleared his throat carefully "—that was no doppelganger, that was I." Handing her the white bag with a little bow, he deposited himself on her couch.

"Oh?" The professor never did anything without reason, such as visiting her twice when once would have done.

"Yes, I...it suddenly occurred to me that there was a matter necessitating my most urgent attention, and so I tiptoed away again, hoping not to disturb you."

"Oh." Obviously that was all he was going to tell her. Alison glanced down at the bag in her hand, changing the subject, then smiled as she guessed. "It isn't—oh, it is!" She inspected the pair of croissants nestled in baker's tissue, her delight beginning to fade as her stomach awoke to the possibilities. "How nice of you, Forrest! I'll just start some tea to go with these."

In her closet-sized kitchen, she filled the kettle and stood scowling absently down at the gas flames as it heated. Forrest knew her weaknesses, all right; so there had been no change of heart on his part. He was just buttering her up, making it harder for her to say no in their forthcoming battle. Damn him!

He was up and browsing through the books on her desk by the window when she returned with the tea. Replacing her much-thumbed Janson, he pulled out the small volume next to it and she bit back a sigh. He didn't read French. It was how they'd first met, back in her undergraduate days, when he was still teaching at Boston University. Forrest had wanted a translation of a magazine, and the placement office had found her for him.... Funny the way your life turned on little events. But for that, she'd have probably become a high-school French teacher. He'd coaxed her into his survey class on modern painting and she'd been hooked.

"Here you go." She set his tea on the desk beside him. It was the same brand Forrest had served that first time he'd called her into his office to discuss a paper she'd written. Something on neoclassic draftsmen, Ingres mostly. She had gone in almost shaking, expecting criticism, perhaps outright rejection, the sort of reception her father gave her ideas at home. Forrest's exuberant praise had been like an unsuspected door swinging wide in a dark room, sunlight beyond lighting the way out. By heaven, there was something she *could* do, something she was good at, after all! She had never looked back. And she'd been drinking English Breakfast Tea since that day.

Forrest's lips moved, silently shaping the uncooperative syllables. He could get one word in three perhaps, and the letter he was looking for was eight pages farther on, but why tell him? Alison tore a wing tip off one of the croissants and wandered glumly back to the kitchen to start the window fan, the flakes of pastry melting on her tongue. They'd all melt today. Another scorcher. It would be cooler up at Shady Breeze....

"Aha, here 'tis!" The professor presented her with the open book—the opening salvo in his argument.

"I've got the translation typed out here someplace." She'd made it months ago. Forrest would be needing it for his chapter on Minot's lost paintings.

"No, that's all right, my dear. Just go ahead and read it to me." Forrest settled on the couch again and began nibbling his croissant, his small bright eyes on her face.

This was hardly necessary. They both knew the letter nearly word for word. She stared down at the open page and licked her top lip. *"Mais pour Renoir, je l'aurais tuée, Paul..."*

"'But for Renoir, I would have killed her, Paul, I swear it. We'd gone out, Renoir, his little shadow, Gilbert, and I, to compare the cafés of Paris with those of Marseilles. Returned at sunrise to find my bitch, Marie, had made a bonfire of the work I'd brought back, my marvelous *Alicia* paintings.'"

"Why couldn't he just have said 'all'?" Forrest groaned. "*All* my *Alicia* paintings? Then I could sleep at night!" He bounced to his feet again and started pacing, but three strides brought him to the front door and he swung back, pointing the croissant at her accusingly. "And even if he does mean she torched his entire summer's oeuvre, how badly was it burned? To ashes? To charcoal? All of it? Or could perhaps *one* of the paintings have escaped with a scorching, perhaps just a bit of smoke damage?"

"He says bonfire, Forrest," she reminded him gently, "and I imagine oil paint burns very nicely, once you get it going."

"How could the bitch do it? Burn the nine most significant paintings in all of France? How?" He was bobbing away down the room again, addressing this tirade to the ceiling.

And yet that question she could have answered from firsthand experience; she knew exactly how Marie had felt—that first breath-stopping incredulity growing slowly, inexorably, minute by heartbreaking minute to unshakeable conviction. Besides, deep down inside, she'd probably known it all along. Then that cold, still conviction poised in her mind for perhaps minutes, perhaps days or months, at last suddenly flowering—erupting—exploding into red rage. No, Marie would not have needed a match to light those paintings of the beautiful stranger. One look must have done the trick nicely.

"Go on."

"Huh?" Forrest was standing before her, utterly unscathed by the hellfire that moments before had been writhing up from her carpet.

"Proceed with the translation, Alison."

"Oh...right... 'My marvelous *Alicia* paintings. My God, Paul, I've had enough! First Alicia betrays me and now my wife. I'm done with painting, done with women! A pox on them all! I'm off to find a world blessed with neither. Perhaps Australia...'"

Forrest was off and pacing again. "So off Minot huffs to Australia on a German grain ship, and for all anyone knows, doesn't set hand to paintbrush for the next twelve years!" He whirled to glare at her again.

But she was taking no blame for that, and anyhow, he *had* kept his pencils. Alison collected her teacup. Minot's drawings from that period almost made up for the lack of paintings, to her mind. Her dissertation was based on his sketch books, those delicate, incredible delineations of life aboard a nineteenth-century wind-driven grain ship—the ports, the storms, the sunsets and the dawns, the ship herself and all her crew from the captain down to the rat terrier who ruled below decks.

"And by the time our prodigal returned to Paris, the Impressionist movement was in full cry." Forrest was into his lecturing rhythm now; she'd first heard these very words in his course on French painting, 1850-1920. "When Minot painted in that style, he was considered just one more Johnny-come-lately, just one more painter to jump on the Impressionist bandwagon, when in reality it was Minot who'd built the bandwagon! Minot who'd dreamed it, built it and shoved it thundering down the hill when he painted those nine revolutionary paintings of the exquisite Alicia, twelve years before in Marseilles!" He stopped and, turning toward her, drew himself up almost on tiptoe. "The paintings," he snarled in a savagely precise stage whisper, "that Renoir and the student Gilbert had seen, the afternoon of the day they were destroyed!" With that indictment, he lowered his chin slowly over his bow tie, breaking eye contact with his audience.

It took an effort not to applaud. This was where he always ended this particular lecture, Alison recalled, and come to think of it, this was her cue. She shouldn't take it, but Forrest was waiting and would be all the crabbier if she didn't play her part. "So all you need is the proof," she prompted over her teacup, her eyes gently mocking.

"Yes, the proof," Forrest agreed heavily, rousing from his trance. "The proof we all believed had gone up in smoke, until thirty-five years ago, when Drew Harrison made his world-shaking announcement in *ARTnews*." Sitting down beside her, he picked up his cup. They sipped companionably, both of them considering that letter....

It had happened before her time, but Alison had caught something of the uproar from reading art magazines of the period. Harrison's bomb had not shaken the world; by 1947 it would have taken a bit more than one rediscovered Impressionist painting to impress the poor old world! But that tiny, intense and far-flung community of the art historian, the curator, the artist and the collector had indeed been rocked by his news—that Professor Drew Harrison of Columbia University had discovered a brand from the burning, one of Minot's lost *Alicia* paintings, a painting that Harrison called by the odd name *Alicia, After*, and that would rewrite the history of art, vindicating Minot, and at last raising him to his rightful place as the father of Impressionism.

Then, just as the art world's first stunned astonishment was overwhelmed by the rising clamor for his proof, instead of producing it... "You know..." Alison hesitated, but decided to say it, anyway. "I've often wondered if that was an accident.... Harrison's position at Columbia was on the line before he wrote that letter. He had such an incentive to make a stupendous discovery. It's almost too good to be true, don't you think?" Whatever Forrest thought, he wasn't saying. Perhaps he wasn't even listening as he disposed of his pastry, then eyed the rest of hers on its plate on the side table. "Perhaps he made it all up out of whole cloth, perhaps someone *did* show him a painting, as he claimed.... It might have been a fake Minot, or could have been some perfectly honest and perfectly awful unsigned piece by some amateur, but Harrison had to have a miracle to save his job just then, so...Isn't that probably just what he saw?" Alison had Forrest's attention now and wasn't quite sure she wanted it, but she slogged on in spite of those slowly bristling eyebrows. "So...then...a few days later Harrison comes to his senses...realizes he has no proof for such an outrageous claim... and yet he can't back dow—"

"You think Drew Harrison killed himself?"

"Well...I...know he was your friend and faculty adviser... but isn't it just pos—"

"Impossible, my dear! Slanderously, preposterously impossible!" Forrest shook his head majestically. "He'd have *never* chosen a beer truck! Drew loathed the stuff. Never touched anything but Scotch. And never before ten-thirty."

"Yes, but—"

But Forrest's displeasure was fading to gentle nostalgia. "Never before ten-thirty. His morning lectures were legend..."

Oh well, she'd tried. "And his afternoon lectures?"

"Legend of quite another sort," Forrest admitted ruefully. "I fear the chancellors had looked the other way quite as long as they dared. Poor Drew's days were certainly numbered."

Indeed, they certainly had been. "And what time of day was the accident?"

"Ahh...I was just leaving my 2:10 class when I heard," Forrest mused, stroking his tie. "The bell on the clock tower was still tolling." He sighed gently.

So Professor Harrison had devoted perhaps four hours to his beloved tipple by that afternoon, when, no doubt floating on clouds of glory, redemption and

Scotch fumes, he'd tried to cross Madison Avenue without consulting the traffic lights.... And he'd taken his secret with him, for no one had come forward after his death to produce the fabulous painting.

Thirty-five years later, only a handful of experts within the field remembered a painting called *Alicia, After*, and most of those dismissed it as myth, the delirium tremens of a failing academic. If most old soaks see snakes on the wall, was it so strange, after all, that an art historian on the sauce should see paintings?

Forrest alone had kept faith, and kept searching.

They both jumped at the knock at her door.

Carey from down the hall would still be at class...so who, then? "Just a moment, please," Alison called out, rising. She hadn't liked this kind of surprise for the past two years. "Who is it, please?"

"Miss Eriksen?" A young man's voice came through the door. "I have a package for you."

"Oh..." A glance over her shoulder assured her that Forrest was still there. Not that he'd be much help in an emergency, she reflected wryly, unlocking the door.

True to his word, the smiling redhead in the hallway held a package. Her answering smile died as she saw it. Oh Lord, not again! That long white box could only hold one thing. How had Don gotten her address this time? The registrar, the art department, everyone had instructions not to give it out. With no phone, there was no address in the phone book to give her away....

"It's flowers, miss," he told her, his grin fading slowly at her lack of response.

"Yes...thank you." She took the box automatically as he held it out to her. It was heavier at one end.

"Its...not quite the usual order, miss," he told her, groping instinctively for some form of reassurance as he studied her face. "I had to go out special to get part of it." He smiled again uncertainly.

Oh, no, something special. The day the divorce went through it had been roses, one dozen dying roses, shriveled and stinking from the black spray paint with which they'd been coated. "Well. Thank you. Thank you very much." She shut the door gently on his worried face.

"Flowers, how nice," Forrest observed as she set the package down on the desk and stood gazing at it. "I debated bringing you some myself, but I concluded the croissants would be of more use."

And cheaper, of course. Silly to get so upset. He meant nothing to her anymore. But why couldn't Don just go his merry way and let her go hers?

*Just treat it as a joke, whatever it is.*

The lid lifted off in her hands to reveal a sheath of roses. Not black or red, but pink and radiantly alive. Not Don...then who? Beneath her tentative fingertips, the petals were soft and flushed as a baby's cheek, and suddenly her palms tingled, remembering: that velvet impact of falling petals. The tingling spread slowly up her arms toward her shoulders. *Oh, please, no. Not him.*

At one end of the box, a tissue-wrapped cylinder waited, garnished with pink ribbon. Postponing all thought, Alison concentrated on unwrapping it. White tissue gave way to a familiar white-and-red label. Campbell's chicken soup. *Who takes care of you, Angel?*

The tingling had reached her spine, and wave after invisible wave washed across her shoulders, her hips and down the backs of her thighs—every place his body had touched hers. Damn! She smacked the can down on the desk and jumped at the noise it made.

"Good heavens, how curious!" Beside her, Forrest picked it up again. She could feel his eyes on her face.

"Yes, isn't it!" She plucked—almost snatched—the can from his fingers, scooped up the box of flowers as well and started for the kitchen. "It's just a joke!" On her, damn it!

The trash was the logical place for the soup. She held it above the basket for a long moment. *This is ridiculous. You're taking this too seriously. Undone by a can of soup. That fever did fry your brains!* Fever— that brought back another shimmering wave of associations, damp skin sticking to skin, her dizziness, the green heat under the trees: everything she'd locked out of her mind these past four days.

"Alison?"

"Just a moment, Forrest." It hadn't been that significant, that intimate. It was just her fever that had made her feel so open and raw. She'd been too ill to keep her walls up. But she'd done nothing, shown nothing that she need regret now. It had all happened inside her head.

"Alison?"

"Coming, Forrest." Panicked by a can of soup! Turning, she set the can on the pantry shelf with angry deliberation. But she couldn't just shelve the roses; they would dry out in no time. Sighing, she filled a ceramic pitcher with water, found her scissors and turned back with the lot to the living room.

As she entered the room, Forrest glanced up from her camera. Normally it lived in the bookcase; right now it dangled by its strap from his short neck. He looked down at it again; her determined casualness was wasted on him. Relaxing a little, Alison sat down cross-legged on the rug.

"Thank heavens you have a decent camera," Forrest murmured, twiddling the focus. "The first thing I'll want is some photographs."

Clenching her teeth, Alison selected a rose and clipped a diagonal two inches off its stem. The scissors made a satisfying snick. How to say it? "Forrest..." She chose a bud and frowned down at it, as if it might unfold while she waited. "Mrs. O'Malley hasn't hired me yet, you know." And with each passing day that no letter came, her hopes rose a little higher. But then, it wasn't enough for Harriet to decide against her. She must write and tell her so, give her some proof to show Forrest, to get him off her back.

"Well...as a matter of fact..." Something in his voice brought her eyes up. His intense gaze skittered away from her face and flicked across the room, then down to her camera again.

"Yes?"

"Ahh..." Lifting the camera, he squinted at her through its viewfinder and turned the focusing ring. "I was...just...wondering how you feel today?"

Beneath the mask of the camera, his smile seemed altogether too jovial. Alison studied him in silence for a moment. "Not bad, aside from a chapped nose. I'm a bit tired..." Or exhausted, rather, at this point. She should have told Forrest the moment he'd walked through the door that she wouldn't continue with his farce. Now she was too tired to pick the fight. "You know..." She pruned the lower leaves off a fourth rose. "You never have told me the details...how you traced the painting to the O'Malleys."

Mercifully, Forrest was disposed to talk—he almost seemed to welcome her diversion. Eyes on her developing arrangement, Alison listened as he paced and filled the gaps of the story.

That he'd been on to something big—perhaps enormous—she'd guessed for the past year from his gleeful hints. But it had been *his* secret—no, his quest and Forrest had told her no more than she needed to know to help him. He had simply put her to work this spring combing Stonington's local newspaper, the *Westerly Sun*, for any and all references to the O'Malleys or to Shady Breeze. And diligent researcher that she was, it was she who had found the gossip-column item concerning Harriet's return to Shady Breeze from a nursing home three weeks ago. And she had been the unsuspecting idiot who had shown Forrest the ad soliciting applicants for the position of companion, just last week.

Now, hearing the complete thirty-six-year saga, she found it was impossible not to admire the sheer, monomaniacal persistence that had kept him on the trail. And impossible not to fear it a little...

"And so Professor Harrison's sister had his appointment diary all along?"

"Yes, may they baste her in Hades for evermore, the old biddy! It was packed away in a trunk with the rest of his papers, up in her attic. Her niece found it for me in two days. Two days!" He stopped and shook his head, appalled. "After Gertrude Harrison had insisted for thirty-five years that it wasn't to be found, that it must have been lost at the scene of the accident!" He shook his head again. "I'll never know if it was senility or sheer spitefulness!"

Alison hid her grin in a rose as the professor stalked past. There was another explanation. Perhaps Forrest had gone too far in his wooing. Begonias each Christmas, chocolates on Valentine's Day and her birthday—perhaps the old girl had been shrewd enough to know it would all end once Forrest got the diary. Or perhaps it had been a game of sorts. Anyhow, she'd provided for him at the last. Her will left him the trunk that contained the diary, and the centerpiece of her parlor up in Camden—the head of a moose shot by Drew Harrison back in '37. Alison grinned again and quickly bent over the pitcher as the professor turned.

But even then, with the long-sought diary in hand, Forrest found himself stymied once more. "'Eliza Channing's daughter, bringing a painting for my evaluation!' That *had* to be the fatal entry, my dear. The date worked—roughly a week before Harrison's letter to *ARTnews*, and the name—my God, you could have flattened me with a feather—Eliza Channing's daughter!"

Eliza Channing—Philadelphia blue blood to the umpteenth generation, with a father in railways and a husband in international banking, a world-renowned collector of Impressionist paintings, and rarer still, a knowledgeable collector, an authority in her own right. She would have to be eighty if she was a day now. Her son, Howard Channing, the elegantly autocratic director of the Washington Art Institute had to be in his fifties, and her daughter had—

"Oh, no, Forrest, Eliza Channing's daughter died years ago!"

"Exactly what I thought, my dear."

Thought? But there was no doubt about it. Glenda Channing, president of the Channing Foundation for the Visual Arts, had died of a heart attack some six or seven years ago; there was not a curator of a major museum in the country who hadn't breathed a sigh of relief at her passing. She had been one tyrannical Lady Bountiful indeed.

"*Glenda* Channing died eight years ago," Forrest agreed triumphantly. "It took me another six months of digging to find that there was a second daughter, the youngest, who disappeared from the face of the earth, as it were, in the early forties. A girl named Harriet..."

Tyler Channing O'Malley, of course! The pieces came together with an almost audible click in her brain. Harriet with her long, delicate bones and that unconscious confidence, that graciousness, which came from years of money—generation upon generation of it. Frowning, Alison nuzzled the blossom she'd been holding—and blinked down at it in sudden delight as she realized she could actually smell for the first time in four days. But...lovely as Shady Breeze might be, it was no mansion. Where were the body guards, the butlers, the mastiffs that went with that kind of fortune? Where were the walls to keep the riffraff away?

"You know the rest of it. I spoke with Mrs. O'Malley by phone before Christmas. She was delightful and utterly adamant. The painting was part of a private collection; she did not care to show it. I ascribed this attitude to holiday vexations, gave her three weeks, and called again. This time I reached her son. He was less delightful and said basically the same thing—cut me short when I tried to explain the significance of the situation. He also failed to inform me that Mrs. O'Malley was, by that time, in the hospital with injuries suffered in the same accident that killed her husband.''

Busy with end-of-semester exams, Forrest had waited another month, then had tried a frontal assault, still confident that, because he was on such a holy mission, no one could refuse him face-to-face; he had merely to explain sufficiently and all doors would surely swing wide.

June Hurley had apparently opened the door to him; the family was not at home. And the opportunity had proved irresistible. Forrest had somehow lied his way inside and had been following her up the stairs to the second floor to view—at long last—the painting, when Tyler O'Malley had walked in....

''And?''

''And?'' Forrest looked down at her haughtily, but his complexion seemed a shade redder. Turning, he paced majestically to her window and stood there inspecting the street, his fingers laced behind him.

Her expectant silence seemed to irk the professor. He rose on tiptoes and bounced a few times impatiently. She waited. His ears were positively crimson now.

''And he showed me the door! Wouldn't hear a word of explanation! The man's a barbarian! It utterly astounds me how quickly good blood can be diluted.'' He bounced again twice and glared down at the street.

End of story, obviously. Alison let her breath out slowly. Oh well.

Forrest whirled and pointed a finger at her. "You'll have to be careful, Alison. O'Malley could be the one spanner in the works if you don't watch out for him.''

"Forrest..." She shouldn't say it just now, but she'd never liked fingers shaken in her face. Alison selected a rose deliberately and looked up past his hand. "Mrs. O'Malley has not offered me the job...and if she does, I will not accept it."

"On the contrary, my dear." Forrest returned her tight smile, his voice equally soft. "You accepted yesterday."

"Wha—ouch!" A thorn bit deep as her hand closed to a fist. The rose flipped upward between them, seeming to leap for safety. "Forrest!" Wounded thumb in mouth she stared up at him, horrified. "You..." Words failed her.

"The letter came yesterday." He was teetering above her on tiptoe, hands clasped behind his back, his expression half triumphant and half nervous. "I thought it merited an immediate response."

"I...you..."

"Alison." Forrest sat on the sofa beside her and leaned down intently. "Before you say anything, I want you to think..."

She was. Oh, she was! His letter would reach Shady Breeze that day. How quickly would Harriet dismiss the rest of the applicants? Quickly. Telegram her regretful change of heart, then? But then she had no address, Alison realized despairingly. She was too tired for this...

"Alison, now just think a moment," Forrest repeated persuasively. "I am a professor of art, a Ph.D., doctor of philosophy."

Yes, she had that.

"Now..." Forrest plucked the offending rose from the carpet near his shoes and sniffed it thoughtfully. "One of the functions—the most sacred duties of a scholar is to ensure the continuity of knowledge. He does this by choosing and grooming his successors, those who will carry on the torch of education once he relinquishes it.

"Those successors must be worthy, Alison." With a sudden twist, Forrest snapped the neck of the rose. Tossing the stem by her feet, he fixed the blossom in his buttonhole. "Now..."

Her head ached abominably, and she knew what was coming.

"What am I to think of a young woman...a doctoral candidate under my direct supervision...who has access to knowledge and yet will not avail herself of it? How am I to take such a student seriously? How could I, in all conscience, accept her dissertation based on incomplete knowledge? For, genuine or fake, like it or not, my dear, the O'Malleys' painting must affect the conclusions of your dissertation as surely as it affects the conclusions of my book!" As always, he ended the lecture on a dramatic peak, finishing it with a mournful whisper. "So we are *both* trapped!"

This blackmail had been implicit between them all along, but somehow they should have avoided making it obvious. It sounded so ugly in plain English.

Alison hid her face in the roses, her eyes suddenly stinging. He'd been such a good friend, in his own way, these past few years. He'd taken her in as a teaching assistant without question when she came scrambling from the ruins of her marriage. He'd coached her and bullied her when she was too shy to lecture in her first sections...

"And besides, Alison," Forrest added plaintively, "I've been searching for this painting my whole life long!"

The peevish tone spoiled the effect of his previous grandiloquent threats, and shaking her head, she hooted softly into the roses. Lord, her head ached! It was so hot. It would be cooler up at—she sat up suddenly, tears glittering on her cheeks. "I *can't*, Forrest!"

His eyebrows jerked reproachfully but his eyes were steadfast. "You can," he said reasonably. "For my— for the sake of truth."

For his sake, he had almost said. Alison nearly smiled as she wiped the tears away. She picked up a rose absently. For his sake... Yes, it was better to think of it in those terms; to convince herself that she would be doing this out of loyalty to Forrest, not selfishly for her own sake, not to save the dissertation that had been the sole focus of her life for the past two years... Yanking the excess leaves off the rose, she jammed it into the pitcher.

And what would her father say if she were to quit now, with her dissertation half finished? Alison paused, frowning, before shoving the last few roses into the water. Not much; he never said much, anyway. But it would be no more than he expected.

Putting aside her own scholastic survival, you could almost—almost—balance Harriet's desire for privacy with Forrest's ambition and lust for the truth. Was there perhaps some way for a tactful person to reconcile the two? Paintings could be exhibited, could be reproduced in books without naming the owner, after all.

She shifted a final rosebud, then leaned back on her hands, sagging tiredly. There. Couldn't be better with those clear pinks almost singing against the blue-gray glaze of the pitcher, a blue-gray almost the same color as his—stop! If she went to Shady Breeze, how was a tactful person to balance her own desperate needs for peace and detachment with the ambitions and desires—whatever exactly they might be—of one Tyler O'Malley? There was no balance, no possible compromise there that she could see. *So you say no! Leave me alone. What's so hard about that?* She had been sick, and unprepared, the last time. Next time she would be neither. Alison sighed softly. *So be it.*

Squaring her shoulders, she looked up and met Forrest's anxious eyes. "So when do I go?"

## CHAPTER FIVE

NO ONE MET ALISON'S TRAIN. It was picking up speed now, its first tentative clunk-clunk, clunk-clunks coming faster as she stared after it forlornly. The last car flicked by her, taking its shadow with it, leaving her almost flinching in the sudden assault of sunlight and color.

The main street of Mystic, the stop closest to Stonington, sprawled before her like a stage set, the river and the business district off to her left, the white and barn-red clapboards of historic houses ahead of her, following the course of the river inland. To the right, cars were parked across the street, busy with late-afternoon traffic. One of the parked cars, a BMW, gleamed dark blue. A flash of red-gold moved in the rear window.

Brown eyes swung her way and, even at this distance, Alison thought she could see his tail waving. Milo. She found herself smiling as she lifted both cases and teetered toward the car.

But there was a second occupant, Alison realized as she dropped her bags by the trunk. The driver's seat was tilted backward, and the long, solid body stretched out in the seat, right arm thrown across the eyes, was all too recognizable. Darn. She'd hoped against hope that June Hurley would be the welcoming party.

Ty was fast asleep, Alison decided, leaning in the passenger window; the buttons on his crisp blue work shirt rose and fell in slow, steady rhythm. She ducked as Milo aimed a kiss at her mouth; he caught her ear instead. She fended him off, laughing silently, but incredibly Ty was still sleeping.

Even when he slept, his lips held that faint curl she'd remembered, as if he knew a secret. A nice one. He looked so harmless that she almost hated to wake him. His thick brown hair was a shade lighter than she'd pictured and a bit straighter, but then, it had been damp last time. "Ty," Alison called gently.

His wide chest rose in a deep, jerky inhalation. He seemed to hold it forever, then let it out in a long peaceable sigh. His smile deepened a trifle.

"Ty," she tried again.

He snorted and rolled away from her, arm still shielding his eyes.

Marvelous. Releasing Milo, she came around the front of the car and stared doubtfully down at him. "Tyler?"

Gingerly Alison reached out to touch the open palm of his right hand.

But she'd forgotten his speed. The hand closed like a trap, catching her fingers. "Ty!" His arm dropped away, taking her with it, drawing the back of her hand slowly down across his cheek, its roughness sending an almost electric shock jolting up her arm. Wide-open eyes looked right through her. Softer than his cheek, much hotter, his lips moved slowly, hungrily across her knuckles. "Ty!"

He froze, mouth open in midkiss against her skin, and was suddenly awake, his eyes changing from soft focus to knife sharp between one blink and the next. Ty stared up at her face, then down to the captive hand pressed against his mouth, and his eyebrows slanted suddenly. Calmly completing the kiss, he released her. "Sor—" He coughed, swallowed convulsively and tried again. "Sorry," he said hoarsely. "Dreaming."

"My God! What happened to *you*?"

His grin was the same, anyway. "*You*, Ang—" The second word ended in another fit of coughing. He shrugged helplessly, then got out of the car. "Bags?" he rasped.

He put them in the trunk, slanting her a look of mock horror as he hefted the suitcase that held her books and dissertation notes. Once he was in full sunlight, she could see the fever flush on his cheekbones. "Good Lord, Ty, you ought to be in bed!"

He shot her another amused look and jerked his chin at the car.

They were both silent on the way out of town and, with time to think, her shyness reasserted itself. What in heaven's name had he been dreaming about, back there?

"Why didn't—" He shook his head angrily and swallowed, "Why—"

"Try whispering," she advised him, remembering one of her own tactics for a sore throat.

"Really?" he whispered skeptically, but his look of delight as the word came out clearly was almost comical. "Hey!" His side glance had a suddenly renewed purpose that warned her she might better have left him mute.

"This is Stonington?" she asked quickly. Ahead of them the salt marshes and inlets on the right were giving way to civilization. A small peninsula, seemingly ready to sink at any moment under the weight of the close-packed town that filled it, jutted out into the blue. At this distance it was a picturesque jumble of clapboard and brick, its chimneys and tall trees dark against the sky beyond, white boats bobbing at moorings close along shore.

"Yes," Ty whispered.

"Then Shady Breeze must be somewhere off there." She nodded toward the higher ground beyond the town to the left.

"Yes." Pulling smoothly off the road, he stopped the car, and silence washed in through the windows. A sea gull yelped suddenly, then another. Milo left the roadside window to thrust head and shoulders out toward the water, sniffing lustily, his tail approving.

She shouldn't look at Ty. That was what he was waiting for; she could feel that as clearly as she could feel his eyes touching her cheek. On the other hand, he was driving her nowhere until she did. Sighing, she turned.

"That's better," Ty whispered. He'd half turned and settled back against his door, obviously prepared to wait her out. He looked very tired and very alert. Dark mirrors to the water at her back, his eyes traveled slowly across her face, feature by feature, as if he were taking inventory. That lurking smile seemed to creep a little closer as their eyes met. "You haven't changed,'' he decided, ''except for the Day-Glo nose...''

''It's *your* turn for that now.''

He nodded ruefully. ''Well, that's just another thing on your account. Why didn't you wait for me?''

''Ahh...I...'' It was so hard to think, pinned in that level gaze. ''I...was afraid I'd miss my ride. I thought I'd better go on...''

''Who picked you up?''

''A...friend...''

''In a white Volvo?'' Soft as the questions were, they had an edge to them.

''I...don't know car types very well,'' she evaded feebly. ''It was white...'' How much had he actually seen, how much simply guessed?

''You're a history major at Brown, grad student, aren't you?''

The change of subject made her blink. ''I was...'' Blast Forrest and his lies, anyhow!

''What was your specialty? What period and where?''

Oh, Lord, she'd never even thought of that! Never thought much about history at all. Ty's smile was coming slowly out of hiding as he watched her face. ''Civil War!'' she threw out.

His smile widened a notch. ''Which?''

''Which what?''

''Which civil war, Angel? Most countries have one or more of those in the closet.''

''American,'' she pronounced icily. ''And the name is Alison.''

Ty neither agreed nor disagreed. He studied her silently, smile slowly fading back to its hiding place.

"Get the flowers?" he asked finally.

"Yes." But by now she was in no mood to thank him.

He waited patiently.

"Thanks," she muttered, defeated at last.

Milo leaned between them just then to nudge her shoulder. Catching his collar, Ty hauled him off, then distracted him with an ear tickle. "Was funny," he mused, smiling down at the panting dog, "getting your address..."

But hadn't he simply taken it off the résumé?

"Called the History Department at Brown, asking for it.... Secretary had never heard of you..."

She smiled blankly, reddening under that ironic gaze. "Ahh..." It was no good. She was trapped. What would Ty say if she simply admitted everything? What would Forrest say? But that she knew—only too well. "It's—" Her voice came out in a squeak and she stopped, suddenly furious. Trapped!

Milo groaned and twisted his head up at a ridiculous angle, leaning into that knowing touch and releasing her from that speculative stare as Ty looked down at him.

The answer came to her. A humiliating answer, but all the more plausible for that. "I...I told you...I decided not to complete the program, Ty. I guess I...sort of dropped out of sight toward the end there."

"You?" Those hawk eyes flicked up again. "You—cutting classes? I find that hard to believe."

"So try a little harder!" It was bad enough to have to lie, but worse yet not to be believed!

Ty's laughing response turned into another hacking cough.

Good, let it hurt him! "Why don't you believe that?"

"Not—" He stopped, fighting for air and weakly fending off a solicitous Milo. She caught the dog and pulled him away. "You're not the type."

"What type is that?" She frowned, tugging the retriever's ear absently. Moaning his satisfaction, Milo almost collapsed into her hand.

But Ty shook his head. "'Nother time. I'm losing it." He swallowed painfully.

"Okay," she agreed, more than willing to drop the subject. "Isn't your mother expecting us by now?"

The sudden slant of his eyebrows suggested she not press her advantage too far, but Ty nodded agreement. "Last question."

"Mmm?" Refusing to look up, she rubbed Milo's hair backward, making it stand up in a cowlick atop his silky head.

"Know a man named Forrest Osgood?"

Her hand froze. Oh, murder; he knew! Did he? He must.

All Milo knew was that she'd stopped. Turning, he kissed her nose.

"Yuk!" She shoved him away, laughing, grateful for the distraction and thinking furiously. "Forrest Osgood? The head of the Art Department at Brown? Why, everybody knows him! Why?" She met his eyes with a confidence she didn't feel, but Ty didn't return her smile. Had she spoken too quickly?

"Just wondered," he answered belatedly. "Met him recently..." He turned back to the steering wheel, brows pulling together in the faintest of frowns. After a moment he started the car.

Ty didn't speak again until they'd parked in what must have once been a small stable at the back of Shady Breeze. "Bricks?" he suggested, heaving her larger bag out of the trunk.

"Books... I figured I'd have time to read." But would she dare to unpack them now, with Ty sniffing after her connection to Forrest? Well, with any luck, she wouldn't be here long enough for that to prove a nuisance.

The back hillside was as lovely as she'd remembered. Each terrace was formed by a wall of native granite, its gray stones stippled with moss and draped with ivy and roses from the flower bed above. Trailing up the stone steps behind Ty's long strides, Alison recognized pansies, marigolds, violets and phlox. "This is heaven!" she exulted, catching up with Ty just below the steps to the deck.

"So you'll feel at home," he concluded, deadpan. "Welcome to Shady Breeze." Gravely he held out a rose.

It was a young one, just opening to its glory, looking almost absurdly fragile between his fingers. "Thank you." Alison accepted it casually, trying to pretend that the giving had been as casual. She slipped it into the top buttonhole of her blouse, then regretted that impulse as Ty watched in open fascination.

He glanced up, eyes glinting wickedly, and she could feel her cheeks deepening to match the rose. Damn!

"Angel?" he whispered above her.

She sniffed aloud, telling him just what she thought of that name, but Ty pushed on painfully. "Aside from...Grant, who was your favorite general...on the Northern side?"

Side? Her eyes widened suddenly, throwing the rose out of focus. In the Civil War, did he mean? Oh, Lord...besides Grant? Who else was there?

"Mmm?" A warm finger hooked under her chin, tilting her head up to meet his laughing eyes.

Damn him! Here she'd been worrying about fending off a pass, when all the time he'd been setting her up for this question!

General...Lee—no, wrong side. J. E. B. Stuart—the same. Patton, MacArthur—wrong war, even wrong century, idiot! If he'd just stop grinning like that!

"Well?" he taunted. His finger smoothed down her throat an inch or so, then feathered up again.

If she gave up now, would he drive her back to the train station? But then, she might as well stay on the train. She'd get no welcome back in Providence. And the thought of Boston beyond stiffened her backbone. Suddenly she had it.

"Stonewall!"

The teasing finger dropped away. "Who?" He looked genuinely puzzled.

"Stonewall Jackson," she repeated, trying to hide her triumph. "I always had a weakness for him." Or his name, anyway. Perhaps the granite back there had reminded her. But what would save her the next time?

Ty was coughing again, his shoulders shaking with the effort to contain it, and when at last he could stand straight, he seemed satisfied.

He took her around to the front door, where the pines above the porch were nodding to the wind off the ocean. *Shady Breeze*—of course! At the top of the steps she turned automatically to the sea and filled her lungs slowly. It was like inhaling sunlight.

"Alison?" Harriet's clear voice came from around
the corner to the south. Leaving the bags by the door,
Ty followed her.

Seated in a white wicker chair, her long flowered
skirt fluttering around her ankles, Harriet looked like
some fragile escapee from a Victorian tea party. She
even had the porcelain teacup, Alison noticed as she
came forward shyly, but there was nothing fragile
about her handclasp.

"Welcome to Shady Breeze, Alison," she said
warmly, smiling up at her.

"Thank you...Harriet." If she could have sunk
through the porch at that moment, Alison would have
pressed the down button. It was all very well to trick
Ty—he could look out for himself! But deceiving his
mother was another matter entirely.

"You belong in bed, Ty," Harriet pronounced
firmly. "I haven't seen you this sick in years."
Lounging back against the porch railing, Ty gave his
mother a lopsided smile and no reply, and she shook
her head in amused disgust. "All right, then, be useful if you won't be smart. Why don't you show Alison
her room? I'm sure she'll want to change out of that
suit before dinner." Her eyes came back to Alison.
"And don't feel you have to dress up," she warned. "I
was simply in the mood for a skirt."

Alison's first impression of the interior was a distracted one at best, since Ty was at her heels. The front
door opened on a large, square hallway. To the right,
a wide and intricately spindled archway of varnished
oak framed what must have been the living room beyond, a room much lighter and brighter than she had
expected in a house of this period. Pale blue and cream

fabrics, the gold of oak floors and unstained furniture, the fresh greens of Boston ferns beckoned the eye with a cool and soothing airiness.

That small and sunny room on her left would be the library, judging from the floor-to-ceiling books flanking the bay window and fireplace. Her pulse leaped, then settled again, as she spotted the seascape above the mantle. Even at a glimpse, it was not Minot. The paint was applied too smoothly; the colors were not vivid enough.

Directly opposite the front door was a corridor leading to the back of the house. Beside it, a wide staircase rose to a landing, and edging around her, Ty nodded toward the stairway, then led the way up.

It took a moment to guess the purpose of the metal track that ran up the stairs beside her, but the chair waiting at the landing explained it. This was how his mother went up to her bedroom, on this sort of portable escalator. With Harriet's fierce independence, she must despise this contraption.

Ty indicated the tracks. "Don—" He stopped and swallowed with effort, his eyes holding hers with an urgency that seemed almost angry. "Don't use...in a fire..."

In a fire...yes, the electricity might fail, trapping Harriet on the stairs. Good heavens, wasn't he carrying his protectiveness a bit far? But she nodded soothingly. "Yes, Ty. I see what you mean."

He shook his head bitterly. "You're... so...small...."

No doubt his ideal spinster companion would have been built like a gorilla, able to sling Harriet over one shoulder like a sack of potatoes in an emergency.

Really, why was he worrying so? "Look," she said briskly, "I'm stronger than I look, but if it'll make you feel better, then get me some weights. I'll start pumping iron tomorrow."

That almost won a smile from him.

"Here, I'll show you! Give me those bags."

Suddenly amused, he shook his head and retreated up the stairs before her. As she hurried behind, her heart sounded louder than her feet on the blue-and-white Oriental runner. Forrest had said the painting was somewhere upstairs, hadn't he? Any moment, her search might be over; this rotten farce would come to an end, for it was going to be a fake, Alison had decided. Minot had been many things in his day, not all of them commendable, but never a fool. If he said the paintings had burned, well, they had burned. Therefore, whatever Harriet had here, it could not be one of the *Alicia* series; she'd held fast and fierce to that conviction these past few days. Once that fact was established and photos taken to prove it to Forrest, she could go. Perhaps even tomorrow. A dreadful way to treat Harriet, but better for all in the long run.

At the top of the stairs, Ty turned toward the back of the house, and Alison's steps slowed as she saw the first painting. It was a watercolor—a beauty—of sailboats racing, their spinnakers bulging like multicolored balloons as the whole fleet burst from a fog bank.

She didn't know the artist. At the end of the hallway, Ty opened a door and glanced back at her. She was supposed to be a history major, not an art historian. Alison hurried past a second piece. Even from the corner of her eye she could tell it was not a Minot, but her heart skipped a beat. A nineteenth-century Japanese woodcut—now that had cost some money.

Halting in the doorway of her room, Alison forgot paintings. So this was what it was to be rich—to own peace and sunlight and such a view! She came forward slowly.

The windows faced west and south, and with the sun going down, the white walls glowed golden. On the oak floor, an Indian dhurrie rug gave back the light in simple geometrics of cream and rust, with sparklike touches of yellow and blue-gray; her feet sank into it. The bed was a massive pineapple poster; the sunlight slanting across it picked out the nubby arabesques of a medallion design on its white bedspread.

Numbly she turned, trying to take it all in…. Dream rooms always had desks, but technically this one was a table, a massive slab of curly maple placed beneath the southern window. But how would she ever be able to write with the sea out there? She turned, suddenly remembering Ty's presence.

He was watching her, his lips curled in an oddly tender little smile, and Alison looked away, her cheeks suddenly burning.

She must have seemed like a hick to him. No doubt this piece of paradise was just the back guestroom, no more, no less, to an heir to the Channing fortune.

Behind her, Ty moved and she heard the soft thump of a suitcase being set on the bed. "That's okay, Ty, I can do that!" But he was heaving the big one up beside it as she turned. Somehow it bounced, then toppled sideways as Ty grabbed for it. It crunched to the floor, landing corner first, and an avalanche of books and papers slithered across the carpet.

"Damn," Ty whispered mildly, ankle deep in her thesis notes. He squatted carefully on his heels.

Those were not the books of a history major! "Ty, wait!" She caught his shoulder. "Let me do that." Beneath her fingers, he was as hot as a stove and about as moveable. "Ty, leave it. I'll do it. You ought to be in bed!"

That caught his attention. He glanced up at her, his hands full of books, his chin brushing against her fingers, his eyes gleaming with mischief and fever. "Damn right!"

If she pushed hard enough she could topple him flat on his rear; the impulse was well nigh irresistible for a second. Raging, she knelt beside him instead.

Methodically stacking her books on the bed, Ty inspected each title before he set it down. *Impressionism and Post-Impressionism, 1874-1904.* Klingenders's *Art and the Industrial Revolution*, *The Mirror of Art*...

When he'd cleared a space around him, Ty turned and slouched back against the side of the bed, hugging himself.

Gathering the pages from an exploded notebook, Alison refused to look up. His denim-clad legs tensed suddenly. He was having chills, was he? Good. Served him right. How had that case come open, anyway? Its latches had never failed before.

"You're missing a couple of books," Ty whispered after some thought.

"I am? Which?" She scowled up at his pile, trying to remember all she'd brought.

*Paintings from My Collection* by Abe Lincoln and *Great Artists I Have Known* by General Robert E. Lee,'' he said dryly.

''Ahh...'' Oh, what was the use? He could see all the way down to her lying heart with eyes like his.

''I told you, Ty, I quit history. I'm sick of it. I've never known anything about art, and always regretted that, so I decided to do some reading this summer.'' Astounding how easily the lies were coming now; was this talent what her father had guarded her against all these years?

But glib as it sounded, was he buying the story?

Like an ebbing tide, those ocean eyes took more than they gave. ''You've come to the right place, then,'' he allowed neutrally. ''Mother's an art fiend.''

''Is she?'' Alison asked carelessly. ''That's nice.'' She collected a book that had slid under the bed between them, then gasped as he caught her wrist and turned it to read the book's title.

''You read French?''

''Yes.'' What was the matter with her? Each time he touched her it was worse. Those long fingers might have been wrapped around her throat, to judge from the way she was breathing. ''My mother was French Canadian,'' she found herself babbling, to fill the silence that was growing around them.

''Was?'' His other hand eased the book from her fingers and set it up on the bed.

''She...died when I was thirteen.... Drowned.'' She shuddered suddenly and his fingers squeezed in comforting response. His eyes more than his fingers held her now, but Alison didn't feel trapped so much as supported, surrounded by invisible arms that protected her from a hostile world.

Ty lifted her hand and set it against his hot cheek. "Want half of mine?" He gave her his little lopsided grin. "She's not half—half..." He let her go as he started to cough, and Alison scrambled to her feet. When he could breathe again, Ty looked whipped. Dark head tilted back against the white bedspread, he stared up at her. "Not half bad," he finished ruefully.

"She's wonderful! And you've got a fever, Ty," she told him sternly. "So go take two aspirin."

"Don't think that'll cure it," he replied thoughtfully.

"So go take a walk." *A long one off a short dock.* "I want to change."

He gave a regretful little sigh, telling her he'd rather stay, then stood with an easy, slouching grace. But he seemed to sway a little once he'd reached his height. "Supper at six, Dark Eyes."

"Alis—" But the door closed gently between them. "Alison, you...creep," she told it helplessly.

## CHAPTER SIX

"AND THIS ONE, HARRIET? Is it by the artist who painted the sailboats upstairs?" Alison paused before a small cityscape tucked in a corner of the living room.

"It is. And you've got an excellent eye to guess it, Alison." Settled on the couch that faced the fireplace, Harriet sipped an after-dinner coffee and watched Alison's explorations with gentle amusement.

*Careful, you history major,* Alison reminded herself as she studied the watercolor. But couldn't anyone see that this artist's choice of colors, the almost calligraphic details laid in with a dry brush were as distinctive as a burglar's thumbprint on the silverware case?

"That's Jack Aubrey's work," Harriet continued. "Pat and I always visit—ed...his studio when we...went out to Nantucket." She took a deep, unsteady breath, then smiled apologetically.

How long would it hurt, Alison wondered as she met those brimming eyes for an instant. Forever? And did you pity a woman who missed her husband so, or envy her? Well, there was no way to help, except, perhaps, to distract her. Alison moved on to a small piece above a bookcase. "Now this is—" her voice caught in her throat as she saw it clearly "—interesting," she finished in almost a squeak.

Their faces upturned to the blaze of spotlights, two ballerinas curtsied to an invisible audience. It was a Degas, a shimmering study in pastel of one of his favorite subjects. The sensation on finding it on someone's living-room wall was roughly akin to stepping into a friend's kitchen to find the president of the United States drying the dishes!

"Yes," Harriet agreed behind her. "That's the very first piece in my collection—a birth present from my mother."

Well, no one could fault the Channings for taste, Alison thought wryly. She glanced up as the floor above creaked faintly and somewhere a door shut. That had to be Ty, for June Hurley had gone home to her family after preparing the excellent dinner, leaving them to serve themselves as apparently was the custom. And Ty had never appeared for the meal. Sleeping, Harriet had supposed, and best not disturbed. So it had been easy enough to steer the conversation to art this evening, a topic she'd never have dared broach with Ty in the same room. Thoughts of him reminded her that she ought to work quickly, while she still had the chance. Alison glanced back at the ballerinas. "That's in the—" she hesitated, as if groping for the term "—Impressionist style, isn't it, Harriet?"

"Yes. Most critics count Degas as one of the Impressionists. Do you like them?"

"I *love* them! The Museum of Fine Arts in Boston has a whole roomful. I remember sneaking away from a school field trip when I was twelve, just so I could stay on a bench in that room, staring.''

And later, when she'd been stuggling to reach a decision about Don, she'd gone back to that bench more than once.... Alison shoved the thought aside and collected their empty cups. "I remember my favorite. It was a fishing boat alongside a dock at night, lanterns everywhere—shining through the nets—and the fishermen carrying baskets of silvery fish ashore. The painter was...um—Minot! That was it. I've loved every painting of his I've ever seen.'' She smiled and started for the kitchen, hating herself.

But broad as that hint had been, Harriet must have missed it. She was on her feet, the walker before her, when Alison returned.

"Well, Alison, I'm going to leave you to your own devices tonight. I have a book I'd like to finish, and I'm sure you're exhausted.''

Indeed she was, but what was needed to revive her was the sight of one particular painting. And she'd been so determined to settle the matter tonight!

"Now the television is in the library here.'' Harriet nodded toward it as they moved slowly to the stairs. "And, let's see, you saw the telephone; I want you to use it whenever and to call whoever you wish, wherever...''

"Now that is brave of you, Harriet.'' Why did she have to be so nice?

"Having survived first Ty's phone bills and then my daughter Patsy's—'' Harriet laughed and pressed the button that brought the chair down the track to meet her. "No, you don't worry me very much, Alison....

You're too quiet, if anything.'' She settled carefully into the chair, her smile slowly fading.

"Could I carry your walker?"

"No, thank you. I can manage.'' Harriet's tone was almost distant now.

They ascended at about the same speed, Harriet with an almost fierce detachment, staring outward into space, Alison in thoughtful silence. From the look of her, Harriet had been an active and healthy woman just a few months ago. To have lost her husband and her independence all in one blow... It made Ty's fanatic protectivness a little easier to understand. She'd lost so much and there was so little he could really do to make up for that.

Gaining the second floor, Alison waited, unwilling to leave Harriet until she was safely off the stairs. The sailboat watercolor made a good excuse. "I like this,'' she murmured as Harriet joined her.

"Oh, this one!'' The warmth had returned to her words. "This one used to drive Pat wild. If you look at the masts closely, you'll see the painter exercised his artistic license and left the spreaders off. That's an essential part of the rigging.... Pat used to stand here, scowling, just waiting for those masts to come crashing down....'' Laughter and tears shimmered together in that quiet voice.

"He was a sailor, then?'' Alison asked quickly.

"He was the captain of my uncle's yacht when I first met him.'' The barely audible sigh that followed was that of a young girl.

Good Lord! Alison stared at the magically upright masts as the picture in her mind became a little clearer.

That would be just one step up from marrying the chauffeur, surely, in the kind of world in which the Channings moved? "So your husband liked art, as well," she murmured to fill the lull in the conversation.

"Pat liked to indulge *me*," Harriet corrected, a smile in her voice. "He knew little about art and cared less, for all my efforts, though he had a wonderful untutored eye. I suppose there's only one painting in the house that he actually chose himself.... You said you like Minot's work?"

"Oh, yes! I love it! What little I know of it." *At last, oh finally, at last!* Perhaps she wouldn't have to unpack at all!

"In that case, you might be interested in this painting, if you're not too tired."

"Tired? I...no, I'm...I'd love to see it, Harriet."

"It's a very special painting," she confided softly as they passed the door that led to an office on the north side of the house. "Pat bought it for me in France in '47, as a belated wedding gift...."

Ohh...no. Alison stopped short in the doorway as Harriet limped inside her bedroom. No. This was the painting she had come to prove false? Harriet's wedding gift? Unable to enter, she leaned against the doorframe, her supper rising within her.

Across the room, Harriet flicked on a second lamp, illuminating the long apartment whose windows looked out on the Sound, showing them both the bed and the figure lying across the foot of it.

"*Ty?*" There was a note of real fear in Harriet's voice.

But he moved, his dark head turning to find her. His feet were still on the floor, as if he'd sat down, then collapsed backward under the weight of the package he clutched to his chest.

Ty tried to speak, then gave it up and smiled instead. Lying there with one cheek pressed to the coverlet, his dark hair softly awry, he looked perhaps fifteen and altogether frightened behind that teasing grin.

He sat up as Harriet came to him.

"Ty, darling, what's the matter? You look dreadful!" Sitting beside him, Harriet put a hand to his forehead. "You're burning up!" She looked around. "Alison, if you'll go through that door, you'll find aspirin in the cabinet there and a glass for water. Would you get that for me, please?"

Under his mother's anxious scrutiny, Ty accepted the pills and swallowed them obediently, almost absently, his eyes on her face. Whatever was bothering him, it was not his fever, Alison guessed as she looked down at them both.

Apparently Harriet thought the same. "So what are you up to, darling?" she asked finally.

He sighed and gave her another odd little grin with tenderness, worry and guilt all mixed together. "When's...when's your birthday?" he whispered.

"You don't have to worry about that tonight, Ty. It's in August, you know that. I think perhaps Dr. Freeman ought to—"

"No." He shook his head quickly. "I'm fine. Just working on...on a surprise for you." Leaning forward, he caught her arms gently. "Remember how we...always said your painting...needed cleaning?"

"My..." The word was a whisper as strained as his own. Then her head whipped around to the wall facing the bed. The expanse was bare except for one stark nail and the palest of rectangles on the wallpaper beneath it. "Ty!" Outrage and something close to panic joined in that protest. "You can't do that now! You know that!" She twisted against his hold futilely.

"Takes two months to clean," he whispered reasonably, but his eyebrows were drawn together as if he was in pain.

"I don't care! I don't want it cleaned! I want it now!" Harriet blazed. "Do you hear me?" She flung his hands aside and whirled to the brown-paper-wrapped parcel he'd set on the bed beside them. "Is this...?" But apparently it wasn't, for she dropped it as if it burned her fingers. "Ty, don't do this to me!" The tears were trickling as Harriet made an effort to regain her temper. "Where is it? I want to show it to Alison."

Alison fell back a step as his blue-gray eyes slashed up at her, glinting like knife blades; they softened again as they dropped to his mother. "Can't. It's wrapped for traveling already." Reaching out, he caught a tear on his fingertip.

"My painting is not going anywhere, Ty!" But temper was getting her nowhere, and her tone changed again. "I...darling, it's a wonderful idea, and I do appreciate it, but not now...not this year. Go get it."

Ty shook his head as if it hurt. "Look...I brought something to replace it."

"Ty, don't be an idiot. You know there's nothing else I want." She wiped her cheeks angrily.

"Oh, you'll want this…" Reaching for the discarded package, he set it between them on the bed and then looked up again, the muscles rigid along his jaw.

"I…" Her eyes flicked down to the flat rectangular parcel. "What is it?"

"I was saving it…till you felt strong enough…." He took a deep breath. "You strong tonight?"

"I—" Harriet shook her head and claimed the package. The first rip revealed the bottom half of a framed, blown-up photograph. "Oh, Ty," she breathed, her fingers gentle and slower now.

Squinting in the sunlight, the man in the photo grinned up from his frame. The very large fish pinned across his bent knee no doubt explained his delight; he'd been in the act of unhooking it when the photographer had caught his attention. His hair was thick and dark—well streaked with gray. That nose was Ty's own. A tear splashed onto the glass as Harriet bent slowly over it, her shoulders shaking.

"Mother…" Ty's hand curved across her head, barely touching it.

"Go *away*, Ty! Please go."

"Right," he whispered mechanically, and sat there, his fingers clenching into fists on his knees, then opening stiffly, only to curl shut again.

Stepping lightly, Alison backed toward the door.

*"Go!"*

Ty went, almost leaping to his feet. One hand caught Alison's shoulder as he passed her, and she bit back a yelp as he spun her around to face the doorway. The hand tightened ruthlessly as she stumbled, the care with which he shut the door behind them contrasting absurdly with the violence in the fingers clamped round her arm.

"That hurts!" she snapped, twisting to face him.

"Tough!" Beneath the jagged black slant of his brows, his face was paper white. They both flinched as the first wrenching sob reached them through the door; Ty didn't have to pull as they retreated down the hallway together.

But she was still in custody. He opened her door and swung her inside. Eyes blazing, Alison whirled to face him, opened her mouth to tell him just what she thought of his tactics, then shut it again as she saw his face. His white slashing grin acknowledged her prudence. "You're *right*! Better not!"

Blast him! He would not frighten her like this. Alison sucked in a deep breath, reaching for words—and he shut the door in her face. The softness of its closing was more insolent than any slam could have been. Damn him! Just who did he think he was? If she'd been a man, she'd have punched a hole through the door, or rather broken a hand trying. Chest heaving with wasted adrenaline, Alison stared at it viciously. Not a chance. The damned door was as solid as that gorilla's head! She backed away a step, one hand absently massaging her arm. The room was suddenly too small; pacing it, she stopped on the second lap to kick off her shoes. Why had he been so mad at her? She reached the bed and wheeled, unbuttoning her short-sleeved blouse with shaking fingers.

One careless knock flicked the door behind her. As she spun around, it opened and Ty stepped inside.

"Do you mind?" she gasped.

"Not at all," he murmured automatically. The scowl of a moment before was smoothing out into that expression he sometimes got, as if he were aware of her every thought. His eyes riveted to her hands where they clutched her blouse together, Ty groped for the door behind him and shut it softly.

Her quick two steps backward brought him back to the moment; his eyes sharpened suddenly and part of the frown returned, as well. Turning, he stalked to the bookcase above the desk.

"What d'you think you're doing?" Those were *her* books his clumsy hands were brushing across as if he had to read the titles by Braille. If he picked one up she would brain him with it.

"Gettin' something to read," he rasped, back turned. "Never get to sleep without it."

"There's a library downstairs!"

"Right, but my books're here." He yanked a volume from the bottom shelf, where she'd exiled all the books she'd found in the room.

"What are they doing here?"

"My room," he whispered flatly, turning. "Thought you'd like the view." The look in his eyes said she didn't deserve it now.

*His* room... He didn't have to vacate it for her! She didn't need or want his consideration, if that's what it had been.

"What's the matter?" Ty had halted by the door. Then he was coming straight for her. Long fingers closed over her wrist; she'd been holding her other arm again without realizing it. Lifting her hand aside, Ty was close enough that she heard the tiny catch in his breath, and her eyes followed his.

The bruises were only starting, but already they looked like some example from a criminology textbook. Four perfect finger marks. "Oh...hell," Ty whispered reverently, tossing his book on the bed beside them. Blazing hot, with all the weight of a butterfly, his fingers found her arm and moved hesitantly across her skin. "I didn't...I never..." He shook his head helplessly.

Odd how so light a touch could penetrate. Those gentle fingers seemed to reach right down to the heart of her, as if they soothed some bruise within. The wild indignation of the past few minutes was twisting inside her, turning slowly to something...hungrier... warmer.

His right hand found her chin. Outspread fingers stroked slowly up her jawline, slid softly into her hair to cup the side of her face. His eyes were black and enormous as she met them, his face too near. "Damn you, Angel!" Ty whispered incredulously.

So stop, then! Stop and free them both if he didn't want this; *she* surely didn't! Alison opened her lips to tell him so, but his other hand was at her mouth, tracing its shape as if he didn't quite believe her, as if only touch could confirm her presence. Her words turned into a sigh against his fingertips.

Perhaps she wasn't there. It felt like a dream with Ty's fingers feathering slowly down her throat, exploring its length and slenderness, a dream slowly closing around her with its own absurd and irresistible logic.

The hand in her hair moved slowly around to cradle the back of her neck, urging her gently closer. Arching her back, Alison leaned against his hand, not certain if she was resisting its pull or merely entrusting herself more completely to its support.

His lips with their lurking curve floated at her eye level. What had he to smile about? But the fingers of his left hand were sliding between the unbuttoned edges of her shirt, tracing her collarbone, the soft slope below it, then finally, inevitably, closing warmly and smoothly around her breast.

Air. Even in dreams you had to breathe, but her deep shaking inhalation only made matters worse. Ty groaned, a tiny, entirely male sound of satisfaction, and his thumb stroked inward, found the waiting nipple and circled softly.

That touch broke the spell. What was she doing here, letting him touch her like this? Was she mad? She'd felt this way before; look where it had got her. Did she need that again?

"No!" she answered herself, twisting away from those knowing hands. There was no way to retreat but across the bed in an undignified scramble toward the headboard. Grabbing a pillow, she turned to face the pursuit, her eyes flashing.

But Ty wasn't pursuing. He was standing where she'd left him, his hand in midair, gaping. Hugging pillow to breast, she watched surprise shade quickly to amusement in that expressive face, watched him fight the grin and fail. She knew how she must look.

"How old did you say you were?" It was a rasping, seductive whisper. "Twelve?" Ty sat on the edge of the bed, and she whipped her feet aside.

"Get out!"

His gaze lingered on her feet, then moved slowly upward across her bare calves. Her skirt was hiked halfway up her thighs, but to pull it down now would only invite more ridicule. "Great legs for a twelve-year-old," Ty decided gravely.

"Get...out...of...here. Now."

Ty leaned toward her, then froze as she flinched. The last of his smile disappearing, he studied her face, his brows drawing together slowly. "My book," he whispered finally, indicating it with a nod, then slowly reaching as if she were some small frightened animal.

*"Out!"* She didn't like the concern in his eyes now any more than she liked the laughter of the moment before.

"Right." He stood. Looking down at her with that almost-smile, he sighed—a soft regretful sound, mocking them both—and went.

But he turned at the door. "Sorry...'bout that arm."

Alison shrugged—a small, huffy shrug. He hadn't intended to hurt her, she knew that, but there was no way to say it just now.

But perhaps he guessed it. His tender, teasing smile crept back from hiding. "If you grow up tonight, Angel...I'm upstairs." He ducked out the door just as she heaved the pillow.

# CHAPTER SEVEN

THE THIRD STEP SQUEAKED. Balanced on one foot, Alison froze in the darkness of the black stairwell, ears straining to catch some answering sound from the floor above.... Nothing....

It had taken her half the night to work up her nerve for this foray. At this rate, it would be dawn before she reached Ty's room on the third floor. The next step creaked softly—he'd hear her heart, if nothing else!

Two months.... She'd rammed her head against that cold, hard fact for the past five hours, like a prisoner bashing his head against the stone walls of his cell. Two months before she'd have another chance to see that painting—two months of deceiving Harriet, two months of dodging Ty. She couldn't, wouldn't stand it, though Forrest was perfectly capable of insisting that she try.

So that left tonight; if Ty slept as heavily at night as he had this afternoon in his car, it shouldn't be too risky. As if to mock that conclusion, the next step groaned and Alison froze again.

The painting had to be up there in his room. She'd checked Pat's office about twelve, with no luck, except that a roll of brown wrapping paper, scissors and tape left out on the desk suggested that Ty might have wrapped the painting there for its journey. But if she could snitch it from his room, she now had the means to rewrap it after she'd studied and photographed it. If...

The next tread stayed safely silent. Above her, the dimmest of rectangles marked the top of the stairs. Echoing off the unseen walls, her shallow breathing seemed to fill the stairwell. Perhaps Ty was lying awake in his bed now, shaking with silent laughter as he listened to her stumbling approach. Damn him! He was on to her.... He had to be. It was just too much of a coincidence that Ty should decide to take the painting away the day she arrived....

With each step she took up, the light was growing. The late-rising half-moon she'd seen from her own windows must be shining through some window above.

But on the other hand, if Ty knew she was Forrest's spy, wouldn't it have been simpler to fire her and spare Harriet the grief he'd given her this evening? And why should Ty prevent her from seeing the painting at all, when Harriet seemed so willing to show it? It made no sense, so perhaps it was only a maddening, enraging coincidence, after all. The man simply had a genius for thwarting her. They were natural, instinctive opponents, cat and mouse; that must be the bond she'd sensed from the start.

Quiet as any cat burglar, or mouse, for that matter, Alison reached the top of the stairs and crept toward the moonlit rectangle of an open doorway. The blood thumping in her ears deafened her to any sounds from the room beyond, and it seemed to take hours to tilt her head around the doorframe.

And in the meantime, she'd forgotten to breathe. Her body remembered just as her eyes found him. Her lungs sucking moonlight, Alison stared.

She should have expected that Ty wasn't the type to wear pajamas. And he'd kicked his sheet off—fought the whole bed, by the way it looked, then collapsed facedown on the field of battle. With moonlight silvering the hard, clean lines of hip and shoulder, and with shadow gashing a black valley down his spine, Ty looked like a slain warrior by Caravaggio—a study in chiaroscuro.

The next few steps were easy; she was floating, too busy filling her eyes to worry. But as Alison reached the foot of the bed, Ty groaned and twisted onto his side. One hand groped blindly, searching for the missing bedclothes but failed to find them.

He must be freezing. Not good with a fever. And there was no way to cover him without risk of waking him. No way at all. And then she saw the package.

So he did know what she was. Or at least suspected. The brown parcel was not much bigger than a pillow. It was resting on the bed next to Ty's head, and he'd placed it on the far side; she would have to slide down the foot-wide space between the side of the bed and the wall to reach it. But if this was a dare, she was taking it.

It wasn't so hard, Alison decided, edging into the gap sideways. All you had to do was concentrate... which was...perhaps...a little difficult...facing that moonlit body. Why had Don never affected her so?

Instead of the floor, her foot came down on something soft...and warm. Biting back a shriek as it grunted and lurched beneath her, Alison pitched forward. She caught the headboard, balanced, overbalanced, toppled sideways and caught her weight again on her other hand, not a foot from Ty's shoulder. The mattress bouncing beneath her, she swallowed another yelp as a cold nose found her ankle. Milo!

Raising himself slowly on one elbow, Ty blinked up at her, eyes wide and black in the moonshine.

What do you say when caught doing push-ups above a naked man at three o'clock in the morning, Alison wondered wildly? No doubt there was accepted etiquette for the situation, but it was certainly beyond her experience. All she knew was that once this was over, she had one golden hide to nail to the wall. Beside her, Milo settled to the floor again and rested his chin across her foot.

"Kathy..." Ty murmured hoarsely, staring up into her face.

Oh, God, so he wasn't awake at all! Should she answer?

"Come to bed," Ty commanded. "I'm freezin'." Sagging down again, he curled sideways and threw an arm across the package, as if it were a woman he were pulling closer.

Numbly Alison straightened and backed slowly toward the foot of the bed. Enough was enough.

"Kath?" This time the name was a fretful plea.

Numbness was giving way to emotion. She recognized the ugly little beast as it scuttled across her mind. Jealousy. An old, old companion—one she thought she'd banished for good these past two years. *You've no right to be jealous!* Just because he'd touched her tonight? The man was nothing to her. Nothing but an obstacle...a freezing obstacle.

The blanket was on the floor. Lightly she pulled it up, softly tucking it around his shoulders and stroking it smooth across the hot curve of his arm. Ty smiled and nestled against his package. "Come to..." He slept.

"FROM THE LOOKS OF HER when I took her coffee up, I'd say she had a bad night. Says she doesn't want breakfast. Now how about you, dear? More coffee, and how do you take your eggs?"

"Yes and just one, please, June—scrambled. And what about Ty? Isn't he having breakfast?" Alison was already learning to cram as many words as possible into any gaps in the conversation that June left unfilled.

"Oh, him?" June snorted, crossing the big kitchen with a pot of coffee. "He was just leaving when I got here. Crawling off to die at his place down in Mystic, by the look of him. I haven't seen Ty that sick since..." Her kindly face tightened suddenly into concentration as the coffee neared the brim of the cup.

And the painting had gone with him, of course. Darn! She'd meant to try to get it once more before dawn, but had made the fatal mistake of lying down to wait. Now what? Two months—she couldn't...

A plate that certainly held more than one egg as well as a double helping of toast came in for a landing beneath her nose. Across the massive kitchen table, June settled down to an even healthier portion. The topic appeared to be larks now, how all the O'Malleys were—had been—early risers.

"What about Ty's sister, Kathy? Is she a lark?" The question had crossed her tongue before it even reached her brain.

It stopped June cold. "Kathy?" she repeated, a forkful of egg poised in midair. "Kathy's not Ty's sister—that's Patsy. He talked about Kathy?"

Why had she ever started this? "He didn't *talk* about her exactly, the name just sort of...came up..."

"Well, glo-ory be," June mused with an odd look of satisfaction. "I'd just about decided we'd never see the day."

"Who's Kathy, June?"

"His wife."

"Oh." The word might have been Swahili. Meaning and nausea arrived together, and she put the slice of toast back on the plate. She should have known. No one like him could possibly be unmarried. "Where is she?"

"Oh, dead," June said simply. "Do you remember that big hotel fire out in Denver about five years ago?"

Oh, Lord. Oh, Ty..."No."

"She was there for her best friend's wedding. Ty was too busy to go. He was wild about that afterward, as if he could've done anything, the way *he* sleeps, but you couldn't tell him. It wasn't the flames that got them all; it was the smoke."

*"In case of fire,"* he'd said last night.... The coffee wasn't helping her swirling stomach but she gulped it down anyway. *"Kathy, come to bed."* "So he's still grieving," she murmured. However sorry you felt for yourself, there was always someone who had it worse. Why couldn't she ever remember that?

"Grieving?" June frowned over the word for a moment. "Well, it's certain sure he won't talk about her, but then I'm not so sure I'd...well...yes, I guess he is, in his own way."

"What way's that, June?"

"By chasing everything in a skirt that moves, these past few years!" June stood and collected their plates. "Now, that's not really fair. His taste's as good as ever it was, from all I hear—my Tom sees him down in Mystic with 'em sometimes. It's just the *quantity*. And I suppose it's only natural; he's just making up for lost time...."

"Lost time?" Alison brought the cups over to the dishwasher.

"Well, he was married to Kathy for nearly five years, and he didn't even know there was another woman left alive on the planet, back then. Bad as his father that way, he was. And then the first two years after she died, I swear he'd have become a monk if he hadn't been too busy working himself to an early grave. Used to drive his father crazy, but Harriet just said let him be, and she always had the last word."

So he was still grieving, if he couldn't speak her name aloud, if she still came to him when he closed his eyes. Alison's hand clenched shut as she remembered that kiss in the car. So that hadn't been for her, either. Well, this explained a lot of things.... The way he looked at her. The intensity of his pursuit. She was just part of the cure, one more female face he'd use to try to blot out his Kathy's. Anger, pity and scrambled eggs made an indigestible breakfast.

"Now what's all this fuss about where her painting is? I haven't seen that off the wall since they moved here and I was the baby-sitter, and Lord, if you think Ty's a handful now..."

"Which painting, June?"

"That red-haired hussy Harriet keeps up in the bedroom. Give me a Rembrandt any old day, but, my Lord, did she dote on it! Used to find her just sitting there mooning over it, and these past few weeks, since she's come home of course, if you could wear out a painting by looking... But then I suppose it's worth a lot. We had some kind of con man try and steal it a few months back, and wasn't he a slick-talking little devil? Kicked like a little bullfrog when Ty brought him down the stairs with one hand on his collar and the other on the seat of his trousers, and I've never seen Ty so mad in all my life! And if *that* wasn't enough of a treat, the fellow tripped head over heels over Milo on his way off the porch! And oh, that reminds me, Ty asked me to ask you to keep an eye on Milo for him. And that'll be the first time I've seen him leave that dog behind since Kathy died. Hard to believe that big moose is the same puppy Ty gave her the month before..."

Alison escaped to the front porch to silence, sunshine and a crisp blue sea crinkling with the first hint of the breeze. Leaning out over the porch railing, she let the day wash in through her eyes, let it sweep through her lungs like a wave rolling through an empty shell, taking the sadness with it. Oh, Ty... Did he ever stand like this, filling the emptiness within with this ocean? The water was bluer than his eyes today. A patch of gold moved in the trees at the foot of the hill—Milo, trotting back from some canine expedition, and a successful one, judging from his tail.

"Good morning, Alison." Maneuvering her walker with care, Harriet stepped down onto the porch and joined Alison at the railing.

"Good morning," she answered shyly.

Shadows bruised the fair skin beneath the serene and lovely eyes that met her glance for a moment, then turned to the sea. Ty was not the only one who could use its healing. "So he left Milo behind," she mused. A smile flickered across her face and vanished.

"Yes. How closely should I watch him?"

"Oh, June will feed him. You just give him a pat once in a while," Harriet assured her. "Shall we go say hello now?"

"Certainly." She couldn't help glancing at the steps down to ground level.

"If you'll lend me a shoulder, we can manage," Harriet told her briskly, as she leaned her walker against the railing.

She limped down the stairs painfully slowly, head regally high, only the clamp of her fingers on Alison's shoulder and her unsteady breathing hinting at her fear. At the bottom they both looked back at the steps with doubled respect and more than a touch of triumph. "Whew!" Harriet pronounced softly. Her sidelong glance gleamed with mischief, and Alison laughed aloud.

"I'll get the walker."

They strolled slowly across the short clipped grass at the crest of the hill, then stopped to watch the retriever. "This is marvelous," Harriet decided, including the entire hillside and the sound beyond in one sweeping survey. "This is the first time I've been off the porch without Ty's help since I came back from the hospital.''

"Ty...won't mind, really, will he?"

"Oh, most likely he will. I don't know how I ever hatched such a worrywart. But he's out of our hair for a few days, I'd say, poor darling. Milo! Come here, boy." She stretched a hand toward the ambling dog. "By the way, I'm sorry I threw such a tantrum last night," she murmured casually. Catching Milo by one ear, she gave it a gentle tug.

"Oh, really, Harriet, you don't have to—"

"It was just a bit of a shock," Harriet pressed on determinedly, "Finding it gone like that. That painting has always been my dearest possession, not so much because it's so lovely as because Pat was so proud of it. He found it in France in '47 when he went over to inspect a ship he thought he might buy for salvage." Milo being about to collapse in bliss toward the ear she was pulling, Harriet transferred her attention to his other ear. "It was my wedding gift—three years after the fact—and a debt of honor, as Pat so gallantly put it." Her lips twisted in a sudden, aching smile. "To replace a painting I'd...had to sell in '44—Minot's *Girl with Violets*. Do you know it?"

Did she know it! That lyrical little portrait with the singing blues and violets of the flowers reflecting off the child's throat and picked up again in the shadows around her wide eyes? Harriet had owned that? What a ransom it must have brought, even back in 1944. "I've...heard of it, I think."

"It was donated to Yale a few years back. Perhaps we'll drive down for a visit later this summer, once you've got your license."

"I'd like that," Alison murmured absently, stooping to distract the dog before he succeeded in knocking Harriet off her feet. And so Pat had replaced that delicate little painting from Minot's last mellow years—a most suitable painting for a young lady—with a portrait of Alicia, Minot's tempestuous mistress from his bravura years. "The red-haired hussy," as June had described her. Alison frowned down at the dog, trying to remember Minot's exultant first description of Alicia in a letter to his brother, Paul. "Eyes like a cat in the torchlight, hair like a river of burgundy." So Pat had brought her back a grown-up's work to replace the chaste child's painting Harriet had sold, and it had hung at the foot of their bed ever since.

And where had Pat got his painting? France in '47—that had the ring of truth to it. The war had rolled across Europe like a tidal wave, churning its civilization to the depths, swallowing families and fortunes whole, sweeping away collections of art that had been generations in the building. And whirling long-lost or forgotten treasures up to the light of day again. Including, perhaps, Minot's red-haired treasure? Maybe, just maybe, the painting wasn't a fake, after all....

And Harriet should know, shouldn't she? She knew her art, all right, and she had been born into the finest collection of Minots in America....

*And you won't know for sure for two months,* Alison reminded herself as she gave Ty's dog a last thump on the ribs. Harriet had moved on. At a distance she looked like a graceful, white-haired girl leaning out over her walker, facing the sea. Following her gaze, Alison saw the white triangle of a sail slicing patiently across the glittering blue.

Two months of this? Well...perhaps.

# CHAPTER EIGHT

"DEAR RIC..." And then what? The sheet of stationery on the clipboard before her was as blank as her brain. Sighing, Alison reached out for Milo and found he was gone. A quick scan of the green slope below her gave no sign of him; gone back to the house for water, most likely. "Dear Ric..." How strange to have been so close once and now not to know him at all. He wasn't the wise-mouthed kid that she'd bullied into wearing a clean shirt each day, tireless at his computer, exhausted when faced with a sink full of dirty dishes.

"How about 'Having a wonderful time. Wish you were here'?" suggested the first male voice she'd heard all week.

Her cheek touched his leg as she glanced around. Looking straight up, Alison found herself squinting up the long denim-clad length of Tyler Channing O'Malley. "Hello," he said softly.

He even looked good upside down! She blinked as a fingertip dropped out of the blue, touched her between the brows and stroked down to the tip of her nose, where it balanced like a dragonfly. A jerk of her head sent it flying.

Undaunted, Ty dropped down beside her. "Who's Ric?"

She'd pictured him as the tragic young widower all week, hiding his broken heart behind that lurking smile. But Ty was hiding it awfully well today, looking healthy and not so much happy as extremely alert.

"The cat's got your tongue again," Ty decided, slouching sideways onto one elbow.

"I see he's given yours back!" *More's the pity.* Why was he always just a little bigger and brighter in real life than in her memory?

"And about time," he agreed, plucking a long blade of grass between them. "Played the merry devil with my schedule all week, being mute. You pack one helluva wallop, Dark Eyes." He put the blade in his mouth at a jaunty angle.

"Alison." She showed her own teeth as she pronounced it.

"Al-i-son," Ty repeated obediently, turning her name to a slow, caressing murmur. His eyes glinted with laughter.

"Your mother's not at home." She finally filled the expectant silence. "Mrs. Winthrop collected her for bridge and dinner out afterward."

"Yes. She told me last night when I phoned."

And yet still he'd come. Biting his grass stem with slow, almost delicate, precision, Ty let her work that out. All right, then. It was time for her little speech—topic today: sexual harassment.

"Who's Ric?" he asked just as her lips parted.

Darn him, did he do it on purpose? "My brother."

"That's right, you have a brother." He looked suitably impressed.

"I have two."

"You do? Where are they?"

As if she had one in each back pocket of her shorts!
"Jon's an undergraduate at Harvard. Eric's a physics
professor out in California. At Stanford."

"You're kidding!" Ty flipped his grass blade
downhill. "Patsy's husband's there. The English department."

Oh, murder! Why had she opened her mouth?

"So Ric's the oldest."

"No, I am," she told him irritably. He looked as if
he were settling in for the rest of the day. "Ric's
twenty-three."

"Twenty-three? That's awfully young to be a professor, isn't it?"

Time to stop talking, before he pried out something incriminating.

But if she didn't speak, he would simply sit and
stare, and that woud be worse.... "Yes, it's
young...but Ric's brilliant. And my father's been
coaching him since he was two."

She could watch the wheels going around without
the least idea of what would come next. "And who
coached you?" he asked softly.

"I suppose I was my mother's pet," she murmured, straining to make the stiff words sound casual.

"But she died when you were thirteen," Ty pointed
out. He waited, his eyes at their sharpest.

"She did." Rising in one swift movement, she
brushed herself off and turned for the house.

Three strides and Ty was stolling beside her, her
forgotten clipboard tucked under one arm.

Grimly Alison held out a hand for it. Eyes crinkling, he balanced it on her palm.

But as they reached the house, Ty touched her shoulder blade. "I want to show you something, Ali. Round back."

Ali. No one had ever tried that before. It ought to have been offensive but somehow wasn't.

Ty's show-and-tell was a car, a freshly washed, freshly waxed, somewhat battered red station wagon, complete with smiling golden retriever hanging out the back window.

Ty opened the driver's door. "If mademoiselle will sit...."

Mademoiselle would and did, wincing as Milo snuffed the back of her neck. Tied to the steering wheel was a pink, rather clumsy bow, a small folded card dangling below it.

"When's your birthday?" Ty leaned in beside her.

"September 14," she muttered, staring at the card. *Oh, please, no...*

"Virgo—I should have known." Reaching across her, he opened the card. "Alison"—that was all, penned in bold, masculine script. "Consider this a late present, not an early one, then. We'll see if I can't do better by September."

For some reason it was hard to swallow. "I've...never had a car, before...."

"Well, it's not much of a car. But I wanted a tank, something heavy enough to bounce off trees or—God forbid—other cars, and let you come back smiling," Ty explained quickly. "And you won't have to worry about the fenders. I've had them precrunched to save you the trouble. We'll trade it in for something sportier when you're ready."

"It's not *really* mine, is it?" she appealed, turning at last. This was so much worse—and better—than roses. "I just work for you. You can't go giving me cars, Ty!"

Their noses were nearly touching, and his grin reassured even as it teased. "So consider it the company car, if it makes you feel better, Dark Eyes. Now scoot over, and I'll show you how to use it."

It felt strange, coming down from the hill for the first time all week. There'd been so much to do: exploring house and woods and garden with Milo; slowly getting to know Harriet; staring out to sea; staring at the incredible little collection of artwork Harriet had gathered over the years. And then sorting through a lifetime of Patrick O'Malley's misfiled papers in his upstairs office—a chore that Harriet had gratefully relinquished after Alison found her crying among his 1950s' tax returns. Alison, though, was perhaps even more grateful for finding some way to be useful. She'd also organized the next phase of her dissertation, written the bad news to Forrest and received the expected reply—in a discreetly anonymous envelope with no return address—see that painting, no matter how long it takes! And somehow, sometime, in these past few busy days, without her even realizing it, Shady Breeze had changed—from an uneasy exile into an island of peace. So it was a little unnerving, swooping down this road through the summer woods, back to the real world.

Or perhaps her uneasiness was due to something—someone—more immediate, Alison admitted.

Her attention divided between the smooth play of hands and feet controlling the onward rush of several tons of red metal—*her* car—and the passing country-side, Alison snatched a fleeting impression of green fields, elms overshadowing the long narrow lanes and historic and modern houses slowly converging to edge the blue fingerlike inlets of the still-distant sound. The car hummed over a low bridge that curved above the railway tracks and a boat yard.

"And this is the borough."

"The borough?" It was the town she'd seen from a distance, the day he'd brought her home. They were driving straight through the most wonderful architectural hodgepodge she'd ever seen.

"The village of Stonington as opposed to the county," Ty explained, stopping the car to let a woman as beautifully preserved as the Greek Revival house beyond her follow a most determined Yorkshire terrier across the narrow street. She glimpsed ivy on stone chimneys, geraniums in a window box, white clapboard and black shutters and gingerbread lacing the porches. The gemlike village green opened out to the left with a copper-roofed stone library at its heart. But the car swung to the right.

Behind the main street, historic preservation came second to a more recent preoccupation with the stunning view. Plate-glass windows looked seaward. Converted warehouses sprouted balconies, slate roofs had grown decks, and a small parking lot thrust out into the water to form a wharf. There, lobster pots were stacked head high and Jaguars were parked next to pickups. Beyond them a line of docked fishing boats webbed the open sky with their stubby masts and upraised outriggers. Ty stopped the car. "Your turn, Angel."

Despite the teasing, he made a good coach. One arm hooked over the back seat, smile barely hidden, Ty drilled her patiently as, stopping, starting, shifting to park, cutting the engine, then starting again, they crept slowly across the parking lot. "Stop.... That was smoother. Now shift to reverse."

It was easy, so easy. Why hadn't she done this years ago? Alison stopped this time before Ty spoke, and he cocked a brow at her. "We're awfully near the edge," she explained, nodding toward the water on one side.

Ty's swift amusement vanished as quickly as it came, and he nodded gravely. "I see." Some twenty feet away, the fishing boats surged gently against their dock lines, bumping slowly back and forth against the wharf and their neighbors. A gull swooped past so low that she could hear his feathers flapping.

"Hey!" Ty's hand closed over hers on the shift lever, moving the pointer up to Park. "Look at that!"

With her hand trapped against the lever it was hard to look, much less see. All her senses seemed to be spiraling inward around those rough, warm fingers. "What?" she murmured stupidly.

"That little dragger there—the *Amy M.* out of Point Judith. That's where it all began!" He slipped a little closer along the seat, still staring intently past her.

"It?"

"The family fortune. That was Dad's first boat—that he owned, that is. He was captain of some might fancy yachts before the war, but that's the little tub he bought a share in when the navy discharged him." He shook his head, his chin just brushing her shoulder. "I can't imagine putting out to sea in that with two feet, much less one!''

''One?'' She glanced up at him, but at this distance, it was like facing a blue-gray breaking wave, and she turned to the window again.

''One, Ali. He lost the other in an accident aboardship, so the Navy discharged him in '43. He limped back here and scraped together enough to buy a half share in that boat. The *Harriet Bea*, he and his partner called her.''

''So he was a fisherman.'' Worse, even, than a yacht captain—the Channings must have died!

''He was for a while,'' Ty agreed. ''Till Mother put a stop to it.''

''How'd she do that?''

''Mmm...proposed to him, married him, came up with a nice little chunk of money and persuaded him to use it to buy three more boats outright. But the deal was he had to manage them from ashore.''

*''A painting I had to sell in '44.''* So Harriet had sold her *Girl with Violets* to get her man safely ashore and on his way to a successful career. And whether her father in international banking had approved or not, it looked as if she'd made a good investment.

His arm behind her along the seat curved closer, encircling her shoulders; a gentle, tentative finger stretched up to touch her bottom lip, stroking along its soft underside. ''What are you thinking just now?''

''I was wishing you wouldn't touch me like that.'' Lies came so easily, nowadays!

''Hmm...'' Ty studied her tight face for several heartbeats—they were easy to count, just now. ''Well...how 'bout like this?'' The hand still trapping her finger feathered slowly down to her wrist; a warm thumb circled the soft skin above her sputtering pulse in a lazy, hypnotic caress.

How could he know all her right spots? But then, weren't they the same for all women? Don had known them, too, and for the same reason. Practice. "No, thank you." The struggle to keep her voice steady gave it a touch of ice.

"Hmm." His hand withdrew slowly, with none of the roughness Don would have shown such a rejection.

His look was one of bemusement rather than irritation, as if she were some gift-wrapped package with a hopelessly knotted bow, and he was without a knife. *But then for a brush-off to hurt, you have to care.* This pass, like all of his, was probably pure reflex. *Everything in skirts.* She yanked the gearshift into Drive.

When they reached the end of the parking lot again, Ty claimed the wheel. Eyebrows barely drawn together to make that winged frown of his, he gave her an almost silent tour of the town, finishing with the beach at the end of the point and its sweeping prospect of three states. Watch Hill, Rhode Island, crowned its long curving sand spit to the northeast, and to the southwest, the granite slab fingers of Connecticut jabbed into the blue. "And the island out there—that's Long Island, isn't it?"

"Nope. Long Island's twenty miles beyond that. That's Fisher's Island, part of New York."

"And what's the monument over there?" She nodded to a tombstone shape at the very end of the point.

"'Eighteen-twelve—brave men of Stonington chase off brave men of HMS *Ramillies*, come to burn the town,'" he recited dryly.

"They'd have burned a town like this?"

His smile deepened a trifle. "Guess it looked more like a bunch of old houses and less like a historical treasure a hundred and seventy years ago, Dark Eyes." Reaching out, he laid a taunting forefinger on the tip of her nose. "And don't history majors know that all's fair in—"

Her color rising, she flipped his hand aside.

"War?" he finished softly, his eyes as bright with laughter as the sun-swept bay beyond. "And now...back to work."

He took her to Lord's Point, a rocky, ragged little hand reaching out into the sound just south of Stonington, and gave her the wheel again.

"You don't trust me!"

"How can you say that?" One muscular arm braced against the dash, the other hooked firmly over the back of his seat, Ty tried to look wounded and failed. "That red thing's a stop sign."

"Why, so it is!" she agreed blithely. He couldn't have chosen a prettier place to explore. Narrow, winding little roads followed the granite fingers seaward, and wavelets danced and sparkled and jiggled the lobster pot markers in the coves between each ridge. After the restored elegance of the borough, Lord's Point seemed delightfully funky rather than lordly, its houses a cheery collection of salt-silvered summer cottages and converted beach houses. Along the edge of the land, occasional outsize boulders looked like wading elephants just stepped ashore to dry. "This is *another* dead end!" She glared at Ty accusingly.

"Why, so it is." His grin was utterly unrepentant. "May I recommend reverse?"

"That's what I like. Good, solid advice!" She had never felt so free, so floating before. It could go on forever, for all she cared. "Let's drive across country. I've always wanted to see California."

He bent to inspect the gas gauge, his dark hair brushing her wrist. "We'll have to fill up first."

"No problem—I've got three bucks at least. Oh, Ty, look at that house!" Someone with ingenuity and daring had sliced into and added onto the standard summer cottage. The result was an airy, surprisingly graceful hybrid of new and old, with a fantastic view southward. "Don't like it, huh?" she murmured as Ty glanced at it and turned back silently. She'd been so sure that he would. Sighing, she gave the car a bit more gas.

He let his breath out slowly. "Glad you like it. It used to be mine. Watch the dog!"

"I see him." After pulling out carefully to pass the slow trudge of a bassett who evidently owned the road, she shot a wary glance at her passenger.

Staring seaward, he was biting one knuckle. Milo nudged his shoulder just then, and Ty reached backward blindly to tousle his silky head. "Sold it five years ago," he continued in that same blank tone, as if that explained everything.

And so it did. It must have made the perfect starter house for a young couple. Plenty of lawn for a golden retriever pup and even the 2.2 kids. Oh, Ty... "Pull over," he commanded tonelessly. "We need to find you some hills."

Once they were up in the back roads, they changed places again and Ty withdrew once more into silence and immobility, leaving her to choose the way and the speed. All right, if that's the way he wanted it. But it was hard to stay depressed; her spirits rose as inevitably as the winding, dipping, steadily climbing road, rose with the increasing confidence with which she handled the turns and the narrowness of the pot-holed country lane. A streak of scarlet snapped through the oaks to the left, marking the flight of a cardinal; the darker, frizzled greens with the stringy bark would be cedars. A stone wall, or what was left of it, snaked down a rock-scrabble pasture toward a perfect New England farmhouse, white clapboards and massive central chimney. The road corkscrewed up and around a poised boulder that dwarfed her station wagon; the lichen and leaf shadow patterns across its craggy surface were lovelier than any canvas by Jackson Pollock.

Ty stirred and stretched long legs beside her. "Slow down, Ali. There's a break in this wall to the right soon...."

"So we're not lost, after all." That seemed a pity somehow.

"Almost but not quite. Take it slowly."

The gap between the tumbled walls revealed a rutted track winding up a rough-mown hillside and out of sight. And she'd wanted to get lost.... Brush scraped the underside of the chassis. The car jounced on its excellent springs and humped over the top of the hill, and the track faded out in a wilderness of cedar and granite. Below them, the rock-spined hills rolled dark and green to the west. "Dead end!" she protested.

"Why so it is." Reaching across, he turned the car key. "Come on. I want to show you something."

She shook her head quickly. "I'm starving, Ty. Let's go back now."

"Lunch! I nearly forgot." He was out of the car already, leaning in the back door. Milo shouldered past him and bounded away, and Ty hauled a small cooler from behind the seat. "Come on."

What now? Still bereft of this morning's sexy sparkle, Ty looked merely hungry and a bit impatient as he glanced back over his shoulder at her.... And he hadn't brought a blanket after all, as Don would have.

She had to scramble for her lunch, up a whale-backed slab of granite to where Ty sat waiting. "What did you want to show me, Ty?"

"Listen."

Silence. She turned her head slowly. Nothing but a breeze off the distant sound stirring the trees to a slumbrous whisper, then dying away again. Then faintly, barely audible to the west, the murmuring insistence of flowing water—a brook somewhere down there in the trees.... More silence followed her own soft savoring sigh. Earth and sky breathing. She glanced at Ty in sudden gratitude, and his answering smile was a part of the design.

They ate in silence—Vermont cheddar and a stick of pepperoni sliced with Ty's big pocket knife, a coarse black pumpernickel slathered with butter, red grapes and cold German beer. One golden retriever edged closer and closer with tragic eyes.

"And that's the last of it!" Ty warned, as the dog plucked a cheese chunk out of midair.

"He didn't even taste it!"

"Oh, yes he did. He's got the fastest tastebuds in the east, haven't you, Milo?"

Lounging back on her elbows, eyes shut, Alison tilted her face to the sun. *If you could just stay like this, keep this somehow...* Life hadn't been so sweet in a long, long—

"Sunflower woman. That's what you are."

"Mmm." A drowsily neutral response, but her skin began prickling awake at the sound of his lazy voice, and her blood stirred in a slow, sleepy, sun-warmed tide.

"So you raised your brothers?"

He just wanted to talk—good. Let him. "Mmm..."

"And there was no time to learn to drive, I suppose?"

"Nor money for a car if I had learned...."

"Hmm... What's your father do?"

"He's a professor at M.I.T.—astrophysics." She took a quick, blind sip of her beer and leaned back again.

"That should pay enough to have let you have some wheels."

"No." She shook her head lazily. "Not really. And every spare penny went for Ric's education. He was just too good for the public schools."

"And what about you?"

"Can't all be geniuses, I s'pose." But it was the only coin her father recognized. So she'd simply made do with second, no, make that third place in his heart, and dreamed her idiotic girl dreams of a man who would hold her first someday. Picturing Don, she had to fight back the ironic laughter.

"So...did you live at home while you went to college?"

"Mmm." Why did he have to know all this?

"The better to make the beds and do the dishes and the shopping and cooking and mending, et cetera, et cetera?"

"Jonnie wasn't even in his teens then. Somebody had to do it." She flinched slightly as he moved, but a squint through her lashes showed him safely sitting now.

"And your father wouldn't—excuse me—couldn't spare the cash to hire a housekeeper to give you some time and freedom to be just a silly college kid?"

Though she'd asked herself that often enough, it was irritating to have him ask it. "No...." It was water under the bridge now, anyway.

"So...is that why you're like this?"

"Like what?" she drawled coldly. But there was no hiding her reaction as a warm hand closed over her kneecap. Muscles wrenched from sun-dazed looseness into full alert as her eyes opened wide, then narrowed in the hot light.

"Like that," murmured the dark shape above her. The reasonable tone didn't hide the laughter beneath it. "All jumpy and prickly. Not easy with men." His fingers moved lightly across the back and inside of her knee. "Did you just miss out somehow, Angel?"

No. That was not how she'd started out. She'd been naive—dreadfully, fatally, naive, but not...prickly. That was how Ty saw her? Not a sunflower but a cactus woman? It had just enough truth to hurt, but his hand was down to her calf now, cupping its soft curve, and she caught his wrist. "Let's talk about something else, shall we?"

"Such as?" The quirk of his mouth suggested gentle amusement; the pulse in his wrist suggested something else entirely.

"Anything." She didn't quite dare to toss his hand aside, so she freed it gently instead.

"Mmm...the Civil War?" His voice was too smooth.

Oh, murder. So much for her lovely day....

"Or how about that dear little old lady you cared for in Providence...according to your résumé?" The emphasis on the last phrase was unmistakable. Hypnotized, her eyes followed his hand as it dropped to her ankle, lifted her foot and balanced it on his bent knee. "Or, I know...I'll tell your fortune."

"Most people read hands," Alison observed acidly, and now she was learning why, as he explored her instep. This was too intimate; the wiring was too direct.

"Ty!" But her attempt to pull away merely brought him closer as he followed her foot home and resettled himself knee to knee with her.

"Look at that!" he marveled.

"What?" The stone beneath her thighs seemed hotter now.

"What a long life line!" As he traced a line like a slow match stroke across her sole, the muscles in her legs hardened.

"Ty, don't be a dope!"

"No...you're right..." he decided, squinting down at it. "It's *not* a life line...it's a liar's line." The hand on her ankle tightened gently as she jumped. "See...it comes up here...circles your big toe twice...then heads...up country." Following the invisible line across the top of her foot, his fingers found her shin bone and started a slow ascent. "Wonder how high it goes?"

On the way up, it apparently circled her kneecap. Ty's fingers tracked patiently after it, then tiptoed on slowly, relentlessly, up the inside of her thigh.

"What d'you mean...lying?" Her breath was coming too fast now; if he'd only stop staring at her throat.

"Why, look at that! It comes out way up there again!" One warm finger found the hollow at the base of her throat, nestled there for a moment, then stroked slowly upward again. His face was too close as she tried to swallow against his touch. "End of the line!" he announced as his fingers reached her lips.

"What d'you mean?" she whispered against his fingertips.

"I mean the day Stonewall Jackson fights for the North is the day Milo whistles Dixie, Dark Eyes!" Delicately he outlined her mouth. "I mean your story smells like one of Milo's little black-and-white sweethearts. I'd say some of it's true, some of it's false, but I'm damned if I know which is which." He traced her lips again—clockwise this time.

"If you're so sure I'm lying, why did you hire me?"

"I didn't. I wouldn't have. You're Mother's idea, not mine." His finger pressed gently between her lips.

She nipped harder than she'd meant to, then grinned in spite of herself as his hand jerked back. "Then maybe you should mind your own business, Ty!"

His dark brows slanted with amusement. "I find that...difficult, where you're concerned." His hand came up again warily and curled softly around the back of her neck.

"Don't!"

"Why?" As he leaned forward, his breath feathered her cheek.

"Because I don't want you to! Will that do?"

"There you go lying again." The words finished against her lips.

Lying? It was he who was lying, kissing like this! His eyes were too close, sky-wide, peering down into hers, but shutting him out, she found herself trapped in the sun-reddened, moving darkness behind her eyelids, found herself caught between the fingers raking through her hair and the slow-moving hunt of those lips. He was lying, to kiss like this, with no real emotion behind it, but oh, what a counterfeit! Sweet silken dampness of tongue against tongue—a deep, melting, meaningless kiss, as once Don's had been, only this one was so much gentler.

Don... She opened her eyes to a black blur of his lashes aquiver against gold skin. Did he see Kathy when he shut his eyes? Taste Kathy? That would account for this tenderness.

"Don't!" She wrenched her head sideways.

"Ali?" Sun-blind, Ty reached for her shoulders.

"Don't!" She flung his hands aside, bounced to her feet and staggered. Her vision returning with the blood to her head, she stepped backward as he grabbed at her ankle. Whirling, she stumbled down the rock.

"Ali, for God's sake, what's the matter with you?" Still sitting, Ty scowled down at her.

"I don't need that!" She had enough problems of her own. She didn't need him turning her head around!

"I'd say that's just what you do need, lady!" Standing in one fluid motion, he brushed off his jeans.

Sure, sex could save the world! That was how they all thought. *"Men!"*

But his grin was wolf white. "*One* would probably be sufficient...Angel."

*And when pigs fly, that one will be you, T. C. O'Malley!* Head high, feet smarting, she stalked to the car.

There was just room to back and then turn it, if she was careful. But it took a moment to recall which pedal was which as she slid behind the steering wheel. And her knees were still shaking.

But no such problems troubled Ty, apparently; he was whistling something bright and sassy as he opened the back door. Milo leaped in, the cooler and her sandals followed, and Alison recognized the tune as Ty stopped by her door.

"Dixie." The Confederacy's battle song... All right, if it was war he wanted...

"I've figured out one thing, Angel," Ty murmured, crossing his forearms on her window frame. "You didn't fall from heaven; they gave you the bum's rush. Now scoot over."

When Irishmen flew, she would! "It's my car, isn't it?" The engine rumbled awake as she turned the key.

"Yes, indeed it is." Ty smiled gently. "But I'll drive."

"*Will* you?" The car jerked as she eased into reverse, and Ty straightened.

"Alison, don't do that." The warning rang bell-clear as she started backward.

Twisting to look behind, she put a casual elbow down over the door lock, then twisted a little farther to press the back one down. "Whyever not, Tyler? Don't you trust me?" Stopping the car, she shifted to drive.

He was moving slowly toward her. "With one beer under your belt, and you in this kind of tizzy? No way, Dark Eyes."

Through the glass of her closing window, she gave him her sweetest smile. "So...*walk*, then!"

She started off slowly, giving him time to release the door handle.

"Alison!"

A brisk trot down to the paved road would do him a world of good. Whatever hell he gave her after that would be worth it. Eyes on the twisting track, she stepped on the gas.

A flicker of motion at the corner of her eye told her he was still there beside her. Faster. The lane narrowed even further up ahead, with a slight drop-off to the left, boulder on the right.

Out of nowhere, Ty flew in from the left, landing hip first on the hood. Twisting lithely onto his stomach, his big hands clamped over the windshield wipers. "You!" He was not amused—and he was blocking the view. "Stop—right—*now*!"

So let him ride. She peered over his shoulder. The ledge—where was it?

"Now. Alison." Ty rapped the glass in front of her nose.

"Keep down!"

"Stop!" He tapped the glass again just as she found the ledge.

The car tilted left, bouncing heavily, and Ty slid away from her, still scowling, finger still pointing, the windshield wiper in his right hand unfolding as his weight hit it.

The brakes! As the right fender met granite, the brakes caught and Ty toppled, still looking more astounded than frightened as he disappeared. Then she heard the leisurely, seemingly endless sound of folding metal as her forehead bounced off her hand where it gripped the steering wheel, and the scrabbling sound of Milo climbing up off the back floorboards. Then— silence. Earth and sky were breathing, not giving one damn. The engine was dead. And Ty?

Not two feet in front of the tire, Ty sprawled like a broken toy, eyes shut, blank face to the sky. "Oh, *God*, Ty!"

What to do? Heart? Beneath her shaking hands, it was fairly hammering, yes, but breath? Warm and heavy against the curve of her palm. So then what? She touched his bare throat uncertainly. Head? Neck? Back? So many bones in that big, fragile, beautiful body, so many things to go wrong. But his chest rose in a sudden, massive inhalation as his lips moved.

"Ty!"

His eyes stayed shut, but his lips moved again as she leaned above him.

"Ty?" It was a coaxing, pleading murmur, which turned to a yelp as an arm looped around her ribs. Yanked down across his chest, Alison found herself eyeball to eyeball with a most wide-awake man. His heart was still hammering—against her breast now.

"I said," Ty pronounced bitterly, "that you ought to be spanked!"

"Me?" She tried a push-up on the rising squeak, but his arm simply flexed. "It's your own fault! If you hadn't—"

"And you're not even sorry! You do deserve a spanking." His other hand found her hips and cupped lightly in delicate menace.

"Cut it out, Ty! Stop kidding!" If she could just work her forearms between them...

"Kidding?" His brows shot up. "Who's kidding? You nearly killed me! I can't think of anything you deserve more than a good sound..." But he took a deep breath, lifting her as his chest swelled. "Well, actually..." His free hand stroked slowly up her spine to the back of her neck. "Come to think of it..."

"Stop it!"

"Why the hell should I?" he asked reasonably. "Don't I get any reparation for your breaking my leg?"

"Your leg? You mean you're—" Twisting, she stared back at their tangled legs, but his grip only tightened. "Ty, let me see!"

"Uh-uh, why should I? You're no doctor."

"Ty, I want...to...see...your...leg!"

But her sternness made no impression. "In the games I used to play, the doctors never looked like you, Ali. You look more like a nurse to me." One hand walked slowly down her spine again.

"You *are* kidding." She growled as his smile broke from hiding.

"You'll never know," Ty murmured dreamily, shutting his eyes and rearranging her slightly. "Be nice to me, nurse, I'm dying."

"Ty, damn it! I'm serious!"

"And that's just the problem!" His eyes snapped wide. "Can't you stop being so serious and just relax?" This time the hand that curled around her neck was not so gentle.

"I don't want to relax!" It would be impossible to get free, but she tried, anyway, arching her back against that infuriating hold. "I don't want to be kissed. I don't even like men, so *cut it out!*"

"Whoa... What was that again?" Ty stared up at her.

"Cut it out," she repeated bitterly.

"Before that... You don't like men?" He would have looked at a Martian that way.

"Forget it," she muttered sullenly.

"In a pig's eye, I will!" Rolling to one side, Ty brought her down to the ground beside him, still face-to-face. "You're not serious, are you?"

At that moment, she could have shot the whole sex. Seriously. "Forget it."

"So what do you like? Women? I don't believe it." He touched her eyebrow with an oddly tentative finger.

"Forget it. You just made me mad." She was getting madder by the minute and felt like some small, wild animal in a box trap. The walls were squeezing in as his arm pulled her closer.

"No, I'm not about to forget it. What do you like?"

"I like to be left alone!" For just a second, something snapped; the animal inside fought the trap, bounced off walls and ceiling, not knowing or caring who or what was hurt in its frenzy to be free. Her fingers spread against that wall of a chest as Ty rolled gently on top of her, pinning her flat and panting beneath him.

"Hey...hey...Ali, hey...Ali-angel..." The words brought her slowly out of it, low soothing nonsense words crooned in her ear. "Ali-Ali..."

Slowly she opened her eyes. Her mouth was pressed to the side of his throat, where his deep steady pulse surged against her parted lips. She tasted salt on her tongue, noticed the scent and warmth of the man and the feel of him as they breathed as one.... In... rest...out...rest...

"Ali?" Ty lifted his head slowly to stare down at her.

"Mmm..." It was very important not to think just now. His eyes were the same color as the sky.... How long had they been lying like this?

"You in there?" Freeing her shoulders, Ty's hands slid slowly up to frame her face as he raised himself on his elbows.

"Mmm..." she murmured finally, reluctantly. He needn't look so worried.... She was fine, as long as she didn't think.

Lacing his fingers in her hair, he traced the arcs of her eyebrows with delicate thumbs, inner edge to outer, inner to outer, making another rhythm to mesh with their breathing. "Ali...are you a virgin, by any chance?"

Idiotic question. Why couldn't he just be quiet? "No, you dope." *Please shut up. Please.*

His thumbs soothed her eyebrows again, and she could feel his muscles slowly tightening. "Ever...been raped?"

The chance to hurt him opened so suddenly—like a door in the trap—that she took it instinctively. "Not till now. No."

She felt her blow thud home through every inch of her, every place they touched, and then he was still again. Too still. "Sorry." He rolled off her carefully and sat up.

This sudden abandonment was so shocking—as if she'd been safe in bed and someone had peeled the roof back. The sky was darker now. How could she have said that?

"Ali, I'm sorry. You know I'd never—"

"I know that, Ty." But he couldn't just sit on people till they gave up their secrets. It wasn't fair. Especially when those secrets could mean nothing to him. Less than nothing... "That's not what I meant."

"I know, I know, I know...." He stood up suddenly, all his weight on one side, and limped toward the car.

"You *are* hurt!"

Leaning against the hood, he straightened and bent the leg several times. "Just bruised. Hit the rock, I think." He glanced down at the boulder.

It was the size of a hippopotamus, and her lovely car would never be quite the same again for meeting it. Ty would never have been the same if he'd fallen two feet to the left. Suddenly sick to her stomach, Alison sat and watched while he backed the car a few feet, then beat the fender away from the tire with a rounded stone.

"That'll do for now." He stood carefully.

"Ty, let me drive!"

He almost smiled, or so it seemed in the twilight. "I'm not *that* sorry."

# CHAPTER NINE

AT THE FIRST SPLASH, Alison looked over her shoulder. "No way! Don't you dare! Out of here!"

But giving her a blandly pink-tongued smile, Milo put a second paw in the blue wading pool.

"Go on!"

He simply stood there, tail waving, looking as hot as Alison had been before she'd discovered the dusty children's pool folded away on a garage shelf that morning. In a fit of inspiration she'd found a spot on the lowest terrace, well hidden from all sides, and inflated and filled it there. She'd spent the morning like a studious crocodile, her back in the sun, her book propped in the grass beyond.

To repel this invader she was going to have to sit up. To sit up, she would first have to retie her bikini top. "You creep!" she declared as Milo waded all the way in and dipped his tongue for a slurp. He was about as stoppable as his master, and where was Ty? For he'd taken Milo along with him, after that first disastrous driving lesson four days ago.

With an ecstatic little groan, Milo collapsed beside her and laid his chin across the rim. Marvelous, sunbathing with a dog.... But he looked as if he'd died and gone to heaven, and if she heaved him out, he'd simply squelch back again. Giving his ear a half-vengeful tweak, she turned back to her book.

> Marseilles, March 12, 1864
>
> Dear Paul,
>
> You will pardon my silence when you know its sweet reason. She has eyes like a cat in torchlight, hair like a cascade of burgundy.... Alicia...I paint and I love and I paint, that is all—but then, what else is there?
>
> You would not recognize my work now. It is the light down here, I think—that and my boundless delight. No contour could confine or define it. Color is all....

A faint whir sounded from above; so that's what Ty was up to—cutting the top terrace. Head raised, she listened, seeing in her mind's eye the heave and lunge of his big body against the thick grass. He would be shirtless in this heat, slippery with sweat....

And in the meantime, down here, she was cool, calm...and stranded. For she had no intention of parading past Ty in bikini and beach towel to reach her room, no way would she face him half-naked, remembering as she did the feel of his body pressed against hers. Shivering suddenly, Alison turned the spasm into a shrug.

They hadn't spoken again, once they'd come down from their hill that evening. Her anger had slowly rekindled as it became apparent Ty had not been seriously injured.... Rape, he'd asked. It hadn't been that far from rape.... Did he have any idea at all what he was doing to her? She'd begun to be so happy this past year, having finally begun to put the pain and anger of her divorce behind her. She'd begun to build a serene and self-sufficient little world for herself—to be happy, damn it! She shifted restlessly, then stopped as her thighs slid across the rubbery floor of the pool.

He was taking a can opener to her psychic armor, that's what he was doing, with that insatiable drive of his to find out what was underneath. And even if he did succeed in slicing through her shell, there was no guarantee that he'd like what he found inside. There was every guarantee that he would not, because whatever, whoever she was, she was not and would never be Kathy.

Beside her, Milo whimpered, dreaming, and Alison nudged him in the ribs. Kathy's dog...just as Ty was still Kathy's man in spite of what June called his skirt chasing; that had been plain enough when they'd passed his old house. So women, to Ty, had to be just a sweet and temporary way of forgetting, just balm for the pain....

Well, whatever Ty thought, she had no intention of being drafted for that role; she'd been second too many times already. *Never* again.

"I've heard of strange bedfellows before, but this takes the cake!"

Oh, Lord! At that teasing baritone comment, her body contracted. Goose bumps skittered across her thighs and shoulders. Dropping her book, Alison folded her forearms on the rim of the pool and buried her face against them. *Go away!*

She could feel the light footfalls of his approach through her stomach where it touched the ground. "Lady?"

*I don't need this, I don't want this. Go away!*

"Lady?" He was kneeling beside her, his breathing suddenly audible. "I have this bo-kay for you, lady. Special delivery. Complete with written apologies."

*Complete with string attached, you mean!* Blindly, Alison shook her head. *No, thank you.*

"Lady?"

There was just no fighting him. "You can give it to my social secretary there," she growled against her arms.

"Uh-uh. I was told to deliver this direct."

"Come back tomorrow. Or next year would be even better."

"'Fraid this is your last chance, Angel. The roses are past prime already. I had to scrounge for these."

"You're breaking my heart!" she mumbled, then jumped as something soft brushed her arm.

"Glad I've got company." He stroked her arm with the blossoms again, then twirled them slowly against her cheek and ear.

Damn, oh damn the man. She sniffed in spite of herself. The fragrance was a color in her mind and the air around them suddenly glowing, all pinkness and sunlight.

"It's awfully hot out here...." Ty murmured suggestively.

It wasn't all that much cooler in the pool, despite the water lapping against her sides.

"Can I come in?"

She'd as soon share a hot tub with Genghis Khan! "Uh-uh."

"Love my dog, love me...." he wheedled.

"He wasn't invited, either."

"Party crashers, that's us." The water splashed, then lifted her slightly as Ty dropped down beside her, and hunching her shoulders, Alison ducked tighter against her forearms. "Ali, don't worry." His voice lost its bantering edge for a second and sounded as soothing as the fingers that touched the back of her head.

Don't worry, he said. So what about panic? She ought to get up now, but to do so, she'd have to tie the bikini.

Softness tickled her ear. "C'mon, little girl," Ty coaxed. "Take a rose. It won't hurt at all."

Huh! "Those things have thorns, you know." It was hard to keep her voice steady while warm, gentle fingers arranged the flower behind her ear.

"Not now they don't. I'm dethorning them. Have another rose." Like it or not she had one, behind her left ear this time. The third blossom was wedged in the crook of her elbow.

"That's more than enough, thank you! Give the rest to my blond friend."

"The blonde's a dog, lady." Ty slipped the fourth rose inside her other elbow. "And, anyway, I picked these for you."

"Thanks heaps."

"You sure make it hard for a man to aplogize, Angel." Underwater, his hand closed around her foot, squeezing gently as she flinched, then stuck a rose between her toes.

"Oh, that's...what are you doing? I thought this was some new sort of assault," she gasped as he caught her other foot. "The Connecticut Flower Man, pouncing from behind tall bushes...."

"Raincoat and roses, that's me," agreed Ty sunnily. "Turn over. This one's for your belly button."

"Stick it in your ear."

"Mmm...got a better idea." One teasing finger tickled the back of her leg, and then a rose stem slowly insinuated its way between her close-pressed knees.

Oh, Lord. "Ah..."

"Say something?" He inserted the second rose a few inches above the first; her temperature rose a few degrees along with it.

It would be so simple just to spread her legs and let the flowers fall. Simple and utterly impossible with that big hand stroking up the back of her thigh. The third rose drew a line of slow fire between her legs as he slipped it into place. "Tyler!" Closing her teeth in one forearm, Alison squinched her eyes even more tightly shut.

"Mmm?" His breath seared the backs of her legs as he leaned above her. Just inches below her hips, Ty positioned the next rose, gave its stem a slow, taunting twirl and then pushed it slowly...slowly home.

*"Ouch!"* Roses flying, Alison pushed up and whirled half-around when the sensation registered as pain. "Hey!"

"Damn it, Ali!" Ty was staring down at her leg. Slipping his hand under it, he lifted it slightly to see better. "God, Angel, I'm sorry! I missed a thorn." Glancing up at her in almost comical remorse, Ty froze. Alison looked down to see her small breasts, her bikini top dangling below them by its string.

"Ulp!" She flopped flat in the water again, blazing forehead pressed against the rim of the pool.

That left Ty still in possession of her scratched leg and laughing. Gentle fingers examined the inside of her thigh.

"Ow!"

"It's okay now, darlin'. I just had to pull out the thorn." A hand settled soothingly across the back of her waist as he raised the injured leg higher.

"Damn it, Ty, that hurt!"

"I know...." His lips found the cut, and with deliberate, unbelievable tenderness, he turned the pain into heat once more.

"Better?" Murmured against her skin, the word was a laughing growl.

"Uh-uh, worse!"

"Hmm." He licked her again thoughtfully. "Okay...then see if this helps."

"*Hey!*" Alison squirmed helplessly as lips, then teeth, found the soft inside of her other thigh and strung a series of tiny, red-hot nips up to the bottom edge of her bikini. "What the hell do you think you're doing?"

"Distracting you. Does it still hurt?" Unfazed by the fabric of her swimsuit, he nibbled gently up the swell of her hip.

"Yes! I mean *no!* If you *don't* mind!"

"Mind?" He laughed, his lips brushing slowly across the small of her back. "Lord, Angel, I don't mind at all!"

"Well, I do," she gasped as he straddled her legs. Turning her head on the rim of the pool, she could just see him kneeling above her from the corner of her eye. His tongue found the hollow of her back and licked slowly higher. "I *do* mind, Ty!"

"Do you?" he murmured skeptically, his mouth making a warm, lazy side trip along the edge of her shoulder blade. "You sure?"

Sure of nothing, she shuddered convulsively while he traced the other shoulder blade. "Yes, I'm sure."

Ty put a hand down either side of her shoulders and leaned above her, his chest nearly grazing her back. "Why, Ali?" He nuzzled her ear.

Why? Why indeed, when her whole body ached for him, when it took every last ounce of her willpower to stop herself from pressing her back and hips up against the waiting, welcoming warmth above her.

"Why?" His lips brushed her ear again.

"Because..." Because Ty would break her heart just as surely as Don had done, though he'd be so much kinder, gentler and nicer in the breaking of it.

"Ty? Alison?" From up on the back deck, June's voice reached them easily.

"Don't answer!" Ty whispered as she turned her head toward the sound.

Was he kidding? "Yes, June?"

"Lunchtime, you two! Come and get it before I feed it to you know who!"

You know who recognized a lunch call as well as the next dog. Lurching to his feet beside them, Milo dripped out of the pool.

"Look out!" Ty cowered against her as the retriever stopped to shake himself.

"Yipe!" Laughing, Alison ducked, while above her, Ty took the brunt of it.

"Aagh!" Rolling off her, Ty collapsed back down in the water beside her and wiped his face with a forearm. "I needed that."

"Here." Collecting one of the roses floating between them, she held it out to him as a peace offering.

"Thanks." He clasped it with both hands to his chest, funeral style, and squinted skyward. She dropped another rose on the black line of hair curling down toward his navel. His lips twitched, but he didn't turn.

"It started out as a nice apology..." she ventured finally.

"Mmm."

"I think I'd better quit."

That brought his head around and his dark brows together. "Why? Because of me?"

Cheek against the soft rim, she nodded solemnly.

His eyes seemed bluer than usual, reflecting the pool around them, as his frown slowly faded. "Wouldn't do any good, Ali."

"What do you mean by that?"

"You're a smart girl. Figure it out." He sat up abruptly. "Now, c'mon. June's going to be hopping."

"Right." Fumbling for the ties to her top, she flipped them across her shoulders, then flinched as his hands touched her nape. "I can do that!"

"I'm sure you can." But he didn't let go. Brushing her curls aside, he started the bow.

She should quit. That threat had been a bluff, but she should really do it. It was getting worse each time he touched her. "Where's Mother, by the way?" he murmured absently. "Upstairs?"

"No, she had a doctor's appointment in New London this afternoon. Mrs. Winthrop's taking her, and they decided to have lunch out first."

His fingers stopped. "That's funny...I spoke with Mother yesterday. I told her we'd drive her down and give you some highway practice at the same time." He gave the ties a final tweak.

"Guess she forgot...." Strange, Harriet was hardly the absentminded type. Starting to sit, Alison glanced down at her top. "Hey, that won't do. It's too loose."

"So I'll fix it." Shoving her gently flat again, he was even slower untying it, as if he were savoring the simple action.

"All right, you two, this is the absolutely final last call!"

"Be right there, June!" Ty yelled back, but his fingers kept their own lazy, caressing rhythm. "Well...in that case, if Mother's taken care of, let's drive down to Essex."

"What's down there?" she murmured drowsily.

"One of our boat yards. We've got a new travel lift that I haven't seen yet."

"Boat yards? Thought you owned fishing boats...."

"Oh, we do." He pulled the strings gently, and the top tugged softly at her breasts. "That tight enough?"

"Mmm..."

"Dad was an Irish hustler," he continued absently. "If it was connected to saltwater, he gave it a try. Fishing boats, marine salvage—got a few boat yards cheap just after the war.... One thing sort of led to another." He finished the bow, then simply held it. "We've been getting into party boats these past few years. Got two out at Montauk, and we're building another."

"What's a party boat?" she mumbled dreamily, not ever wanting to move again.

"A big boat that takes parties of wild-eyed, wild-drinking fishermen out to where the fishing's good. Want to try it sometime?"

She shook her head mutely, her hair brushing his hands, and then tried to sit up. After a second's hesitation, his hands dropped away. Avoiding his eyes, she checked the bow with her fingers.

Beside her, Ty stood. "What grade do I get there?"

"For bow tying?" She glanced up at him.

"For restraint." He held out his hand, and reluctantly, she took it.

"B minus," she decided as he lifted her.

"Well..." That hidden smile crept a little closer to his mouth and eyes. "That's a start."

"THE ONLY PROBLEM was that, in those days, Ty didn't wear pajamas. He was quite the hit of my bridge party." Flashing her son a mischievous smile across the dining-room table, Harriet held out her glass for more wine.

His face about the same shade as the rosé he was pouring himself, Ty shook his head. "Uh-uh. When you start exposing the family...jewels, it's time to cork it." Setting the bottle down just beyond her reach, he gave her a meaningful stare but the quirk of his lips spoiled its effect.

Undaunted, Harriet turned to include her in the family squabble. "Alison, my dear, when you have children, arrange to have your daughters first. Men who start out as big brothers are ruined for life; they take their responsibilities far too responsibly.... Tyler, I'm not tipsy—I'm happy. I've had one-half a glass so far, and I intend to have the other half!'' Her chin lifted slightly.

"Never cross a redhead with intentions...." Ty measured out exactly half a glass, his smile slowly curling. "That's probably the best bit of advice Dad ever gave me."

Above her triumphant smile, Harriet's eyes suddenly glittered in the candlelight.

"So when did Ty stop sleepwalking?" Alison hastened to ask. "Or did he?"

"Well, let's see, the time that he devastated my evening bridge party... He was almost seven then, and I suppose he kept it up, off and on, for another year or so. The midnight monologues continued until he left for college, and I imagine they continue unto this day, don't they, Ty?"

Her son shifted restlessly. "Don't ask me! I'm always asleep."

Who should she ask then, Alison wondered, inspecting his profile through her lashes, above the tilt of her wineglass. He had been gone from Shady Breeze for half a week this time, going over the plans for the new boat being built up in Rhode Island. He'd dropped in for a driving lesson and then dinner this evening, but he hadn't come straight back to them. June's husband, Tom, had sighted him on the street in Mystic late last night. Talking with a blonde—"a blonde to knock your eyes out, my Tom said, though his eyes fall out so easy it's a mystery to me why he hasn't gone stone blind these past twenty years or so!"

Perhaps the blonde would know if Ty still talked in his sleep. Though she herself could testify to that. *"Kathy, come to—"*

"Earth to Ali..."

"Ahh...yes?" Looking up, Alison made the mistake of meeting his eyes. Toes curling in her sandals, she blinked, but it was too late. The warmth of his gaze surged across her body in one dizzying wash of heat; her nipples were suddenly taut and aching.

"Want some coffee?" he asked, with a hint of a smile just for her.

Dishes cleared, they settled in the living room. Returning from the kitchen with the cream, Alison found Ty leaning against the mantel, his eyes on the Degas. "What about this?" He threw a quick half teasing, half serious glance at his mother. "I never liked these ol' ballerinas much, anyway."

"You'll sell that over my dead body!" Harriet assured him warmly. "You can do without your boat yard, Ty. You've got enough already!"

"But I want this one," he said reasonably, still staring at the painting.

"Well, find another way to finance it."

"I will," he promised serenely and strolled over to the coffee tray.

"Speaking of paintings, Ty—" Harriet's voice took on a certain precision "—just when will my *Alicia* be ready?

Above his coffee cup, Ty's smile seemed a bit forced. "Just in time for your birthday."

"I don't see why it should take that long!"

"I understand this guy's the best. I expect he's got quite a waiting list of paintings to be cleaned."

"Who is he, Ty?" Alison asked casually. Forrest had so many connections. If she could just locate the painting, it was possible that the professor could contrive to see it.

"Why?" Ty's polite interest seemed just a touch too innocent. "Do you know any professional restorers?"

"Ahh...no, I just wondered—" Jumping guiltily as the phone rang across the room, Alison breathed a sigh of relief. Saved by the bell!

Phone to his ear, Ty laughed. "Well, hello yourself, stranger!" Turning to his mother, he mouthed the name, "Patsy."

The younger sister in California.

"No, I'm just mooching some home cooking tonight. So how's Bill? What? Oh..." Dropping into the easy chair behind him, he slouched back, stretching out his legs. "Okay, I'm sitting. Shoot." Eyebrows cocked upward, he glanced across at Harriet, and then his amusement vanished. "You're *what*?"

On the sofa beside her, Harriet had caught the change in his face, as well. "Ty, what is it?"

But gesturing for silence, Ty hunched forward over his knees, his face slowly hardening to an expressionless mask. "I...that's wonderful, Pats," he murmured dazedly. Eyes wide, he was staring a hole through the carpet at his feet. "I...no... No, that's... wonderful."

*Is he trying not to cry,* Alison wondered suddenly, as beside her, Harriet got slowly to her feet.

Ty swallowed carefully. "That's terrific, Pats. I'm proud of you. Now Mother's dying to talk. You take care of yourself, all right? Bye." He dropped the phone on the chair and stood. "For you." Face a frozen blank, he patted the hand Harriet had laid on his arm and turned away. "Back later." Four long strides, each one longer and quicker than the last, and he was gone. The front door clicked softly shut.

Still staring after him, Harriet lifted the receiver. "Darling? What's your news?" Then her face lit up. "Oh, baby, that's marvelous!" She sat down carefully, still beaming. "No, darling, he's fine. You just...took him by surprise. You know he's thrilled for you." She glanced toward the front door. "No, Patsy, that *was* the way to break it. He wouldn't want you to tiptoe.... Now when are you due?"

So Patsy was pregnant. Why had that hurt him so? And what could she do to help? Nothing, nothing at all, Alison told herself bleakly. She should leave the room, give the expectant grandmother a little privacy, but Harriet finished as Alison rose to go.

"That was Patsy," she announced proudly. "She's pregnant."

"So I gathered." Alison grinned. "Congratulations, Grandma!" Harriet had crossed the room without her walker, she realized.

"She's tried twice before and miscarried each time," Harriet explained, rising shakily. "So this time they waited to tell us. She's five months pregnant, and the doctor said today that he thinks she's out of danger."

"That's wonderful, Harriet!" Alison collected the walker. "Do you want this?"

"Why don't you bring it along and lend me a shoulder?"

They moved slowly to the front hall, Harriet keeping her balance with the lightest of touches on Alison's shoulder. "Did Ty leave?"

"I'm not sure. I didn't hear the car."

Harriet studied the door for a moment, then sighed. "Alison, would you do me a very great favor?"

"Of course, Harriet. What is it?"

"Go find him."

Simple words, but somehow they had a weight and a resonance out of proportion to their simplicity.

"And bring him back?" Alison asked carefully, trying to decipher that mute appeal...if it existed at all.

Harriet shook her head. "Not necessarily. I'm going up to bed now. But I think Ty might be in need of a little company just now."

But why expect *her* to provide it? Alison wondered as she stepped out on the front porch. It was not that she wouldn't do anything in the world for Harriet— not just because of the guilt she always labored under, but because Harriet was Harriet—but still...

The pines above the porch stirred gently. Ty was not on the porch but his BMW was still parked down the hill, Alison noted as she came down the steps. Out on the lawn, she forgot him for a moment. Head thrown back, she turned one slow, full circle, taking in the stars. In the blue-black dome above, they seemed to be shimmering in time to the crickets song. Lonely, lovely... Where would Ty be?

Pacing along the crest of the hill, she scanned the darkness, then stopped. Something big and light bobbed uphill toward her—Milo. He stopped for a pat, then wandered off to the house. Peering downhill again, Alison spotted a rocklike shape where no boulder should have been. Arms clasped tightly around his knees, Ty stared out to sea. His head jerked slightly as she dropped beside him, but he didn't turn.

And now what? She hadn't thought past finding him. In the dark, his breathing was slow, deep, almost shaky.

Automatically hers slowed to match it. Out... in... Out on the sound, a buoy winked one red eye—on...off...on...out...in...while two tiny lights, green and white, glow-wormed steadily across the dark.

"Fishing boat coming into Stonington," he muttered. His voice had a ragged edge to it—swallowed tears? "Watch..."

Green light, white light—then a red light blossomed and she laughed under her breath. "Magic..."

"Just made his turn," Ty explained huskily. "We're seeing him head-on." Silently they watched as the green light vanished and the red and white crawled shoreward. Beside her, the grass rustled as Ty lay back, hands clasped behind his neck.

Something as old and irresistible as gravity was tugging at her shoulders, telling her how easy it would be to lie down across his chest, rest her ear against his heart.... But staring up at the stars, Ty was elsewhere, shut in with his sadness, thinking of—

"June told you about Kathy?"

What should she say?

"Oh, don't worry," that low, toneless voice continued. "I knew she would.... Guess we all use June to say the unsayable."

The unsayable... So that's what Kathy's death had been—still was—to him.

"Well, there was something else." His voice pushed doggedly on against her silence. "Something I only told Dad. And, of course, he told Mother."

He was silent so long that she leaned above him, trying to make out some expression in his upturned face.

"She was pregnant."

It took a second for those flat little words to hit home. "Oh, Ty..."

"We'd found out the day before she flew out there. We'd decided we'd give a little dinner party for our parents, champagne and all, and make the announcement...when she came back...."

*And she never came back....* Starlight gleamed on his cheek for a moment, and Alison stroked the tear away with her fingertips. Never, *never* would she feel sorry for herself again! She had merely wasted her time and her love; Ty had lost his. Beneath her fingers, she felt him smile. Then, warm and gentle, his hand closed around her wrist, moving her hand till it covered his mouth. Trying not to shiver, she sat there, cupping his breath in her palm, holding his life and feeling it seep through her skin to mix with her blood and join the crazy rush of it up to her heart and back again to his touch. Warm lips moved against her palm. A word or a kiss? Then lifting her hand, he moved it down to his heart.

She felt a slow, steady drumbeat, slower than her own heart's stuttering. He wasn't feeling what she was feeling at all. Though her hand was warm against his body, the rest of her was suddenly cold and she shuddered.

"Cold, Ali?"

"No."

"Don't you ever tell the truth?" Half sitting, he hooked an arm around her waist and pulled her gently down. She squirmed, but Ty didn't let go, only loosened his hold enough to let her wriggle onto her back, her head nestled against his shoulder.

Defeated, she sighed and felt his arm rise with her rib cage. Overhead the stars quivered brighter and nearer; she shivered again and his arms tightened. Turning, he buried his face in her hair.

"It was like waking up in a strange land," Ty murmured against her, "once I finally realized she was gone.... No one to talk to.... I couldn't speak the language, couldn't understand it...."

Putting up a hand, Alison laid it against his cheek and he snuggled closer. "Sometimes it feels like I've just been talking to myself these past five years...."

And so he'd searched, and was still searching, woman after woman, for someone to talk to. Not one of them spoke his language...for not one of them was Kathy.

*And neither was she!* Ty pulled her closer, and she shivered again. Under her fingers, his head turned restlessly and his mouth found her palm; she could feel the hot, damp stroke of his tongue throughout her body. Her hips slowly tightened, fighting the aching urge to rock upward.

"Dark Eyes..." The hand at her ribs smoothed slowly higher, and her thighs and stomach tensed, as well.

"Ty..." *Don't. Please don't.* But his hand was sliding gently up around her breast, his thumb teasing the upstart nipple, and she caught her breath in a gasp, her back arching, her breast swelling to fit his palm. Then she froze again. If she started moving now it was over. All over.

"Ali, what's wrong?" His thumb circled in sweet persuasion, and she sucked air between clenched teeth again.

Wrong? What was wrong? *Everything*—to feel this way, knowing how badly he could hurt her and *would*, if she were fool enough to let him love her. For she wasn't Kathy. Her muscles were shaking with fatigue, the trembling made worse by the shivery dance of the fingers upon her breast. If she ever took on a man again, he would have to love her. No one else. *Her.* "Stop!"

His fingers froze. "What's wrong, Ali? I thought you came out to find me."

"Your mother sent me."

His hand jerked against her breast, then lifted away. "I see..."

Without that sustaining touch, her body lost its hard, urgent curve and sank slowly, limply beside him.

"And that's the only reason you came?"

If she widened her eyes enough, stared hard enough at the stars, she would not cry.

But Ty's fingers caught her chin and swung her gently to face the pale blur of his face. "That's the only reason, Ali?"

The only reason she would ever give him. "Yes."

"My...mistake, then. Somehow I thought—" Ty sat up without completing that thought.

If she stared hard enough at the sky, she would not cry. But the stars were smearing across the darkness, and she couldn't stare them dry again. Rolling over, she pushed to her feet. "See you later, Ty."

"See you," he muttered bleakly, staring out to sea.

He could talk to himself, once she was gone. Or even to Kathy.

## CHAPTER TEN

"AND HOW MUCH RAPPORT are you developing with the dear lady?" Forrest inquired while buttering his third slice of the freshly baked French bread their waitress had supplied.

"We get along very well." That was actually the fourth slice, Alison decided. "As you see, she leaves me pretty free to come and go as I please during the days." She glanced appreciatively around the dim, elegant restaurant that Forrest had chosen for their lunchtime rendezvous in Stonington. As much as she'd grown to love Shady Breeze, it was nice to come down from her peaceful hill for a change. Nice to take a break from Pat's papers—she'd just discovered a new cache this morning—and nicer yet to take a break from her dissertation. Harriet had promised they'd do some sight-seeing, once she got her license, but to do that she first had to satisfy Ty that she was ready to try for it. And he hadn't returned to drive with her since the night of Patsy's phone call, three days ago.

"Do you anticipate any difficulties in persuading her to let me view the painting, Alison, once it's returned?" Forrest broke into her reverie.

Alison shrugged. "I don't understand why she refused you that first time you called, Forrest. Harriet's hardly the neurotic-possessive type.... Are you sure that you only asked to see it, that time you phoned her?''

"Absolutely."

"She has quite a...sentimental attachment to it, you see, especially since her—especially now, so if you asked her to lend it for an exhibition, yes, I can see her refusing you.... But just to view it?" Perhaps Forrest had rubbed her wrong, though he was usually at his most charming with women. Or perhaps Harriet had simply anticipated that pleas for a public revelation would follow the rediscovery of *Alicia, After*. As indeed they would have. Still... "I don't know. Harriet seemed almost eager to show it to me that first night."

"That confounded, infernal nuisance of a son of hers!" Spoon poised, Forrest glared up from his avocado. "I'd like to...to..." But apparently the desire could not be specified in mixed company. Shaking his head he scooped viciously into the soft green.

Alison hid her grin in her water glass, then straightened her face as the professor glanced up. "Another thing that puzzles me is why *Ty* would want to hide the painting from me, if Harriet has no objections to showing it," she said hastily. "Or could that have been coincidence, his taking it just then?"

Forrest dabbed at his lips with a flourish of the white linen napkin. "You're quite convinced he suspects you?"

"Oh, he knows I'm lying, all right." She nodded gloomily. I'm just not sure he knows *why* I'm lying.'' Why hadn't Ty tried harder to find out? Or had he?

"Presume for a moment that he does know why," Forrest hypothesized. Lacing his fingers, he propped them against the tip of his nose. Above them his eyes examined her beadily. "Presume that he did, indeed, recognize my car the day of your interview... and so, ascertaining that you are a spy for me, he removes the painting. What does that signify?"

"That's what I was wondering!"

"One." The professor raised one forefinger on high. "It signifies that the piece is genuine, and that the younger O'Malley wishes to avoid the fame and assorted hoopla that will inevitably follow my worldwide announcement that the painting has been located, and that it is indeed one of the lost *Alicia* series." His eyes gleamed brighter at the thought. "Or, two." His opposite forefinger shot up to form a peak with the first. "The painting is false."

"That's a good alternative," she agreed wryly.

"Answer me this, Alison," Forrest commanded, eyeing her from behind his finger steeple. "Who stands to inherit the Minot once Mrs. O'Malley...passes to her reward?"

"She's not that old, Forrest!"

"Could it conceivably be our muscle-headed young friend? What would happen to the value of that painting, should we prove it false and announce that to the art world?" Forrest asked softly.

*And more important, what would happen to Harriet?* "It would become worthless, or at least worth *less*, depending on who the artist really was..." she concluded reluctantly for him. "But you think it's going to be authentic."

"Since Drew Harrison thought so thirty-five years ago, yes, I am most sanguine," Forrest agreed briskly. "And furthermore, that last theory credits O'Malley with what I conceive to be an excess of foresight, to presume that he's guarding the painting's future value." The professor paused, his small eyes dreamy as he nibbled a black olive from around its pit. "So let us consider some short-term motives our impetuous young friend might have. Suppose, *just* suppose, our friend were in need of money, right now..."

Her eyes flicked up from the tablecloth as a low teasing voice echoed in her brain. *"What about these old ballerinas?"*

"Is it possible that, at this very moment, *Alicia* hangs on some ecstatic new owner's wall?" speculated Forrest softly. "There are umpteen private collectors who would give their firstborn male child plus a few spare millions for one of the *Alicia* Minots."

"Ty would never do that to Harriet! Never!"

"Even if he had reason to believe the painting was a fake and that we were about to expose it? Might he feel he was protecting his mother by converting the painting to cash, thus leaving some new owner to be caught holding the bag?"

Would Ty do such a thing? He could be fiercely protective, yes, but still...

"Or here's yet another possibility," Forrest purred relentlessly. "Suppose O'Malley needed a short-term loan—say, for two months? Paintings have been used for collateral before, with banks, and certainly with private lenders. But again, that deal would fall apart the minute the painting was proven counterfeit."

"Or perhaps he's simply having the painting cleaned, damn it! You make things seem so sinister, Forrest."

The professor's smile was superior—man-of-the-world to ingénue. "Life often is." He bent over his avocado.

"So the gist of all this is that you have no more idea than I do what's going on," she growled.

"Quite. Therefore the inevitable conclusion is that you stay put, my dear. Sooner or later he'll have to produce either the painting or a damned good explanation for his dear mama. Either way, we're that much closer to the truth, with your little foot in the door." Leaning back as the waitress cleared their plates away, the professor smiled to himself. "Thirty-five years..."

"Can I bring you something else, sir?"

"Yes, my good woman. We'll have two Viennese coffees, if you'll be so kind." Flourishing his napkin again, Forrest turned away. "And now, my dear, how goes the dissertation?"

"Rather well, actually, Forrest. I've come up with an interesting theory about Minot's use of interlocking compositions. I tried it out on Harriet and—"

But the professor's face had settled into an indulgent smirk. "And you needn't look like that, Forrest. She's more knowledgeable than half the professors I've encountered at either B.U. or Brown! She married too early to go to college, but I didn't need to bring a book with me. She has all mine and quite a few more I've found useful, and they've all been read to tatters."

"Well, I suppose it's hardly surprising," Forrest conceded. "Her mother did write the definitive treatise on the Post-Impressionists, to say nothing of..." His voice trailed away as those bird's nest eyebrows drew together. "But if Mrs. O'Malley's in a position to comprehend the earthshaking significance of her Minot, why hasn't she—"

"Why, Tyler O'Malley," a clear soprano fluted gaily from the entrance lobby across the room.

Forrest's eyes bulged. "Oh...my...dear merciful heavens!"

Beyond a departing foursome, Alison could just make out a pair of broad shoulders and that unforgettable profile. The girl—woman—clinging to Ty's forearm and beaming up into his face with such sweet provocation was a blonde...a beauty...and Alison hadn't felt so sick since...since—

"Au revoir, my dear!" Nearly tipping his chair as he bounced to his feet, Forrest bolted toward the rest rooms, his forgotten napkin fluttering from one fat hand like a flag of surrender.

If she didn't look his way, Ty might not see her. Alison fixed her eyes on the window, her stomach churning in time to the waves, her ears straining to catch the eager piping of the blonde. A blonde... Would this be the same one June's husband had spotted in Mystic? Or another? What did it matter? If the blondes were lined up two abreast all the way around the block, waiting their turn, what the hell did it matter to—

"Where's your friend?"

"Ha?" No need to fake surprise as she jerked around; how could the man move like that? He seemed taller today as she tilted her head back to meet those glinting eyes, as if he were poised on the balls of his feet like a fencer.

"I said, where's your friend?" Ty dropped his hands on Forrest's chair back.

"My friend?" Alison thought she could make out from the corner of her eye a slim shape lingering in the lobby doorway. What about *his* friend?

"The friend Mother said you walked into town to meet," Ty elaborated levelly, his finger tapping gently against the polished wood.

"Ahh...you just missed him." Was he angry?

"Him who?"

Yes, he was angry. And beyond him, Ty's own inquisitive friend still watched. Or waited, Alison realized, as a sensation like heat lightning flickered across her stomach. "My friend," she repeated perversely, as if Ty were just a trifle dense.

His half whisper was savagely precise. "I guess I was after a *description*." Yanking the chair out, he dropped into it. "Young? Old? Married? Single? How long you've known him? How well?"

"And I guess I wasn't in the mood to give you a description!" she shot back. The high-handed, arrogant—

"Oh, well, in *that* case..." Ty shoved back his chair, then froze as the waitress appeared beside them.

"Here you are," she warbled, placing the coffee cups before them. Her smile vanished in confusion as Ty sliced a glance up at her—as if the amiable frog of a few minutes before had changed to an ill-tempered prince. "Oh..." She took a step backward. "Oh, and here's...this." She dropped the check midway between them and fled.

The check. And she'd brought no money, knowing that Forrest was apt to stick her with the bill if she did. Arms crossed, Ty was leaning back in his chair, looking, by that first sneaking quirk to his lips, as if he just might enjoy this, after all.

Alison stared down at the bill again, her face slowly heating as she pretended to check the math. So now what? Offer to wash dishes? Drag Forrest from the men's room to pay up?

"Pass the cream?"

She lifted it absently, then froze, pitcher in midair, as over Ty's shoulder she spied the plump, fleeting form of the professor gliding toward the exit.

Before her, those blue-gray eyes sharpened. As Ty started to turn, she smacked the pitcher into his still-outstretched hand and let go.

"Hey!" But his fingers caught it automatically as he snapped back around. "Careful there!"

"Sorry." Biting her bottom lip to stop the laugh, she met his glare wide-eyed.

He studied her for a second, then whipped a glance over his shoulder. But the doorway was empty now. No blonde. Professor long gone.

And that left guess who to pay the piper! She glanced down at the bill again.

"If you want help, you'll have to ask." He put Forrest's cup down, his eyes alight, and licked a stray drop off the corner of his upper lip. "Well?"

It cost a lot to find the proper tone of humility. "Well...would you?"

"Well...I don't know..."

"Damn it, Ty!"

"What's the magic word?" he teased.

"Please?" she growled.

"Beg pardon?"

Heaving a sigh, she gave in. "Please."

"Consider it done, Dark Eyes." Plucking the check from her fingers, Ty studied it while he sipped his coffee, his eyebrows slowly rising. "Exotic taste you've got there," he concluded at last. "Avocado stuffed with goat cheese, shrimp and sun-dried tomatoes?"

"No, I had the chowder and the spinach sal—"

But the sudden flash of his grin told her she'd fallen into a trap, though just what it was she had no idea. "I *see*," he murmured with obscure satisfaction, and leaned back in his chair, suddenly completely relaxed.

For a moment they studied each other in silence, his apparently amiable, hers wary. But Ty had forgiven her for deserting him the other night, it seemed. So her presence could hardly have meant that much to him, then. And she had tossed and turned half that night, hating herself for running when he needed her... needed someone. Anyone? Softly, she sighed. Most likely he'd gone back to town and found a blonde. What color hair had Kathy had, she wondered.

"Nice blouse," Ty decided as he finished Forrest's coffee.

It was her favorite, too—cream linen with a low, square-cut neckline, but she was in no mood for compliments. "Thanks." Ty was dressed as casually as ever—navy polo shirt and khakis. Did he even own a business suit like other men?

"Yes?" Across the table, Ty was watching her like a cat. Abruptly reaching out, he rested three fingertips in the valleys between the knuckles of her hand outspread on the tablecloth. They fitted exactly.

"Don't you ever work?" She snatched her hand out from under.

"I like that!" He left his hand before her, just inches from her ribs. "I started on the books at five this morning, so I'd have time to make you safe for the highways this afternoon."

"I'm driving today?" Why couldn't he move that hand? She had an odd impulse to touch it, to find out if her fingertips matched the hollows between *his* knuckles.

"You're driving, Angel—it's your last chance for a week. I'm off to Miami tonight. Want to come?"

Not bothering to smile at the joke, she shook her head.

"I have to raise some cash, and fast," he answered the question in her eyes. "One of Dad's oldest backers has retired down there. I'm going down to sail with him for a few days and then we'll talk money."

And perhaps art? People, even old friends, didn't give money away for nothing. But Ty wouldn't, just wouldn't, sell Harriet's painting, would he? "What... why do you need money, Ty?"

"There's a major boat yard coming up for sale down on City Island." His fingers tapped restlessly before her. "We could have *just* swung it before Dad died...but he wasn't quite...planning to go when he did, and the estate got nailed for the taxes." Pulling his hand back at last, he sighed gently, "I'll have to put together a syndicate, if I want it now."

"I'm...sorry. I didn't know you were having trouble."

He gave a cheerful little shrug. "Trouble's a relative term, Angel. I haven't exactly hocked Milo yet."

Or Harriet's painting?

"You'll get used to it. The O'Malley fortunes are like a roller coaster, but we've got the luck of the Irish," he concluded in Hollywood-Irish brogue. "Let's go."

"NOT BAD," Ty decided, glancing back at the car parked behind them. Opening the car door, he looked down at the curb. "Not bad at all, Ali."

Why should a little praise bring her so much pleasure? Alison shoved that question aside. "Shall I try it again?"

But Ty shook his head. "You've about worn out this spot. Let's find something more exciting. There's a little old lady down on the next block who always parks her Silver Cloud in front of her house. You can park next to that."

"I will not!" Alison exclaimed, laughing. Checking her rearview mirror, she pulled slowly out from the curb.

"Where are we going?"

"I don't know. I'm just the chauffeur."

"Okay, go straight," Ty decided.

That route dead-ended at the little town beach on the end of the point. Well, she'd circle it once and head back into town.

But Ty had other plans once they'd bounced out over the potholed sand. "Park here, Ali. I want to watch the waves."

As long as that was all he watched. She swung the gear shift to Park, but left the engine running.

Ty reached over and shut it off. "That's better."

That depended on how you looked at it. She decided not to. Stretching her legs out, Alison crossed her arms, tilted her head back against the seat and shut her eyes. It wasn't so bad when they had something to distract them, such as the parallel parking, but at times like this, you could cut the tension between them with a knife. Shifting restlessly, she tried to focus on the screams of the gulls blowing in through the windows with the sea sound, and the nose-wrinkling tang of sun-dried kelp.

"I'm going to sell you to a sideshow," Ty decided beside her. "The Amazing Knot Lady!" he declaimed, barker style. "Watch her loop those lovely limbs into a bowline, a clove hitch..."

Opening her eyes, Alison looked down at herself. She'd crossed her legs as well now, and had indeed pulled herself into a tightly drawn knot of rejection. "Granny knots," she joked feebly, unwinding her legs. "That's all I know. They'd never take me."

"Oh...I think we could find you a taker," he murmured, sliding around on the seat to face her.

She didn't turn, but stared out to sea through the spokes of the steering wheel instead. Don had taken her...taken her for everything she had to offer.... And yet Ty could take her for so much more...hurt her that much more; she *had* to keep remembering that.

"Okay...we'll change the subject," he agreed, though she hadn't spoken. "You got some mail today. I checked the box on my way out."

"I did?" Still she couldn't turn.

"Mmm." Something soft stroked across the underside of her chin—an envelope, her name and Benefit

Street address typed on it, then forwarded by the post office to Shady Breeze. No return address.

Grateful for the distraction, she grabbed it. ''Thanks.'' But inside was not the advertising come-on she'd expected, only a single sheet of stationery, covered with that slashing, blatantly male handwriting she'd hoped never to read again. But it was too late now.

Sweet Lips!

Was passing through town the other day and decided to look you up just for laughs and whatever else I could get. It wasn't that hard to get your address—that little swivel-hipped redhead in your art department office was most obliging. But she tells me you're off on vacation. With who, baby? And is he as good as me? We both know, don't we? So, till next time.

Oh, and don't bother to change apartments, doll. You know I can find you when I want you!

All my best,
Don

Conscious of Ty's eyes on her face, Alison folded the letter on its original crease lines, twice. Did she look as green as she felt? She folded the letter again, careful to line up the edges exactly. It was an empty threat, meant to disturb, to intimidate, but he hadn't the persistence to follow through on it; she'd be out of his mind as soon as he left town...wouldn't she? Halving the letter again, she pressed down the crease precisely. He'd just never forgiven her for being the one to leave. Alison took a deep breath. It was simply meant to remind her of the hold he'd once had on her, to bring the past back in all its vivid, unhappy detail. Sexual assault by U.S. Mail. How could she have ever, ever loved him? Grasping the perfect little square between thumbs and forefingers, she started to rip.

The paper twisted and stayed firm, and she stared down at it stupidly. Too thick. She'd have to unfold it once to—

"Here." Large fingers plucked it out of her grasp, and Ty tore it neatly in two. "Will that do?"

Alison shook her head. Shreds. She wanted shreds.

He tore each half in two again and glanced at her questioningly.

How could she have ever thought that he was like Don? "Again, please," she whispered.

Putting three squares on the dash, he ripped the fourth with some effort. "That's as small as they go, Dark Eyes." He handed her the pieces, ripped the other quarters one at a time and dropped them into her cupped hands. "Shall we eat them now?" His eyes crinkled.

Smiling, astounded that she could smile, Alison shook her head. Clutching the shreds carefully, she elbowed her door handle up and nudged her door open against the push of the sea breeze.

Standing sentry on top on the garbage can, a sea gull took wing at her approach, his derisive yelp echoing behind him. Lifting the lid, she deposited the confetti precisely on top of a half-eaten hamburger. *Farewell to thee, Don. You can't hurt me anymore.* As the wind whipped her hair into her eyes, she returned to the one who could.

When she slid behind the steering wheel, Ty gave her an unreadable assessing glance, then turned back to the waves. "Got anything you want to tell me?" he drawled, his eyes on the horizon.

Her breath caught for a second. "Such as?"

"Oh...say...who and what you are?" His level gaze swung her way and stayed this time as the color burned slowly up her cheeks, climbing right up to her hairline. Eyes watering with the blush, teeth clenched, she stared back at him, cornered.

Finally, he sighed. "Okay, okay... Sorry I asked."

So was she. She started the engine. But a hand closed over her fingers on the key and turned them back gently. "Just one question, Ali. Is Ericksen even your real name?"

Her hand jerked and his fingers squeezed gently. Ericksen...her father's name...It was as real as any she'd ever have. It had been Harris for a while there; she'd had to beg a judge to give her back her own name—as humiliating and painful as the rest of the sorry episode. She glanced up at him sideways. "Of course it is!"

But she'd waited too long. His fingers slipped out of her fist. "God, you're a rotten liar! You ought to know better than to try by now."

"It is!" So much for his wonderful understanding!

"If you say so." Swinging away from her, he squinted out to sea, the muscles rock hard along his jaw.

And finally, just to fill that chilly silence, she started the car.

## CHAPTER ELEVEN

SILENCE STILL PREVAILED when Alison and Ty came up the front steps of Shady Breeze a few hours later. Except for the briefest of directions and questions, the driving lesson had been a mute one since the beach, but if Ty thought he could force her confidences that way, by withdrawing all his warmth and support, he had another think coming. Two could play that game.

"Ty? Alison?" Harriet's voice came from the sunset side of the house.

"Coming, Mother."

But she met them at the corner. One hand poised just above the porch railing, she walked steadily toward them, her face stern with concentration.

"Mother, for God's sake!" Ty's steps quickened. "Where's your walker?"

"In the house." The briskness of her reply in no way concealed the pride bubbling just below the surface of her words. Turning slightly, she moved her elbow out of range of her son's hovering hand.

"And what would your doctor say to this?"

Her chin lifted slightly. "Congratulations is what he'll say, or I'll find one who will!"

His sigh was closer to a snort, but the smile that had been missing all afternoon seemed not so far away. "Congratulations, in that case, before you disown me.'' Brushing her chin with one careless knuckle, he turned aside and, behind his back, Alison's eyes met his mother's in gleaming amusement. ''What's this?'' Ty scowled at a pitcher on the wicker table. ''Lemonade?''

''It is, but none for me, thank you.'' She walked slowly back along the railing, one hand at the ready.

Handing Alison a glass without looking her way, Ty watched gloomily as Harriet reached the corner and came back again. ''You're making me nervous, pacing like that,'' he complained, dropping into one of the wicker easy chairs.

''Well, I'm nervous myself.'' Without raising her hand to the railing this time, Harriet turned and prowled slowly away. ''Mother called.''

''Ah...'' Ty's hint of a smile was directed down into his glass. ''And what does Eliza want?''

''She's driving up to Boston next week. James has finally decided to retire, and she's taken a new chauffeur on approval. I suppose she wants to road test him.'' Stopping, Harriet turned glumly to lean out over the railing. To the west, a red-orange sun was trying to squash its way past the green-blue resistant horizon. ''The official reason is that she's attending the opening of the Bonnard exhibition at the Museum of Fine Arts. And there's some young sculptor up in Marblehead who's caught her eye. She plans to inspect his studio before she decides whether to give him a grant or not.''

''And let me guess.'' Ty smiled. ''She's commanded your attendance on this little jaunt?''

Back turned, Harriet nodded shortly.

"She just wants to see you, you know," he said gently. "The rest is just window dressing."

"Well, I don't want to see her!" Harriet cast him a stormy glance, then started away down the porch again.

It was time to vanish. Putting her empty glass on the table beside Ty, Alison turned to go, but two fingers hooked over the back of her belt, checking her in midstride. "Stick around, Ali" Ty ordered under his breath. "You're family." Without releasing her, he filled her glass again and put it in her hand. His fingers nudged the back of her waist in a teasing salute. Then his hand slipped out of her pants just as Harriet turned.

Backside burning, Alison retreated to sit on the railing, turning to glower back at him. But all Ty's attention was for the approaching Harriet. "She had some kind things to say about Dad...at the funeral," he told her. His mouth quirked suddenly. "At least they were meant kindly!"

But Harriet was not impressed. "It's just a little late for that now, wouldn't you say?"

"Better late than never, Dad would have said," Ty retorted softly.

Eyes flooding with sudden tears, Harriet whirled to face the sunset again, and this time she moved with the awkward, unconscious grace of a girl.

"He always admired the old gal, you know," Ty continued, "even if she did scare the bejesus out of him."

"She didn't scare him!" Harriet declared fiercely.

"Well, she sure scares me!" Laughing, Ty rose to lean on the railing beside her. Silhouetted by the sun's afterglow, their profiles were a rough and a finished casting from the same mold. "But I think you should go. It's a good idea."

"I don't want to go!"

"I bet you'd enjoy it." Draping an arm around her thin shoulders, he started her slowly toward the front door. Passing Alison, he put a hand to her back to bring her along, as well. "Take Ali along to protect you."

"I wouldn't inflict that on my own worst enemy, let alone Alison!" Harriet declared. "She's not tough enough."

"Oh, nonsense, Harriet! Of course I'll come." If Harriet needed moral support, it was her place to give it, after all.

But both of them were looking at her as if she'd lobbed a cherry bomb off the porch. Then Ty laughed quietly. "You see? With Alison riding shotgun, what have you got to fear?"

"She doesn't know Mother..."

"I could show you *The Fishermen*—my favorite Minot," Alison coaxed. Ty was right. An excursion was just what Harriet needed.

"I'd love to see it with you, Alison," Harriet returned warmly. "And someday we will. But I suppose, this time...I've got to face Mother alone."

"Bravo!" Ty applauded. "I wish I could be there to see it, but I'm down in Florida till Thursday, and then I promised Jake and Lena I'd be here Friday." In the dusk, his hand smoothed up Alison's back, then dropped as he reached for the door and ushered them both inside.

I OUGHT TO BE WORKING, Alison told the man silently.

*What? On a day like today?* That's what Patrick O'Malley seemed to be saying as he laughed up at her above his trophy-size fish. The sunlight from the window behind her reflected off the glass covering his photograph, and those deep-set blue eyes—bluer than Ty's—squinted up at her through the glare of two suns, one trapped forever within the frame, the other rolling slowly up the sky outside toward twelve o'clock. *There are better things to do than study on a Friday afternoon,* Ty's father insisted cheerfully.

Yes, there were, but she had no one to do them with and was too blue to do them alone. Ty must have returned from Florida late yesterday. Somehow she'd thought he'd stop by, but... *Guess he had other fish to fry,* she told his father sardonically.

Pat's grin seemed to widen a trifle, but he had no comment to share. Seated at the foot of his bed, she studied him somberly, searching for the missing son in that laughing, weathered face. The shape of the forehead, something elusive but unmistakable about the nose, and then, of course, the capable set of those wide shoulders... There were hints and portents for her, but Ty was no carbon copy of this earthy Irishman.

*Ah, but the temperament's my own!*

That seemed likely. Harriet, for all her charm, had a fragility, a nervy brittleness that Ty lacked. His easy confidence, his...unflappability, must have come from this man.

Meanwhile Patrick appeared to be sizing her up. *So you're Alison,* he concluded, smiling. *It's high time he found a new girl.*

*It's not that simple,* she protested. *He still loves his Kathy.*

But Pat was not worried. *Give him time.*

If it were only that simple! Standing, Alison smoothed the bed, then turned back for one last look. There was something about the curl of the lips, as well...

*Give him time,* Pat seemed to repeat. *And now, young lady, I have this fish to unhook.*

Smiling in spite of herself—at herself—she left him to it, shutting the door to Harriet's—and Pat's—room softly behind her. If only it were that simple. But if Ty hadn't recovered in five years, why expect him to recover at all? Look at Harriet, still pining as if she'd lost Pat yesterday.... Ty had inherited a gift for loving from both parents, it would seem. That could prove a curse as well as a blessing.

Drifting moodily down the hallway, Alison returned to her room. Harriet wouldn't be back till late tomorrow. In her absence, Alison had written herself to a standstill on her dissertation, and so had spent the whole morning winnowing the last of Pat's papers— and then had gone to tell him so. Now there was nothing left but Minot. Six months ago he would have been companion enough....

"Miss me?"

The low, laughing words whirled her around to find a familiar shape lounging in her doorway. "Why, no. You mean you've been away?" But the silly grin on her face belied that breathless taunt.

"Damn right I've been away, you dark-eyed liar! Do you still remember what a triangular yellow traffic sign means?"

"Yield," she answered automatically.

Ty simply stood there, his eyes holding hers as her color rose. "Right," he murmured finally. "Let's go take that driving test."

"Now?" Was he crazy?

"Now. Your hour's at hand, Angel—I'll meet you downstairs." He turned, then spun back again. "Bring a sweater and wear tennis shoes."

"Why?" But he was gone.

"I DID IT! I actually, actually, really did it!" Alison chortled for the third time. Too excited to sit in one place, she bounced on the car seat, then clasped her hands simply to keep them still.

"What did I tell you?" Smiling to himself, Ty pulled the station wagon out into the line of traffic waiting for the drawbridge to come down.

When it lowered, they crept over the Mystic River and into the bustling town. "I actually did it.... Sure you don't want me to drive?"

"Can you fly and drive at the same time, Angel?"

"Oh, absolutely! If I can pass that test, I can do anything!"

"Glad you're finally figuring that out...but we'll be there in a minute. Why don't you just sight-see and I'll play chauffeur for now?"

"Where are we going?" Alison turned to admire old brick mills and once-shabby warehouses converted to glass-eyed condominiums and offices. And a pleasing amount of grass and trees had survived the development.

"You'll see," Ty promised serenely, turning down a drive that wound around a granite ridge toward the water. They parked next to a familiar blue BMW in the small lot beside another converted mill, this one an upright, surprisingly graceful structure at the river's edge.

As they got out, Alison glanced at him warily. "Is this where you live?"

"Yup." Opening the back door, Ty collected a large damp paper bag.

"What's that?"

"Just a little something I got while you were off observing stop signs."

Ice and bottles from the sound of it. She took a deep breath. A celebration drink, at his place? Much too dangerous.

Ty turned away from the building and headed across the grass toward the river. Scampering after him, she fell into step. "Ty, where are we going? I can't *believe* this mystery routine!"

"Not so amusing when you're on the wondering end, hmm?" That shut her up. She followed him out one of the finger piers past a long sleek power yacht. Tied behind it was a large dinghy, the rectangular sport-boat type with two big inflated rubber tubes forming the sides and meeting in a point at the bow. Stepping aboard, Ty stowed the bag and turned back to give her a hand.

It was impossible to avoid his eyes as his hand— warm, utterly secure—closed around hers. He didn't let go, but stood holding her more with those strange

twilight eyes than his fingers, until the wake of a
passing powerboat rocked the dinghy. "Sit there, Ali."
Nodding at the air-filled rim of the boat, Ty sat across
from her; their knees nearly touched. Turning to the
formidable outboard in the stern, he fiddled with a
lever, yanked a cord and it roared into life. "Cast off."

As they powered downriver toward the Sound, her
heart hummed in time with the outboard. Wherever
they were off to it was wonderful, magical! With the
sun nearing the green hills to the west, the river was a
well of deepening blues. The white-painted pilings of
the docks alongshore and the white boats tied up at
them gleamed pale rose shading toward lilac.

Looking over his shoulder, Ty cut the motor.
"Look!"

Coming up from behind, looking as wide as a small
jet on the narrow river, a swan ghosted toward them
at eye level, his wing tips nearly kissing the water with
each floating downstroke. Soft rush of feathers, a
glimpse of wild dreaming eyes and the perfect snowy
line of outstretched neck...to be run down by a swan—
what a way to—But carving a last-second detour
around them, he found the precise center of the river
again and rustled away. Laughing quietly, unbeliev-
ingly, she stared after him.

A hand cupped her cheek. Still laughing, she turned
into Ty's kiss, soft and strong as a wing pressed
against the air. Wings beat in her throat and her heart
as her lips and tongue answered his, and a wild sweet
sensation feathered across her shoulders and down her
spine—wings sprouting, perhaps? But she was flying
already, her breath coming faster with the effort, as
she breathed him in.

Gentle and sure, he finished the kiss before she'd had enough. He backed off a few inches to study her, his eyes darker than the sky and full of questions.

"Thank you," she half-whispered finally.

An incredulous smile flashed from hiding. "For what, Angel?"

*For making me feel this way!* "For the swan...for the day...my license. This adventure." Smiling, she shrugged, struggling for some lighter note.

The current had carried them downstream, and was now floating them through the open gap of a train bridge, its steel girders black lace against the washed-out sky. "If you want to thank me—" Ty took a deep breath "—kiss me." He was struggling for lightness, as well, but not quite finding it.

"I thought I just did..." she joked feebly.

Slowly, Ty shook his head. "I kissed you. You've never..." His voice trailed away and he tried to smile.

Never kissed him, never willingly touched him. Was it that lonely, then, to be the man, the pursuer? He looked so young and almost frightened, waiting for her to reach out or to reject him.

As desirable as he was, how could he feel that way? Her hands came up without thinking. He shouldn't be left to feel that way. Leaning slowly forward, Alison framed his watchful face with her hands, her palms tingling with the heat and the evening roughness of his skin. "Thank you," she whispered against his mouth.

He didn't seize the lead as she'd expected. Warm and responsive, his lips answered her own, but Ty let her do the soft exploring, let *her* set the gradually quickening pace. Wings, she was definitely growing wings, Alison decided, pulling him closer. Wet velvet touch of tongue gliding across tongue—Lord, this was crazy! Too sweet to pass up, but so crazy; this aching pleasure was a measure of the pain that would follow when she fell back to earth.

Ty's face jerked between her hands, breaking their kiss, and his head whipped around. "Damn! We're almost aground. It's shallow in here." Yanking the cord, he started the outboard and spun the inflatable around, out toward the channel. Lips still tingling, Alison took a steadying breath and willed her heart to slow down, while trying to tell herself that this interruption was welcome. For nothing had really changed between her and Ty. Nothing....

Without releasing the motor's steering handle, Ty moved across to sit beside her, shoulder to shoulder, thigh warming thigh. That last kiss had been a big mistake.

The river had spread to a wide sheet of shining blue as it neared the sound. Granite-fringed islands were topped with lush greenery and opulent houses throwing back the sunset from copper-bright plate-glass windows. In the distance, she could pick out the delicate sunlit verticals of sailboat masts.

"Ali?"

She hunched her shoulders and looked past him, jaw set.

"Want to steer?"

"Me?"

"You. Anybody who can drive a car can handle this. Push this to the left and she'll go right, and vice versa." Once she was given something to worry about, her worries vanished for the moment. It was easy, so easy, humming along like this, one side of her warm from his body, her hair blowing back with the wind.

Ty draped a casual arm around her shoulders and she shot him a wide-eyed look of warning. But his other hand covered her fingers on the steering grip. "Hold on." And he turned the handle.

The outboard's growl rose half an octave. Surging ahead, the inflatable seemed to lift itself almost out of the water as their speed doubled. "Don't make any sudden moves," Ty yelled calmly beside her. "Just a little bit will turn her." His hand dropped away, leaving her in charge of their snarling flight. The boat skimmed between the soft lilac sky above and the hammered silver river below like a zipper welding the two halves into one translucent whole. With engine vibrations shuddering up her arm, Alison's whole body shivered in speed-crazed delight. Ty squeezed her shoulders and nodded toward the east. The first star… *Star light, star bright, just let us go on this way all night.*

"Lobster pot marker ahead," Ty sang out, pointing to the white bleach bottle floating at the end of a line leading down to a trap. "Head to the left—slowly."

They were nearing the boats now, all of them moored or anchored in an outer harbor, all of them nosing into the last gasps of the daily southwester. Ty nodded toward the outermost boat, a dark blue one with two masts. "See the ketch out there? She belongs to some old friends of mine, Jake and Lena Salzman. They're just passing through, on their way up to Maine."

Just what she needed—strangers to deal with. She was having trouble enough dealing with her own feelings. But it was too late to turn back now. A hatch slid back, and the silhouetted head and shoulders of a very large man popped up from below. Ty shifted to the other side of the dinghy. "Better let me bring'er alongside."

Alison studied the man and then the woman coming on the deck as the dinghy idled up to the boat. Old friends of Ty's.... They would have known Kathy, then....

"Welcome aboard!" Enfolding her fingers in a paw the size of a baseball mitt, the bearded man helped her up to the deck, then stood looking down at her with a plainly admiring grin—what she could see of it through a red curling beard. "And so this is Alison."

"Hello." Not a brilliant retort, but it was far better than her usual tongue-tied response. Perhaps she *was* learning....

"So you still haven't trained him to shake and let go?" observed Ty to the petite brunette who was smiling at them from around Jake's awesome spread of shoulder.

"He's untrainable! I learned that years ago." She gave Ty a quick exuberant hug. "Hello, stranger!" Then she turned to Alison. "I'm Lena, Alison, since these lugs have forgotten their manners. And this is Jake." Her hand rested on his upper arm for a moment, then slipped away. "Now come sit down in the cockpit, and I'll fix you a drink."

"All we need are glasses, Lena," Ty told her, leading the way aft to the rectangular foot well, which was surrounded by cushioned benches, and above that, a sheltering curve of varnished mahogany. "I've brought the booze." The "booze" was Dom Perignon.

"My God, we rate that highly?" gloated Jake, hoisting the bottle for gleeful inspection.

"Dream on, friend!" Ty reclaimed the champagne. "I brought *you* some rum." Moving to sit beside Alison, he balanced the bottle lightly on her denim-clad knee. "This is for Alison."

"Oh? What's the occasion?" Lena wanted to know as she returned.

"The occasion..." Twisting to meet Alison's wary eyes, Ty studied her for an instant, as if she knew the answer better than he. That ever-ready smile crept slowly from hiding as she stared back at him, cornered. "The occasion is that Ali got her driver's license today."

"All right!" Jake applauded. "Free at last! So—to Alison and the open road!" Grinning, he clinked glasses with her, and she found herself smiling back.

"Thank you. But the real credit...umm...to an *intrepid* and persistent teacher...." She saluted Ty and the others followed suit.

"Most persistent," he agreed softly. After a long moment, he looked around. "And to old friends..."

"And to new," Lena declared, touching glasses with Alison. Then she dashed off to rescue the roast in the oven. Alison followed her down the ladder.

Her first impression of the interior was one of richness and warmth. Varnished mahogany glowed softly in the light thrown by a polished brass kerosene lamp. The corduroy cushions on the settees along each side of the cabin were almost the same shade as Ty's eyes. On the butcher-block counter in the small U-shaped galley, a crystal vase was jammed full of roses.

"Now's the time to explore," Lena warned while filling a pot with water from a polished brass pump over the sink. "There won't be much room to move around once those two come below."

Forward of the main cabin was the head, with lockers opposite. The forward-most cabin housed a V-shaped double berth with shelves built above it along each side of the hull. A hatch overhead was propped partly open to let in the soft sea breeze. *You could leave it open on clear nights and watch the stars,* she realized. *Just lie there in someone's arms and watch for shooting stars.* A pang of envy bright as any star shot across her soul—for the stars, or for the sheltering arms that seemed to go with them?

A faint, tentative little yodel sounded from above, and Lena chuckled. The sound drifted away, then returned, swelling mournfully to a full-throated howl. "Moon's rising," she informed Alison.

Jake's song rose again; a crooning, oddly haunting plea. Stepping partway up the ladder, Alison peeked out on deck, where all seemed damp, empty darkness after the golden light of the cabin. Then to the east, she found the object of Jake's ecstasy—a gigantic red eye just now peering above the horizon.

The moon song rose again from the stern, and turning aft, Alison could see Jake leaning out from the rigging toward the path of moonshine that was slowly creeping toward the boat. Beside him, Ty leaned against the mizzenmast, hands in his pockets. As she watched, he tipped back his head and added a pensive, bluesy harmonizing to Jake's higher moans. The moon was nearly clear of the horizon; their duet rose to a series of exultant coyote yips in counterpoint, then merged into one last triumphant howl that faded slowly away as the moon broke free. To Alison's ears, the rumbling masculine laughter that followed sounded no more civilized than the previous wolf music, and she found herself laughing in soft disbelief.

Ty's head swung around. Beside him, Jake finished his champagne and lobbed the glass in a lazy, overhand arc out to sea. A final splash amid the moon's glitter, and then it was gone. Alison shivered. Ty was picking his way forward across the deck with long, catlike strides. He knelt beside her silently, and a hand curled round the nape of her neck.

"Hello, wolfman."

"Bite your throat, lady?"

"No, thank you." His eyes were black and silver.

"What's the matter—don't you howl?" Ty asked huskily.

Silently, Alison shook her head. There'd been no one she'd ever really wanted to howl with, before this.

"It's easy. Just hold your lips like so." His fingers shaped her skeptical smile into an open pucker. "Perfect." His mouth covered hers and clung gently as she started. Then his lips shaped a soft, silent howl against her, a wild exultant sound that only they could hear as Ty pressed her closer.

Something shuffled on the deck beside them; glasses clinked faintly. Taking his time, Ty finished the kiss, then looked over his shoulder. "Are we blocking traffic?"

"Oh, not at all." Jake grinned at them. "Not at all. We seem to have lost another glass," he mumbled when he followed Ty down the ladder.

Glancing up from the roast she was carving, Lena gave him a dark look. "That's *four* you owe me!"

On a scale from one to ten, the evening was a twelve, Alison decided later. The folding mahogany table had been cleared except for the brass candlesticks and the crystal, which Lena—no doubt wisely—kept for below. Across the table, face wild in the flickering candlelight, Jake was embarked on yet another yarn. She shifted slightly and Ty's arm tightened around her, as if he feared she were leaving. But no fear of that, for this night was magical, better than any that had ever come before. Probably better than any that would come again, but she'd worry about that tomorrow, back in the real world.

"You've never told me you two were in Paris together!" Lena was protesting.

"I certainly have," Jake insisted. "The infamous Christmas ski trip we took in our sophomore year? To the Alps? The time Ty broke his wrist and I was arrested?"

"And that's a story in itself—" Ty began.

But still watching her husband, Lena cut him off. "I hate to be the one to tell you, dear convict, but Paris is not in the Alps." She reached up to pick a bit of fluff out of his beard.

"We went to Paris first, Lena. I *know* I've told you this. About Ty's painting and the imaginary marquis?"

Ty shifted suddenly and slouched down on the settee, stretching his legs out beneath the table.

"Why, we chased all over Paris, hunting for—" Jake jumped slightly and swung to look across the table, his red eyebrows rising in puzzlement "—hunting for this marquis,'' he continued after a second's hesitation, ''and it turned out—'' Ty shifted again just as Jake's story jerked to a halt. Taking a deep, careful breath, Jake scowled at Ty.

''Have some more wine,'' Ty suggested blandly.

''No...thanks, I'm seeing gremlins under the table as it is, pal.'' Jake shook himself and looked around briskly. ''Now who wants tea and who wants coffee?''

''But what's this about a painting?'' Alison protested. ''And who was the marquis?''

Ty grinned easily. ''Some other time, Ali.... To tell that one properly, Jake has to be either sober as a judge or four sheets to the wind. He wouldn't do it justice tonight.''

Shooting him a quizzical glance, Jake turned away. ''Tea or coffee, Ali?''

Sipping their coffee, they listened to the weather forecast on the *Bluebird*'s UHF radio. Chance of thunderstorms late tonight, clearing by morning. Jake went forward to let out more anchor chain—thunderstorms meant squalls and a wind shift—while Lena stretched and gave them a sleepy, yawning smile. ''Why don't you two stay here tonight?''

But Ty was shaking his head. ''You guys are on vacation, Lena. The last thing you need is a mob scene in the morning.''

In spite of Lena's declarations to the contrary, and then Jake's, Ty stood firm. On the forward bulkhead, the brass ship's clock chimed eight times.

''Why eight bells when it's really twelve?'' Alison wondered.

Jake laughed. ''You've got a lubber this time!''

"Out!" Lena commanded suddenly. "These poor people want to go home and you're in the way."

A lubber *this time*, Alison mused, following a grumbling Jake on deck. Previous times meaning Kathy, or some woman or women Ty had dated since? Brooding over that, she missed her footing stepping into the dinghy.

"Easy!" Hands bruising her waist, Ty deposited her on the far side of the inflatable and turned back for his farewells. In spite of the boat bobbing, *he* had no trouble standing, apparently.

Arms tight around each other's waists, their hair haloed by the full moon at their backs, the Salzmans stood watching Ty and Alison pull away. Jake waved one long arm in a final, flailing salute, then turned to envelop his wife in an extravagant, dancing-bear hug. Beside Alison, Ty laughed. "Like them?"

"Yes." And envied them. Desperately. What would it be like to be that sure of someone, that right with someone? That comfortable and happy? She'd never, ever had that with Don, not for a moment.

"Good." Ty caught her arm. "Now slide back here and hang on. I want to make tracks."

## CHAPTER TWELVE

WITH THE OUTBOARD'S ROAR climbing up the scale, the inflatable lifted up and took off. Behind them, their wake was a comet trail, foaming bright in the moonlight, then smoothing out into two rippling black ribbons veering across the midnight blue. His arm snuggled around her waist, Ty was peering over her shoulder, and shutting her eyes for an instant, Alison gave herself up to sensations—wind in her face, the warmth of his body, the endless, shuddering power beneath her thighs. They were halfway back to town already.... What then? She shivered and his lips touched her ear.

"Cold?"

It happened all in that second. She felt him tense, the dinghy veered wildly to the right and then Ty's arm was sweeping her onto the floorboards as the engine sound changed. The steady purring choked and died just as Ty landed on top of her. The dinghy hit the end of some invisible tether and surged backward, then stopped cold, bobbing gently up and down.

After the speed and the noise, the motionless silence was nearly deafening. Stunned, flat on her back on the floorboards, Alison stared up at the moon, too winded to laugh yet.

"Ali?" Ty sat up with a groan. "Ali!" His hands were shaking as they traveled up her ribs, brushed butterfly light across her breasts, searched her collarbone and then her neck. "Angel, are you all right? Can you sit up?"

"Of course." With his arm around her shoulders, she came up easily, and he leaned her back against one side of the boat. "What happened?"

"We've caught something in the propeller. A lobster pot marker, I think." Ty bent over the motor as he talked. Grunting, he straightened and the outboard pivoted up out of the water and locked into that position. "Right," he panted.

Alison clambered back to lean beside him. At the end of the drive shaft, a dark, dripping wad reminded her of a ball of yarn that had been bested by a kitten. "There's a propeller under all that?"

"'Fraid so."

The knot ended in a single line as thick as her finger, leading bar-tight down into the water. Somewhere down below, a lobster trap and probably some lobsters were serving as their anchor. Ty straightened and stole a glance at the sky.

"So what do we do now? Wait for help?"

"Nope..." Ty scrounged in the pocket of his jeans. "I start chopping." He pulled out his pocket knife.

But it wasn't easy. Hanging out over the stern to reach the propeller, Ty had to balance himself with one hand along the drive shaft and hack one-handed at the knot. From the other side of the outboard, Alison watched him bobbing just inches above the water as the dinghy hobby-horsed in a sudden gust of wind. "What's the sky doing?" Ty muttered, working his knife blade between two turns of line.

Doing? Alison looked over her shoulder. The stars were muted by moonlight, but a starless patch of darkness caught her eye and she understood. *Chance of thunderstorms...* To the west and north a soft margin of pure black now edged the horizon. "Ah..."

A snapping, metallic sound from the outboard whirled her around as something heavy splashed into the water. *"Damn!"* Upended over the stern, elbow deep in the river, Ty struggled for balance. The locks that held the engine in up position had slipped; drive shaft and propeller were now underwater.

"Here!" Catching his belt, Alison hauled him backward until he caught his balance, but he didn't turn.

"Thanks," he growled absently, peering down into the river. "Son of a *bitch*," he finished in a teeth-clenched, vicious whisper and heaved a disgusted sigh. "Lost my knife... I've had that knife since..." He shook his head bitterly, still searching the water as if it might float to the surface any moment.

Since Kathy gave it to him, no doubt. And he still cared that much. Suddenly too tired to stand, Alison slumped down on one side of the dinghy.

"Since I was twelve," Ty continued absently. "Dad gave it to me for Christmas. *Damn!*" Spinning around, he consulted the sky; the black stain had crept a little higher, but had to be miles away still.

Surely she shouldn't have felt so happy. It was nothing to her, who gave him knives. Or it ought to be nothing, if she had any sense at all.

Stalking to the bow, Ty knelt and peered under the rubber splash cloth that covered the first four feet of the dinghy, turning it into a protected crawl space. Reaching under, he dragged out a coil of line and a small anchor, set them aside, then crawled in farther. He backed out a moment later with a screwdriver in his hand. Growling to himself, he returned to the stern, upended the outboard and attacked the line with a vengeance.

Sliding down to sit on the floorboards and lean back against the soft side of the boat, Alison watched the moon and listened to the muffled curses wafting back from astern. Sighing contentedly, she stretched her legs out. There were worse places to be—millions. And worse people to share them with...about two and a half billion.

By the time Ty gave up the struggle, the clouds were halfway to the zenith; the leading edge of the front was a roiling, shifting band of silver lace. "I can't do it." Ty dropped heavily beside her. "I'm sorry, Ali."

"Don't be—it's lovely out here. I guess someone will see us in the morning?"

"Mmm."

Interpreting that growl as a yes, Alison swallowed a smile. The prospect of being rescued offered more humiliation than comfort, apparently.

"You warm enough?" he asked abruptly.

"Ah...yes." If it didn't get any cooler. Catspaws were pattering in from the northwest now, each breeze cooler and damper than the last, and the dinghy was veering slowly around to meet them.

"That doesn't sound very warm." His arm curved around her shoulders. Waiting until the tension in her body had eased a little, he gathered her closer and his other arm wrapped around the front of her waist, locking her in place.

They leaned like that for a long time, heads back and eyes on the sky, feeling each slow, steady breath as the other took it. The shared warmth of their bodies brought a sort of peace. She could feel his irritation slowly slipping away.

Overhead, movement caught her eyes. Faint and tiny, a star crawled across the heavens, a silver ant on the homeward trail. "A satellite, do you think?" she murmured after a minute, pointing.

"I'd say so." His hair whispering against the rubber, Ty shifted. "Ali? Tell me something."

"Something," she joked feebly.

His arms squeezed in punishment, then loosened again. "That letter, the other day...the one we tore up..."

Oh, murder, here it came! And there was no way to lie with his arms wrapped around her like the straps of a lie detector, measuring every leap of her pulse. No way she wanted to lie tonight, here in his arms.

"Who was it from?"

*From nobody! Nobody at all.* She took a deep breath, her ribs expanding against his forearm. "From my husband."

"Your—" It was an explosion more than a word, and his body was suddenly rock hard against her. Catching her chin, he swung her around to face him, none too gently. "Your *husband*?"

"He used to be!" she offered quickly. "I'm divorced now."

"Oh..." Again it was more breath than sound, but the fingers on her chin eased a little. "I believe that's called an *ex*-husband."

With her chin trapped between his fingers, there was no way to nod agreement.

"Or do you feel that he's still your husband?" Ty demanded suddenly.

"No!" She tried to smile. "The other way around, if anything. I feel as if he were never my husband, as if it were all some ugly misunderstanding. A bad joke."

"As bad as that?"

Nodding bitterly, she swung away to stare at the sky. The moon was an opal brooch on the edge of the lace. As she watched, the first threads of cloud looped across its face.

Ty pulled her a little closer. "Tell me about it."

Shaking her head, Alison watched the moon slide under; the thicker knots of cloud lace were black outlined with silver as the gauzy light flickered, then failed.

"Please?" There was an odd note of strain beneath the huskiness of his whisper.

"Why?" Why did he have to put her through this, tonight of all nights? Above them the moon winked through a rip in the black velvet of the thicker clouds and vanished for good.

"'Cause I need to know." Ty cupped her cheek with his palm, trying gently to turn her head his way again.

Resisting that pressure, she leaned fiercely against that cupping warmth. but *why* did he need to know? Just his insatiable curiosity? To protect Harriet? Or was there another reason?

"Dark Eyes?"

In spite of the humiliation, all the anger, she wanted to tell him. Just as a child shows a scraped knee in hopes of that special kiss to stop the hurt. She shivered. Such a mistake, to come looking to Ty for love. Kindness and comfort—most surely—but love?

"Tell." The command was a dark, tickling kiss laid in her ear. "Where'd you meet him?"

All right. She took a deep breath. "In college, just before I graduated. At a student film.... I guess he was just prowling that night. He was eight years older than me. A sales representative with one of the biggest high-tech firms outside of Boston. Selling whole computer systems."

"Successful?"

She nodded tightly and his hand stroked up her cheek and into her hair. "So..." Ty murmured thoughtfully. "A successful salesman.... Then we're talking lots of charm, an expert at persuasion, lots of conviction.... Travel?"

"All over the country." It was too dark to see anymore. Shutting her eyes for a moment, she focused on the slow, hypnotic rasping of his fingertips against her scalp.

"So...sophistication, lots of money if he was selling systems...sounds like a pretty fast handful for a shy little girl who couldn't even handle a car yet," Ty decided quietly. "What did he see in you?"

A damn good question. Depressing that Ty had to ask it, but...she shrugged. "Don was between women, for once in his life. He wanted me. I was too much of a little prig to be gotten without marriage, so..." She shrugged again. Above them the smooth blackness flickered golden and suddenly rough—revealing mile after mile of impacted, jammed and jostling clouds and then smooth blackness again. In the distance, the air seemed to shudder, a shock wave too low for human ears, and Ty pulled her closer.

"I think he thought it was for real, that first half year or so. He'd decided it was time to settle down...raise a son or two." Her laughter was silent and bitter. "It never even occurred to him we might have a daughter...."

"Lord..." The fingers in her hair stopped. "You mean there's a child?"

"No." She shook her head quickly. "I didn't want any."

He drew a sudden, sharp breath. "You—"

Just above, the blackness ripped apart along a thousand golden seams, then vanished in a blaze of light. The black dropped again with a sound like the sky toppling piece by ragged piece around their heads. Cringing against Ty's chest, her ears ringing, Alison felt her face was suddenly wet.

"C'mon!" Ty was scrambling forward, dragging her with him. Half-blinded by the rain, she saw the crawl space before her by a second flare of lightning. Diving under the canopy, they squirmed forward on their stomachs as the thunder smashed down again. Giggling like a couple of lunatics, they reached the bow, which left their legs kicking in the rain from the knee down. "Sweet Lord in heaven!" Ty's hands groped for her in the blackness. Rolling onto his side, he pulled her against him, pillowing her head on his shoulder as his arms wrapped around her. "Don't you have *any* influence upstairs?'' he half-shouted in her ear.

The drumbeat of rain on rubber just inches above their heads made speech impossible. She shook her head, her lips brushing his throat at the V of his shirt. Soft curling hair tickled her lips, and she fought down an overpowering urge to put her tongue to it.

As suddenly as it had come, the rain disappeared, marching off to the east, leaving a disgruntled rear-guard muttering upon their canopy. Though drenched and cold from the knees down, they were damp, warm and increasingly cozy from the knees up. The thunder rumbled again, muted by distance now.

''Whew!'' Ty breathed into her hair. ''Now where were we? So you don't want kids, Ali?''

''I didn't want them *then*!'' She stirred restlessly, felt her breasts rubbing against his chest and stopped. ''I'd been a mother to two boys since I was thirteen. I wanted a breather, a little time to find out who *I* was.''

''Sounds reasonable.'' The intensity had left his voice. It sounded lighter, almost lighthearted all of a sudden.

''Well, Don didn't think so. Oh, he gave me a year, but then he wanted results, and it was fight about it and make up and fight all that second year....''

At the back of her head, his fingers had found a slow, steady stroking rhythm. ''And then?''

Lips against his throat, she sighed. ''And then I found he had a lover.... He'd forgotten a note from her and left it in one of his suit pockets. She was a secretary at his company. He'd known—'' her breath caught in a silent, bitter little laugh ''—*known* her a long time before me.''

Light and warm, his unseen lips trailed across her forehead and then back again. Suddenly, ridiculously, her eyes were full of tears.

"I...was...devastated.... Don was dreadfully contrite. Said it was just a moment of madness, a silly impulse, and she meant nothing at all to him, and anyway, wasn't it my fault, to some extent? I hadn't been loving enough, I didn't try to understand how tough his job was, how much stress he was under, and I wouldn't have his babies...."

"Oh, *Ali*—"

"And I guess I bought it." That painful, soundless laughter shook her again. "I went back to him after a month, determined to make it work. To try harder...and...well, we patched it back together, though it never had quite the same shine to it, and after almost a year, I was just thinking perhaps it was time we had that baby, when..." She stopped, remembering.

"Don...went to a convention in L.A., and the second day I called his room.... He usually called me when he traveled, but for some silly reason, that time I called him." She took a deep breath and the clean, warm smell of Ty's skin was somehow comforting. "And a...woman answered the phone, then hung up on me when I gave my name."

"So...I confronted Don when he came back. He insisted I must have gotten the wrong room, but he looked...funny—couldn't quite look me in the eye."

"I damn well hope not!"

Shrugging, she turned her head slightly to rest her cheek against his throat. "So...I was suspicious, but it wasn't enough to break up a marriage...and I kept telling myself I just had to be wrong—he was being so sweet and tender.''

''Bastard...'' Ty whispered distinctly into her hair.

''But then, after a few months, he started in on wanting a son again, and I just couldn't face it, Ty. I wasn't sure if I was standing on rock or sand; it was no time to have a child.''

''Damn right it wasn't!''

''Anyway, we limped on like that for a while, Don blaming me, me not sure *whose* fault it was, just trying to make it work again, until I received a letter one day...''

''A letter?'' At her waist, his hand moved restlessly, found the edge of her sweater and slid slowly up beneath it.

''Printed in block letters,'' she continued, struggling to keep her voice steady. ''Telling me Don was seeing a woman...the same secretary who'd been his mistress two years before.''

Warm and slow, Ty's fingers were tracing her spine, bone by tiny bone, up toward her brassiere. ''And?'' he murmured huskily.

''And I was tired of all the damned uncertainty. Don was out of town, so I took a taxi out to see her. She admitted it freely. She had no real attachment to him. They just had a lovely time once or twice a month and had done so for years.''

''So...'' Fingering the bra clasp, Ty must have felt her stiffen. His fingers beat a slow, caressing retreat down her spine again. ''So...he'd...never really broken with her, hmm?''

''No...she'd been there all along.... I showed her the anonymous letter, and she was outraged. She was sure she knew who'd written it—another secretary at the same company who she'd suspected for some time was also seeing Don.''

"Oh, Angel!" If he was laughing, it was too kindly to hurt. "You sure know how to pick 'em!"

Nodding ruefully, she hurried to finish it and forget it, once and for all. "So I went home, packed my bags, wrote a letter and left. There was just no way I was ever going to be first with Don. There would always be a Mistress of the Month, if not a couple, and I'd always be the standby. Good ol' wifey. Old second best." Just as she'd been second, no, make that third, with her father. What was wrong with her, anyway?

"And I swore I'd never—*ever*—be second best again, Ty.... I'd rather be alone, be nothing to no one, than stand in someone's shadow again." Did he understand what she was trying to tell him? "I'd *much* rather be alone," she repeated fiercely.

"Ali..." His hand slipped out of her sweater, joining the other to smooth upward and frame her face. "Ali...you're not going to be alone. Not ever again. Can't you see that yet?"

Oh, God, if it were only true! Her eyes were filling again, overflowing. Ty caught the tears with his thumbs and wiped them gently across her cheeks, again and again. If only he meant that, meant it in the way she wanted him to mean it! She blinked desperately, and his thumbs traced the curve of her lashes. "I can't...can't see a thing in here!" she joked shakily.

"Well...let's see if I can shed a little light on the subject, then."

How could a voice be so whimsical and tender all at once? Rolling onto his back, Ty pulled her with him and settled her snugly astride.

"Ty, please..." she muttered, bracing her elbows on either side of his arms and raising her breasts off his chest.

"I will, Ali." His voice was low. "I will please you, if you'll only let me." His hips rocked slowly up against her, hard and inviting, as hot as her own.

"No! It's—" But her voice ended in a throaty gasp as his fingers slid under her belt band and under her panties, to take her hips in a warm, kneading grasp and pull her more tightly against him. "Ty..." Half plea, half moan, it reached him this time, and his fingers stopped.

He took a shaky breath, lifting her as his chest expanded. "What's the matter, Angel? Should I stop?"

Oh, Lord, please, no! With her head and shoulders pressed up against the overhead canopy, and her hips molding urgently against his, she swallowed desperately. What *did* she want? "Ah..."

"Want me to slow down?" he asked tenderly.

She drew a deep, grateful breath. "Yes, please..."

On her hips, his fingers were gentler. "I'm sorry.... I've touched you so many times in my mind that I forget you're not used to it yet."

Oh, but she could get used to this, Alison thought hungrily, slowly relaxing down upon him. As her breasts touched his chest, Ty groaned, a soft, male sound of relief and pure pleasure. His fingers slid farther, brushed once across the melting, pulsing center of her desire, then trailed away toward her waist while she gasped and squirmed closer against his hardness.

"Ty!" she pleaded, but his hands were creeping under the front of her sweater. Stopping just below her breasts, his fingers shaped themselves to the underside of her curves and held her tenderly.

But that wasn't enough, not nearly enough, and he knew it. "Ty, *please*," she whimpered, her legs twisting shamelessly against him. He laughed breathlessly and still withheld the touch she had to have.

"Kiss me!" he demanded.

*Anything* to make him touch her! Swooping down upon that unseen, beautiful mouth, she traced its shape with the tip of her tongue and slipped inside just as the tips of his thumbs found her nipples. Moaning into his mouth, she pressed herself against him, hip, breast and mouth, and still it wasn't close enough— everything in that midnight world shifted and throbbed and swirled around her as their tongues danced together and his thumbs teased again across the swollen peaks of her breasts. For one roaring, dizzy second she tottered on the brink, her body gathering itself for the fall, her lungs seeking air in a series of gasping, stuttering inhalations as her breasts swelled to fit his hands.

And, as if he sensed it, those hands retreated.

"No!" she moaned, as his mouth slipped away from her, too, and his lips found her cheek, her jaw, her ear, the side of her throat. Two years? How had she waited two years? Another two *minutes* would finish her; she was aching and hollow and oh, so ready—

On her jeans, Ty's fingers froze. "Ty, *please*..."

"Shh!" he whispered intently.

Could he hear it, too? That slowly gathering drumbeat within her? She lifted her hips beseechingly, and his fingers slid a tantalizing inch farther before stopping again. An odd, high-pitched whine with a deeper, shuddering backbeat sung in her ears. She was fainting, or perhaps a heart attack? If he didn't come to her soon, she would—

*"Damn!"* Ty breathed, and his hand slipped away. "Of all the—"

The hum was louder, surrounding them eerily. "What—"

"We've got company, Angel." Ty rolled to the side, placing her gently alongside him. "That's a propeller you're hearing." Invisible fingers stroked her face, and he pushed himself backward toward the opening.

"Maybe they won't see us!"

Laughing under his breath, he stopped, grabbed her leg and kissed the side of her thigh. "They can't miss us, darlin'. The channel's narrow here."

Out of the blackness, a spotlight pounced on the outboard, then swept slowly forward to silhouette Ty's head and shoulders as he slithered out to meet it. Squinting against the light, Alison could hear the soft rumble of a boat's engine.

"Hi, there!" a man's voice rang out. "Need any help?"

"No!" Alison muttered under her breath, "We do not!" Teeth clenched behind a sheepish smile, she wriggled feet first out into the blaze of light.

## CHAPTER THIRTEEN

ENGINES MUTTERING SOFTLY in the darkness, the *Hat Trick* backed slowly in toward the dock. Tow line in hand, Ty stepped down off the powerboat and thumped lightly onto the boards, then pulled the disabled dinghy in after him.

The quieter of their two rescuers—older gentlemen who'd been out for a weekend of fishing until the squall caused them to run in for shelter—offered her a supporting hand as she stepped up onto the gunwhale.

"Got her." Ty's hands closed around Alison's waist, and she was lifted gently down beside him. "And thanks again," he called to the skipper up on the flying bridge as his arm settled around her shoulders.

"Our pleasure." The older man grinned down at them, then slowly spun the steering wheel as the boat eased ahead. "You all have a good night now." There was a cheerful, very masculine note of conviction that they would.

"And thank *you*," Alison told the silent one at the stern. He sketched her a smiling, kindly salute. Then they were gone, chugging softly upriver, and Ty was steering her gently but firmly up the dock.

If only they hadn't been interrupted like that, Alison thought unhappily. It was a different matter entirely to walk soberly and cold-bloodedly up this hill toward his apartment, toward his bed, with this silent, withdrawn man at her side. Was he in the present at all, at this moment, or was he off in the past, thinking of the woman who should have been by his side? Glancing up at his distant face, she saw there was no way to know. All she knew was that she felt trapped, as if she were being marched off to some fate she'd neither chosen nor even conceived of yet.

As they passed her station wagon, she hung back against his hold, glancing back at the car longingly. She could even drive it alone now. She could run for it...if only she had the keys. Her steps slowed.

"Ali?" Stopping when she did, Ty was suddenly with her again. His head turned to the car, then back to her in swift comprehension. "Hey, Ali," he murmured huskily. Swinging her to face him, he cupped her chin and cheek as she tried to duck her head. "You don't want that, Angel. A dark house and a cold bed?

"I think maybe I..." But his fingers were brushing softly across her moving lips, and that light touch was vibrating a wire stretched tight within her. Silently quivering, she stared up at him in a sort of hungry, hesitant despair.

"You don't want that tonight, Ali," he soothed. "Trust me. That's not what you need or want." He was right, so right. "Trust me," he whispered lightly, and kissed the tip of her nose.

As they reached the door at last—the only one in sight when the small elevators stopped at the fourth floor—she lost her nerve once more. But snatching a wild-eyed glance back toward the elevator while Ty found his keys, Alison saw its doors close with a soft finality. Over the doorframe, the red light above the number four winked out, and the third floor light blinked on as the car descended.

*Trust him.* Trust him to be one jump ahead of her every time, he meant!

"I have these etchings..." he murmured evilly as he guided her in before him.

He had no etchings, but a savagely exquisite Chinese kite graced the wall of the short hallway that opened into the living room. There were paintings in the living room, mostly watercolors as far as she could make out in the dim light, but it was the gigantic windows arching along two walls of the room that claimed her attention. Outside, the moon had struggled free of the clouds once more. Lovelier than any night scene Minot had ever painted, the Mystic River snaked its glittering, expanding course to the sound.

Behind her, Ty struck a match, and the tiny sound rasped a quivering path across her nerves. Trying not to shiver, she watched him from the corner of her eye as he lit the candle that waited on the end table by his big sofa. He lit a second at the other end of the sofa and she turned away, wandering blindly down the long, high-ceilinged room toward the fireplace.

She and Ty? It wouldn't work. She could see it wouldn't work; he'd lit those candles for too many women before.... Everything in skirts, June had said. She was just part of his pattern of escape.

"Ali?" Ty called quietly.

Fingers jammed in her jeans pockets, her shoulders hunched against the gaze that was heating her spine from across the room, Alison stared unseeing at the portrait hung above the mantel. It wouldn't work.... They'd share a beautiful, heartbreakingly tender night, and then what? She'd wake to find herself trapped in love—she was trapped there already—and Ty would wake to find she wasn't Kathy any more than any of the others had been.

"Dark eyes..." Warm, long-fingered hands closed lightly over her shoulders. "C'm'ere, darlin'." Rocking her stiff body back against him, Ty rested his chin on her head. "It's going to be all right, Ali.... It's going to be *so* all right...." His hands slid down her arms and up again.

Fighting that slow hand magic, she stared fiercely at the painting above the mantel. In the pale light, the woman's outflung hair looked black upon the pillow, as did the nipple of the small, high breast that the forefinger of her delicate hand nearly touched. The bed around her was in total disarray, the sheets sketched in with a beautiful, tumbling brushstroke. The woman's faint smile was inward turning and utterly satisfied—*she* had no doubts as to the benefits of a night of lovemaking. *Alicia, After*—after what, she'd always wondered? Now it was obvious.

Atop her rough fisherman's sweater, Ty was tracing a lazy figure eight around the base of her breasts, and trembling inside, Alison fought the instinctive response of her hips. "So you've had her here all along," she murmured dreamily. There was no need to search for the confirming signature, though even as she thought that she saw the neat, characteristic block letters worked into the tumultuous sheets—*Alicia, après*—and then, a few inches to the right of that, the artist's name—Minot.

"No, I didn't," Ty murmured at her ear. "Honest. I really had it cleaned. Got it back last week...."

"Then why—" But her throat was too dry, and she had to stop to swallow. "Why didn't you bring it back? You know how she's been missing it."

"You know why." His fingertip was following a slow, contracting spiral in toward her tautly expectant nipple, but at the last possible instant, instead of stroking the tip, it swirled away to trace a teasing, melting path around the other peak.

"I...I do?" But she knew nothing now, only that she'd be begging, crying for his touch in another moment.

"Save it, Ali. We'll settle that in the morning." After gently tugging her shirt out from under her belt, his hands slid down at last against the bare skin of her belly, cupping her softness and pulling her back against his waiting hardness.

"But..." There was something about the painting... Something...

"The morning, Angel," he insisted, nuzzling the side of her neck. "Don't lie to me tonight. This is a night for truth telling."

Truth telling... *All* the truths? That she'd lied and faked her way into his household? That she wanted him desperately? That she loved him? "I—" She shook her head wretchedly.

"And the first truth is that you're frozen," he decided whimsically. His hands slipped briskly out of her jeans. "So let's start with a shower." Swinging her off the floor, he carried her out of the room and through his bedroom, which was moonlit, so that its arching windows, looking upriver, revealed the sleeping town. His steps slowed as he passed the king-size bed and then quickened again.

In the bathroom, he set her down on the deep blue tiled counter by the sink, her feet dangling.

Things were moving too fast. "Ty..." But she had nothing to say. Stop? Don't Stop? Don't start if you mean to stop next week?

"Right." He acknowledged her confusion softly, his smile faint and tender. Turning away, he slid open the frosted glass doors of the shower. Water rumbled onto the porcelain, then changed to a rattling spray as steam started rising. "So..." He turned back again and lifted her off the counter. "Get warm..." Kissing the tip of her nose, he backed away toward the door.

He was leaving her, just like that? Not going to undress her? Relief and indignation made a ridiculous combination as she stared after him. His grin flashed for a moment, and then he was gone.

Eyes closed, numb toes beginning to tingle, she stood beneath the shower head, focusing on the hot, delicious sweep of the water down her body, letting the warm, pattering touch of the spray on her breasts and belly and thighs obliterate all thoughts, all doubts, everything but the present goodness.

Finally she roused herself from her trance to find his shampoo. Eyes shut, leaning against the tiles, she worked up a lather, her nostrils flaring as she recognized the faint, balsamy scent she'd come to associate with Ty's hair.

"Save some for me, Dark Eyes."

Swinging blindly toward his voice at the back of the tub, she slipped just as his hands caught her waist.

"Easy there! Sorry, I didn't mean to scare you."

"I...well, you did." She smiled blindly up at him. It was scary—no, terrifying—what the touch of his fingers on her bare skin did to her. She'd have fingerprints on her heart tomorrow.

"But you scare easy, Ali." His fingers were gliding slowly up her sides, stopping to thumb the sensitive concavity of her armpits, following her upraised arms to her fingers buried in her soapy curls. "Too easy." His fingertips massaged her scalp in hypnotic circles.

Not needed, her hands dropped away to hang at her sides, but that didn't feel right. She was taking, yet ought to be giving, as well. Hesitantly she brought one up again, spread it lightly against the hard swell of his chest and felt his deep inhalation.

"Please," Ty said simply. Smiling again, she brought her other hand up to begin a slow exploration of this masculine terrain: the hard planes of muscle under the wet curling softness of his chest hair and the long, delicate hollows between the curve of his ribs.

"Angel?" he murmured huskily, finally, his soapy hand gliding down to cup around her hips.

"Mmm?" Entranced with the hard, tiny shape of his nipples beneath her fingertips, she barely heard him.

"Come closer." He lifted her onto her tiptoes as he spoke, and she felt his hardness butt gently between her thighs. Then she was astride him, gasping with a kind of fright as her hips rocked in to press closer against him.

"That's not..." But she couldn't finish it. Burying her face in the hollow of his shoulder, she locked her arms around his lean waist and rubbed her breasts against him instead.

"Not what, Ali?" Hands kneading her hips, he was backing her slowly into the full force of the shower.

Shaking her head blindly against him, she let him rinse her, the soap slicking down her cheeks while her thighs clenched around him and she rocked forward and back in slow, instinctive invitation.

"Not what, Angel?" Ty swung her out from under the spray and brushed the hair off her forehead.

"Not close enough!" she pleaded, arching up against him. Opening her eyes, she found his laughing face only inches above her own.

"Oh, Angel!" he groaned against her parted lips. "Patient lady!" Pressing her slowly back against the wet tiles, he deepened the kiss as the shower splashed over them, turning his caress to a warm, wet, underwater dance of tongue upon tongue while his hands cupped her breasts.

Eyes shut, she was swirling down, down and around a dark whirl of water, drowning. But it wasn't air she needed now. "Ty!" she pleaded, wrenching away from his mouth.

*"Patience,"* he soothed, nipping slowly down the side of her throat. "We haven't even soaped each other yet."

"Soap be damned!" Gasping as he bit her shoulder, she squirmed closer against him. "It's *you* I want."

"Oh, you'll have me, too, darling!" Licking a lazy zigzag path down the top of her breast, his tongue paused just above its aching, swollen peak. "Every last inch of me." With just the tip of his tongue he outlined the aroused corona.

"Ah—" Hot and wet, his lips closed at last over the yearning peak, licked, sucked and slowly kissed it as she pressed his dark head closer with shaking hands. Turning to the other one, he teased it with gentle teeth, then tongued his way up to her mouth again.

"Ty, please!" She panted as he started to kiss her, and that fierce smile of his suddenly faded.

"Hmm?" he murmured whimsically, and nudged the tip of his nose along her eyebrows. "No soap?"

"No...please." This tenderness was harder to bear than the teasing; shutting her eyes against the tears that had sprung from nowhere, she shivered and hugged him harder.

"Ali?" The end of his nose rubbed slowly down the tilt of her own, and circled her tip in an Eskimo caress. "When was the last time?"

Blindly she shook her head. She didn't want to think about the last time.

"Mmm?" One hand found her breast again and her hips responded instantly, pressing fiercely up against him.

"Two years," she muttered against the side of his throat.

"All right, no soap then," he decided with a smile in his voice, but once out of the shower, Ty was not to be rushed. Trapped between the softness of the deep blue towel he'd wrapped around her back and the golden-brown wall of his chest, she found he preferred to lick her dry, sipping the silvery beads off her shoulders, her breasts, lapping them out of her navel with a hot, slow tongue and a savoring growl deep in his throat.

By the time he reached her legs, her knees were shaking. Kneeling at her feet, his dark, wet head pressed to her belly, he dragged the towel slowly, slowly, down the backs of her thighs.

"Ahh!" She would melt if he didn't stop this sweet torture. He'd have to mop her off the floor along with the bathwater! But he'd lost all mercy as his tongue probed again and again to the center of her throbbing desire. "Ty," she gasped, and his head tilted up.

Tenderness and a kind of exultant wildness warred in the tanned face that gleamed up at her.

"Please, Ty, please...I just need you," she whispered shakily—words she'd meant never to say to a man again, but the fierce joy lighting his face made them all right, somehow.

"Want me wet or dry, darlin'?" Still holding her hips, he rose before her, soaking her all over again with the hair of his chest as he slid up the length of her.

She wanted him any way at all. Anytime. Wet, dry, upside down, inside out. Now. "Give me that!" Laughing breathlessly, she snatched the towel and dried him as best she could with his hands and his lips running constant interference.

"That'll do," he growled after a moment and scooped her up, towel and all.

Damp breasts pressed to hot chest, and heart hammered against heart as he carried her out of the steam into the cooler bedroom. Her fears returned as they neared the bed, and she locked her arms tight around his neck. It was too good, too sweet, too wild to be true, too wonderful to last.

Sitting on the side of the bed, Ty cradled her in his lap, kissing her eyebrow, her ear, the side of her throat when she pressed her face to his chest.

She couldn't look up at him, couldn't bear to see his face. Did he even know or care whom he was bedding by now, with his heart going like a jackhammer against her forehead and the arm under her knees trembling with desire?

Twisting around, he set her gently on the bed and followed her down when she wouldn't—couldn't—let go of him. Eyes closed, she groaned softly as the warm weight of him pressed her into the blankets.

"Ali?" Warm, gentle fingers framed her face.

She couldn't look at him, but pulled his head down blindly, buried her fingers in his thick, wet hair, kissing him with an urgency born of the growing, aching need within her and the fear that came with it. Too sweet to be true: the hot silky slide of tongue against tongue, whirling down a dark river of the mind, the current sucking them onward with a rush as his hands closed around her breasts. "Ty, please!" she panted, her shaking hands molding the damp hardness of his shoulders, his back, his hips....

"Ali, *darlin'*, slow down." But he was catching her fervor, his hands quickening as she strained against him.

"Now..."

"Wild woman!" He laughed breathlessly, but pinning her writhing hips, he entered her with a torturing gentleness even as she moaned and tried to thrust closer. As he came all the way home, his mouth covered hers. Groaning into each other, they started to move.

On a dark rushing river, she was the runaway raft and Ty the castaway, riding her, urging her on with hands and lips. Somewhere up ahead was the shudder of falling water. Rapids, then a whirling eddy as his tongue found her breast, and then the accelerating slide of the current again and the rhythmic pounding of the approaching falls. His hands in her hair, whites of his eyes catching the moonlight and her hands at his hips pulling him closer, they were shooting out over the edge, out into sunlight, crying aloud, falling, floating, locked tight together. And the landing was soft, so soft—white swirling foam and rainbows above the spray, and then a soft, billowing floating away into peace...and gentle darkness.

Miles and miles downriver, mouth pressed to her forehead, Ty groaned softly and raised his head. "Lord..."

"Mmm?" Stretching luxuriously beneath him, Alison opened her eyes and found him staring down at her.

"Ali..." Sliding his weight onto his elbows, he reached for her face and cupped it with his palms. "Are you...?" But the words wouldn't come. Faintly frowning, he shook his head, set thumb tips to her eyebrows and traced their arc.

Smiling sleepily, she shut her eyes and felt the butterfly touch of his thumbs following the curve of her eyelids, inner corner to outer, then her lashes, then back to her brows again.

"I...didn't mean it to be like that...the first time," he murmured awkwardly just above her. "Meant to be...hey...you awake there?"

"Mmm," she purred, stretching again, her hands sliding up to his hips and petting him in hazy contentment.

"Are you all right, Angel?"

All right? *All right?* She felt too good to be true, but even as she thought it, the fear flicked across her mind again. Too good to be true. Locking her arms around his waist, she hugged him closer, inhaling the warm special scent of him. The secret was not to think, just to feel.... As long as she didn't think, she'd be all right...

After a long moment, he sighed and rolled over onto his side, pulling her with him. He lay there a long time, stroking her back with light, lazy fingertips, his deep steady breath warming her hair as she slid down, down a black velvet slide into sleep.

Alison awoke when he sat up. The room was darker now; the moon must have been down. "Ty?"

"Back in a minute, Angel."

It was a long, long minute; the room was black, dimensionless, utterly strange without him. Dragging the disheveled blanket up, she huddled beneath it, trying not to think.

The bed sagged lightly beside her. "Mind if I put a light on?" Ty asked casually. A lamp beside the bed clicked on, the warm glow turning his skin to red gold. He was so beautiful and she hadn't ever told him, but he was looking down at her now, his eyebrows pulled together in that odd, lifting frown, as if she were some stranger he'd just discovered between his sheets. "Want some water?" he asked abruptly.

He kept a hand on the glass while she drank. Unnerved by his faint, attentive frown, she spilled a little and reached to wipe it away.

"Wait…" Catching her fingers, Ty set the glass aside, leaned slowly forward and put his lips to the trickle at the side of her mouth. "Ali…"

A droplet trembled atop her breast. It wouldn't stay there long with her breasts heaving as they were, but Ty caught it just as it started its slide. "Ali!" he whispered again fiercely, sipping her skin, and she was suddenly as hot and liquid as his wandering mouth. Glorying in her power, she leaned slowly away from him, luring him down until the mattress blocked all retreat.

This time Ty set the pace, a pace that seemed to suggest they had hours, days, even years to touch, to taste, to ease in and out, flow back and forth. Moist, warm skin dragged across skin in a deliberate, lazy friction kindling slowly, ever so slowly, to a flame that burned from the inside out, slow but hungry, spreading down her thighs, licking up her backbone, reaching for fuel, consuming it and searching for more. Coals in the belly glowed hotter and brighter each time Ty pressed gently toward their throbbing center, as if to be burned was all he had ever desired. Heat rolled outward, clenched toes prickled with heat, and red coals burned behind Alison's eyelids and between her legs until at last the soft, hot, groaning explosion fused them together…and as one they drifted toward the final soft ashes of sleep.

WITH HER CHEEK SNUGGLED against Ty's shoulder, there was no way to turn and watch the sun rise without waking him, but through her lashes, Alison watched the white wall beyond his chest shade gradually from lilac to rose to gold. She felt the sun rising within her as well, her happiness glowing until she wondered that its light didn't wake him. But, dark hair tousled on his pillow, Ty was sleeping deeply, chest rising slow and steady as his nostrils flared, his secret smile exposed in sleep, a satisfied, happy man, and she the one who had done that to him...for him...with him. A shiver of contentment shook her shoulders, and Ty's arm tightened reflexively as his head turned an inch her way.

"Mmph," he proclaimed softly, eyes closed. His hand slipped away down her arm, feathered across her hip, then dropped away.

Across the foot of their bed, the blue towel was draped, reminding her of bathrooms, mirrors.... It would be nice to brush her hair before he woke, and she was too happy to lie still much longer, so Alison eased up on one elbow. He felt the change instantly—frowned and reached for her, then smiled as his hand found her breast. "Kathy," he murmured comfortably, kneading her softly, "Kathy, love," and sighed, his smile deepening.

Breath frozen in her throat, Alison waited for the words and the pain to penetrate. The pain wouldn't hit home until she breathed, and she didn't want to do that anymore. But already the sunny wall across the room was fading, being swallowed by the slowly expanding darkness behind her eyelids, and her chest rose mechanically, sucking in the pain-filled air. At her breast, Ty's hand felt the movement and responded, turning her insides to one hot, hurting redness, where hunger and rage swirled with disbelief. She had to inhale once more, breathing in more pain as his hand caressed her again.

*Kathy!* All the time he'd lain with her, loved her as she'd never been loved before, Kathy had been waiting to claim him back again! There was no way to compete with this. She'd tried and failed too many times before—and sworn never to punish herself this way with anyone again. Out. She had to get out. Catching his wrist, Alison moved his hand aside. It was like pulling herself apart; his hand belonged there now. Her body ached for its return as he frowned, his empty fingers spreading wide, then curling into a loose fist against his chest.

She sat up quickly and slid backward across the bed, dodging his fingers as Ty rolled over onto his stomach and reached for her blindly. "Love?"

He'd never called *her* love. Angel, Dark Eyes, but never that crucial endearment. Standing sickly by the bed, Alison watched him snuggle facedown into his pillow and subside into sleep once more. She memorized the beautiful, long, lean shape of him, even as she summoned the anger to leave. *Out.* This rage would destroy her—and him, if she stayed....

In the bathroom, she found her jeans were sodden, loathsome against her flinching skin; the shirt was no better. She rolled underwear and sweater into a wad to carry along with her shoes.

The keys...in his pants pocket, hung neatly on a hook behind the bathroom door. He'd said the car was hers, so long ago.

As she tiptoed across the bedroom, her eyes blurred too much to see him clearly, but Ty was still on his stomach, motionless. He'd probably sleep for hours.

Halfway across the living room, she remembered: *Alicia*...the reason for all of this—the heartbreaker with eyes like a cat in torchlight and hair a river of burgundy. She turned.

Above the mantel, a woman with the gray-green eyes of a cat and hair like a fountain of red gold smiled past her, smiled into space, perhaps meeting the eyes of a lover dead eighty years ago.

*"Burgundy is a dark red wine—ruby red, even darker than that,"* a small, conversational voice babbled in her brain as Alison stepped forward. On tiptoe, she was just able to lift the painting down. Through her drying tears the woman shimmered in soft focus. *"You would not recognize my work now.... No contour can confine or define it...."*

It was early Impressionist all right. The artist was still struggling to free himself from the hard-edged contour line; he'd succeeded around the face, certainly with the tumbled sheets, but had lost it with the hand, which was as beautifully and precisely defined as any by Ingres...but then Minot had studied two years in the atelier of a student of Ingres.... Still...

Still there was something not quite...and then there was the hair color.... *Forrest would know,* she thought desperately, *Forrest would know in an instant.* Holding the painting at arms' length, Alison stared at it, eyes narrowed. *And you should know, too! That's why he sent you, because you should know, too!*

The faintest of sounds from the bedroom snapped her head around. Ears straining, Alison waited, but it did not come again. Perhaps he'd turned over.... She had to go. Now...

Her eyes swung back to the painting. Brushwork more delicate than Minot's, not as sure, but if Minot *had* painted this, he'd painted it twelve years before any Impressionist work of his she'd ever seen, so... Still... *Come on, come on, come on, you should know! This is what it was all for, all the pain, all the sadness still to come, just for this moment. To stand here and know. Your head should work, if not your heart!*

Ty's wordless, wrenching groan spun her around. The sound of a nightmare, or of sudden awakening? *Now. Get out now!* Retreating toward the door, her sweater forgotten, she still looked down at the painting between her hands. Who? If not Minot, then who? The style was too good, much too good, to be an unknown.... Opening the door, she leaned in the doorway. Forrest was depending on her. He'd be writing a chapter on this painting, staking his reputation on her verdict, and there'd be no second chance, no chance ever to look again and change her mind.... She wouldn't be back this way—couldn't ever come back—and Ty would never forgive her, anyway, not so much for her lies as for her leaving.

"Ali!"

Or was it perhaps "Kathy" that he'd called? At this distance she couldn't be sure. She couldn't be sure if he was even awake—couldn't stay to find out. Forgotten painting cradled in one arm, she fled barefoot down the hall.

## CHAPTER FOURTEEN

THE DRIVE UP ROUTE ONE to Providence was a nightmare, a series of disconnected, senseless images and random thoughts: a car horn savagely honking when she stopped for a green traffic light in Westerly; a truck that thundered past too close—too close for a timid driver, anyway—forcing her onto the shoulder; red-haired *Alicia* on the seat beside her, smiling, ever smiling.... Cross a Renoir with a Minot and you'd have the style, but no one painted like that. No one she knew...and she should know.... *"Don't you know that yet? You'll never be alone again. Don't you know that yet?"*

Passing the lonely, windswept marshes of Rhode Island's South County, with its twisted pines, she caught a distant glimpse of the ocean, which was almost the same color as his— And all the time, all that wonderful time, it had been Kathy...

As she approached the city, the traffic was stop and go; the sunlight glared off chrome and windshields to jab her burning eyes. Had she gotten onto Route 95, as Forrest had done, it would have been faster, but she'd missed the turnoff somehow.

Forrest...he'd wanted the painting; now he'd have it. For there'd been no returning *Alicia* once she'd taken her in that moment of panic, no way to drop her off at Shady Breeze, when Ty might have been only minutes behind her. Now Forrest could photograph her, study her and get her back to Harriet by this evening.... Somehow... Anyway, she couldn't care less. It was not her problem. She'd started all this for Forrest and now she could let him finish it, make the explanations, the apologies, the excuses, the lousy lies— pick up the pieces however he chose; she did not care. About anything.

But it was not going to be that simple, Alison realized, as she rang the doorbell of Forrest's garden apartment for the twelfth time. Not home. How could he do this to her? Painting clutched to her chest, she squinted up at the sun glinting through the branches of the chestnut overhead. Not much past ten. Even Forrest awoke by ten, but she gave his bell one last despairing push, then blundered back to her car and stood by it, the wheels of her brain spinning uselessly. Gone. Just when she needed him—gone. The man had a genius for avoiding trouble.

For that was what she, Alison Eriksen, unwitting art thief, held in her hands. Trouble. *Big* trouble. And another thought was beginning to impinge on her tired mind. Somehow she'd pictured Ty back at Shady Breeze—in a towering rage, but safely confined to that cool sunny world to the south. But a good driver, in a bad temper, with a fast car...could connect that world with her own in something less than two hours.... Perhaps some part of her had wanted that all along.... Slamming the door on that thought, Alison started the engine.

She drove to her own apartment the way she had always walked it—down Waterman, which happened to be a one-way street running uphill. But by the time that occurred to her she was halfway down. Shrinking from the incredulous stares of the oncoming drivers, she made it to the bottom without encountering the law, made it to her apartment without encountering Tyler O'Malley and parked well out of sight behind the house.

But if Ty wasn't breathing fire on her doorstep, it was only a matter of time before he would be, Alison concluded, tiptoeing up the back stairs. He had her address, or at least had had it when he sent those roses so long ago. Pausing at the landing, she wiped a hand angrily across her eyes. But with any luck at all, right now he was still in Mystic, sleeping or just now waking.

Sleep...that's what she'd like to do. Lie down and sleep...wake up in his arms and start this day all over again. Wake to find that these past few hours had truly been a nightmare....

A shower soothed her sore body but brought no solutions to her aching head. But then, for some things, there were no solutions. There was no way to make a man love you if he couldn't forget— Shutting off the thought with the water, she reached for a towel. First things first. And first and foremost, she did not want to see Ty...ever. So she'd get dressed and get out...and find Forrest. She had to find Forrest. If she couldn't find Forrest— But feeling the panic rising within, she squelched that thought, as well.

Ten minutes later, dressed in a yellow cotton sun-dress—not the soberest attire for an art thief, but most of her clothes were in Connecticut—with *Alicia, After* tucked firmly under one arm, Alison stepped out her door and met the steely eyes of Tyler O'Malley as he came up the last few stairs to her landing two at a time.

That one look was enough to blow her backward through her doorway. Numbly she watched her own hand close the door before her and throw the dead bolt, just as the doorknob twisted violently.

"Alison! Open up." The knob twisted again, then stayed turned as he held it. Automatically she reached for the knob on her side, clinging to it as if the brass could conduct all the strength and anger from which she was hiding. "Alison?"

"Go away!" Somewhere deep within, a sob was fluttering, battering at her lungs like a bird trapped in a closet. Shutting her eyes, she leaned her forehead against the wood; she couldn't get any closer than that.

"The hell I will! Open up. Now!" The knob twisted again.

The bird was up in her throat now, scrabbling with its tiny claws. Wordlessly she shook her head against the door.

"Alison, what do I have to do? Call the cops? Do you want the police in on this?"

No, please, no strangers! No strange eyes staring at her, asking questions when she couldn't even breathe. She couldn't see now either, and shook her head again silently.

"Alison?" The first raw fury in his voice had changed to a hard-edged, implacable conviction. "Open the door...now."

There was really nothing else to do. Nowhere, no one to run to, only this one angry man... Her fingers found the dead bolt by touch.

Through her tears, it was impossible to read his expression, but the care with which he shut her door behind him was as ominous as the click of the dead bolt. "You little bitch." The tone was quietly conversational, too carefully controlled. Lifting the painting out of her hand, Ty stared down at it silently, then moved to prop it on her desk. "So that's what you wanted all along...."

Was it? It was hard to remember now, but she supposed it was.

"Has your twit professor seen it yet? No? Well, that's something, anyway," he allowed, leaning back against the edge of her desk. That blue-gray arctic gaze roamed slowly across her face, flicked down to her bare shoulders, then quickly retreated. "Sit down. This could take a while."

Who was he to give orders like that? It was his fault that all this had happened, he who had chased her down and made her love him, when all the time he had nothing to give in return. *Nothing*... But Ty was looming just above her, his hands heavy on her shoulders. "Sit...down." She found herself folding helplessly into the sofa's softness. Head thrown back on the cushions, she glared up at him through her tears.

Standing between her outstretched legs, he stared down at her, the denim of his jeans brushing the insides of her knees. Finally Ty shook his head. "I can't believe you'd sleep with a man just to get hold of that." He jerked his chin toward the painting.

Then he wasn't a *total* fool. "That—" The word came out in a croaking whisper; she swallowed and tried again. "That wasn't why."

"No? Then what *was* the reason?"

She was not going to discuss this. But Ty's low savage voice prodded on.

"You were a hungry, greedy little girl last night, Ali.... Did you just need a man that badly? The moon was right and there I was?" Dropping on the couch beside her, he braced a hand either side of her shoulders, pinning her in place as he searched her widening eyes. "Did you just mean to use me and run? Was that it?"

It should have been laughable; if she could have swallowed all the tears, she would have laughed.

"Hmm? Is this all you wanted?" Fingers curling around her shoulder straps, he followed them down to the top of her bodice, where his palms cupped her breasts.

"Get your hands off me!" But it was too late. She was molten inside, anger and need bubbling like lava, her nipples rising to the slow friction of those knowing hands.

"That's not what you were saying last night, Angel," he jeered huskily. "What changed?"

Nothing, so far as her body knew. *Everything,* she reminded herself fiercely, wrapping her fingers around his big wrists and pushing with all her might.

The lurking smile had a bitter twist she'd never seen before as, just for a moment, Ty resisted her push. Just long enough to demonstrate that it was not her strength that moved his hands aside. Eyes locked, his blood pumping through her encircling fingers, he breathed raggedly in concert with her.

She watched the next thought form in his eyes as his brows slanted. "Or didn't I measure up to past performances? Was that it?"

A performance... Was that how he'd seen last night? It was a word Don might have chosen.

But eyes narrowing, Ty was taking her silence for answer. "That's it, isn't it, darlin'? You're still carrying a torch for your stud of a husband, aren't you? Faithful little Ali, still pining for the bastard who done her wrong."

Pining? She could have slapped him silly, he was so far off the mark. "Don't talk to *me* about pining! It's not *me* who's stuck in the past, Tyler O'Malley!" Shoving his hands aside, she slid away from him, but he caught her arm again.

"What are you talking about?"

"I'm talking about your ghost, Kathy!" Tearing at the fingers wrapped round her arm, she found them immovable. "I'm talking about the fact that when I go to bed with a man, I want to know it's *me* he wants! I *won't* be some stand-in, just because I'm available and she happens to be dea—"

"*Alison!*" Catching her other arm, Ty yanked her back again and pinned her against the back of the sofa. "Ali, you were *not* a stand-in for *anybody* last night." Nearly eyeball to eyeball, he shook her as if he could shake that thought into her head somehow.

"Oh, I wasn't?" She looked up at him bitterly. Instead of one bird in her chest now, she felt a flock of them, bumping, battling, all trying to take wing at once. "And do you...know what...you called me this morning, while...you were touching me?"

"This...morning?" His brows drew together in that winged frown she'd always loved and it started her tears.

"*Kathy*... You smiled and called me...'Kathy, love.'"

"I...did?" Ty murmured weakly, that faraway look robbing his eyes of their light. "Son of a..." His hands dropped away.

The birds were escaping at last, ripping her chest apart, tearing holes through her breathing. Her voice was in tatters. "So...don't...tell *me*...who you were... All the *time*... When I..." Useless. Absurd. And the pity in his eyes was the last thing she wanted. Twisting away from him, she staggered to her feet.

"Ali, come here!"

Dodging his hand, she ducked into the bedroom and dived for the bed. She should never have woken at all today—then she could have died happy last night. Retreating to the far side next to the wall, she buried her face in the pillow and let the sobs fly.

"Ali...?"

"Get out of here!"

But the mattress sagged beneath his weight, and his arm settled around her heaving shoulders. She shook her head violently, but Ty simply snuggled closer and lay half on top of her, his cheek pressed to her hair, one of his long legs pressed between her own, his hands closing over hers, twining their fingers together, giving her something to hold on to as she cried.

"Ali, Ali...Ali, love..." His face brushed back and forth through her hair. "Ali, *that's* why you ran? Because I...hell...but what about the painting, why did you...Ali, darlin', *don't*, hush..." He kissed the nape of her neck. "Ali, come on, talk to me, Ali..."

With comforting of this caliber there was no way to keep crying for long. Pain receding to a kind of blurry, despairing peacefulness, she lay beneath him, body tensing for each shuddering little inhalation, which she held with her back pressed against his chest, then released in a long, shaky sigh to catch another hiccupping little breath.

"Ali?" He nuzzled her ear. "If you feel like that about...us, how could you steal—"

"Oh, *damn* it, Ty!" She whipped her head blindly away from his lips. "I *didn't* steal her, or I guess I did, but I didn't mean to... I was holding her, and you made a sound, and I just...just ran." The last word rose to a ludicrous squeak. "I'm sorry."

"But you've been trying to get hold of *Alicia* since the day you arrived, haven't you?"

"No!" She shook her face against the pillow. "No, not to get her, just to *see* her, and I didn't even want to do—It's Forrest, Ty—he made me—you don't understand...my dissertation...he can...without him I can't..." She shook her head savagely, fighting back the sobs. *No way to explain it*. No excuse could jus-

tify what she'd done, and she burst into tears again.
"I'm sorry!"

"Ali." Kissing her ear, Ty rolled off her, then the
bed rebounded as he stood. Once she was without
him, her tears came faster and she hugged her pillow
convulsively.

"Here." He was back again, depositing the box of
tissues from her bathroom next to her face. While she
used them, he unbuckled her sandals, then teased the
soles of her feet with a gentle finger.

"Cut it out, Ty!"

He did, but his hand curled around her waist instead. Ignoring her resistance, he rolled her onto her
back and sat staring down at her, his face an odd mixture of worried frown and tender, almost-smile. "Yup.
That's the lady I fell in love with," he decided after a
moment. "The one with the Day-Glo nose."

But she'd stopped believing in miracles some time
this morning. "Cut it out, Ty. It's Kathy you love."

His deep-water eyes considered that gravely. "Awfully hard to love someone when she's not around."

"Just use your imagination. If you shut off the
lights, or shut your eyes, you can always pretend."
Tears pricked her eyes again, and she turned her face
to the wall.

But a big hand cupped her cheek and swung her
back his way. "Ali, if I believe *you*, you've got to believe me... I wasn't pretending last night."

"You weren't pretending this morning, either, Ty.
You thought I was Kathy." And when he neither de-
nied nor defended it, the tears welled again.

Carefully he brushed them away, caught the next ones, as well, then gave it up. "Oh, Ali..." Lying down beside her, he pulled her into his arms and let her cry herself out against his throat while he stroked her hair and shoulders and crooned her name over and over till she ran dry and lay there sniffling feebly against his wet skin.

"Tissue?" There was almost—not quite—a smile in his voice.

"Thanks." She twisted away to use it, but he wouldn't let go and pulled her back under his chin once she was done.

"All right, now listen..." Ty paused for a moment, thinking. "I loved Kathy and I'd never deny it. But she's gone, Ali. Nobody knows that better than I do." Creeping up to her hair, his hand started its mesmeric, rhythmic stroking. "And you can't hug a memory. You can't come home and tell it what you did today; it won't make you laugh, won't hold you when you wake up scared in the middle of the night." The arm around her waist tightened as if with some particular memory and he took a deep breath. "So I've been looking for someone this past couple of years, Ali. Looking hard."

Shifting in the crook of his elbow, Alison pushed away from him a little so she could watch his profile as he gazed up at the ceiling.

"And I was starting to run scared," Ty murmured reflectively, his smile a bit wry. "I'd had something special—*very* special—before...and I couldn't see taking less the second time." His hand slid down through her hair, found her ear and fingered the edge of it with an idle, delicate touch. "Wouldn't be fair to the girl, if I felt, at the back of my mind, that she didn't measure up.... Nothing good could come of that in the long run...."

So he recognized that.... Thank God for that, but—

"And then, after all my hunting, when I'd just about given up hoping, thought maybe the first time was a fluke, that maybe lightning doesn't strike twice...boom! Out of the blue—there you were on the back porch, kissing my dog, just like that."

"Smelling of skunk," she reminded him dryly.

"*And* roses." The corners of his mouth deepened at the memory. "And nothing like what I'd expected or been looking for.... You're so different from Kathy."

"What was she like?" Sooner or later, she'd have to face up to it. As Ty considered the question, she watched his face carefully.

"Oh..." His blue-gray eyes seemed faraway, examining a memory with amusement, love, but no longing whatsoever that she could see. "Long, dark hair...tall...bubbly. She laughed all the time...so self-confident she almost scared people."

Everything that she would never be. Alison shifted restlessly, but his smile returned, suddenly—just for her.

"And then there you were—little, fragile, an angel with singed wings.... And all I could think was, I can teach her to laugh! Just give me a few weeks...or a few years. You've got a mouth made for laughing, you know."

"I do?"

"And for kissing." He outlined her disbelieving smile with a fingertip. Rolling toward her with deliberate and irresistible intention, he put that proposition to the test. "Mmm," he breathed at last, backing off half an inch. "Not necessarily in that order, you understand." His mouth descended again.

With his kiss slowly deepening—silken, liquid—it would have been so easy to give up, give in to the sweet craving, but... Alison pushed up against his shoulders, and after a reluctant pause, his head lifted and Ty looked down at her, his eyes asking the questions. "But this morning, Ty..."

"I know..." Taking a deep breath, he was obviously dragging himself back from action into thought. "I know, Ali...and I know how it must have felt, but I want you to think a minute..."

Fascinated with the shape of his mouth as he talked, she reached up to touch it and he kissed her fingers absently. "No one but Kathy's ever made me feel like last night before—that...well, happy's not a big enough word." He looked down at her quickly, as if to check that she understood. "But I hadn't felt that way for five years, Ali." His fingers moved to brush a curl off her forehead and then lingered. "So this morning, my subconscious, or whatever you care to call it, notices I feel wonderful—better than wonderful—and that there's a woman in bed with me. Therefore, it concludes, that woman must be Kathy." He frowned anxiously. "That make any sense at all?"

Perhaps...perhaps it did. She gave him just the tiniest of nods.

"It...might take a little time to connect that feeling with you," Ty warned softly, his eyes intent on her face as he leaned slowly above her again. "But if we work hard..." That teasing smile crept from hiding, but behind it there was still a question—a question she answered with her own shaky smile and by sliding her arms up around his neck.

It was all the invitation he needed. Rolling gently, hungrily on top of her, he cupped her face. "Oh, Ali!" His lips brushed her mouth, her cheek, her eyebrows. "It's you I'm going to be calling for, Ali, in no time at all, night and day. You're all I want, all I seem to be able to think about, nowadays." That whisper ended against her lips, and as she took him in with a wordless, murmuring welcome, his fingers found her breast. Yearning up against him, she would have sworn that the bed rose a foot in the air and began to spin. "All I've been able to think, these past few weeks..." he muttered, breathing heavily and glaring down at her buttons as he fumbled the last few free, "was that if I could just get you into bed, everything would work out all right."

And so it did.

"You're not a very restful bedmate," Alison complained somewhat later, her face buried in her pillow.

Balancing a tray on the bedspread, he sat crosslegged beside her. "'Fraid this was all I could find..."

He'd found the can of mandarin oranges she'd left in the fridge last month and the stick of cheddar she hadn't finished and— "Crackers?" She wrinkled her nose at the saltines. "You eat crackers in bed?"

"Only the night before I do laundry."

"I'm having second thoughts!" she announced darkly, sitting to brush her hair back, then leaning back on her hands.

"Uh-uh! No second thoughts." His voice was suddenly husky as his eyes caressed her bare breasts. Slowly his gaze climbed to note her spreading blush, then at last trapped her eyes. "No second thoughts, Ali. Just think of it as your first breakfast in bed. I'll do better next time."

Suddenly she was blinking back tears. No one had ever brought her breakfast in bed before. And "next time..."

"Love on an empty stomach'll do that to you." His eyes suddenly tender, Ty wiggled a cracker just beneath her nose.

After a few minutes, they shifted to lean against the wall, knees up-bent before them, thigh pressed to thigh. "So we've answered the main question," Ty announced, passing her another cracker. "But there's a few minor details I'd like filled in."

"Me too. Who was that blonde?"

"Blonde?" He looked almost foolishly pleased and way too innocent. "Which, er, what blonde?"

"The...ah...*slinky* one in Stonington."

"Oh, her?" Ty gave her a teasing, wicked grin. "Just a friend...far as *I'm* concerned, anyway."

"Hmm," Alison murmured dryly. *But if I believe you, you've got to believe....* "I *see*...and how did you know I was working for Forrest?"

"Mmm, well, I was curious from the start." Reaching for another cracker, Ty held it while she took a bit. "Curious about every last inch of you, as a

matter of fact, but especially curious as to why someone with your education would want a job like
that...." He placed the rest of the cracker carefully
between her lips, grinning when she nipped for his
fingers and missed. "But I didn't make any sort of
connection till you disappeared that first day. I got
down to the foot of the hill in time to see his Volvo
driving off, and that started me thinking."

"How'd you know it was *his* Volvo?"

"License plate IQ 303, Rhode Island? How would
I forget that? Did he ask for it special?"

Laughing, she shook her head. "But I'm sure he
accepted it as merely his due."

Snorting agreement, Ty reached for a slice of cheddar and balanced it on her shoulder. "This one's mine.
I'm just flavoring it...." He frowned faintly, searching for the thread again. "Then when I called the
History Department at Brown, and the secretary had
never heard of you... And then you show up with
enough heavy-duty art books to write a dozen disser-
tations, not knowing your Stonewall Jackson from the
tooth fairy..." His smile curled again. "I figured I
knew which way the wind was blowing."

Turning toward her, he put his mouth over the flesh-
warm slice of Cheddar, captured it in the midst of a
slow sensuous kiss, then brushed his lips along the top
of her shoulder, a growl humming deep in his throat.

"So why didn't you just tell Harriet?" she managed weakly.

"Well...there were several reasons. She was absolutely set on you...and *I* wanted to see more of you....
It seemed easiest to just get the painting out of your

sight while I sized up the situation—though *that* was no fun.'' He grimaced, remembering.

''But why did you have to hide *Alicia* from me?'' And from Forrest?''

''You tell me.'' Moving with that suddenness that always left her blinking, Ty was off the bed and back again in a moment with the painting, which he propped upright on her bureau. ''Well?''

''It's not a Minot.'' How had she not known that this morning?

''You're sure?'' But he wasn't surprised. ''How do you know?''

She frowned, thinking how to explain it. There was the hair color, of course, but even more than that...

''If you knew a person very well, Ty...and then he went away for twenty years, when you met him again, you'd know him, right? There'd be a feeling.... Something would ring a bell, wouldn't it? Well, in the same way, if you met a person, and he insisted you'd been friends twenty years ago...after talking for a few minutes, if he was lying, had never met you at all before, you'd know that, too, wouldn't you? Or at least you'd have a very, very uneasy feeling...right?''

''We nonacademic types call that a gut reaction, Angel.'' His fingers smoothed the line of fine, blond hair just below her navel.

''Right.'' She frowned back at the smiling redhead. ''That signature says, 'You know *me*! I'm an old friend of yours!' But all the time, a little voice inside my head keeps saying 'Liar. I never saw you before in my life!''' She glanced at him quickly. ''That's not just a gut reaction, Ty. It's based on knowledge.

Everything you know about a painter—his brushwork, choice of subject matter, use of space, choice of
pigments and their placement—everything you know
and everything you don't even know you know—It's
not a Minot," she repeated, feeling more sure of it
with each repetition. "But how did *you* know that?"

"I didn't know...but I had some pretty strong suspicions."

"Why?"

"Ohh... Well, I've always been interested in *Alicia*." His smile barely hidden, Ty studied the redhead. "It started out as a strictly scientific obsession.
She's as fine a subject for comparative anatomy as a
young boy could ever want."

"Uh-*huh*!"

His smile curved at her tone and vanished again.
"Then, as I grew older and became seriously inter-
ested in art, I began to appreciate her as a painting.
Guess I never told you that, for a couple of years
there, I was going to be the director of the Museum of
Modern Art when I grew up."

"You?"

"Me, Dark eyes... It's in the blood." He picked up
the tin of oranges they'd neglected. "My grandmother would have been thrilled to accept me as a
throwback to the Channing line—blue blood triumphs
in the end, you know. She'd have been delighted to
groom me for the part and probably had the connections to put me there eventually."

"So why didn't you stick with that plan?"

Ty laughed softly. "It was just a way to terrorize
Dad. That's worth a lot when you're seventeen or

eighteen, but it wasn't worth selling my soul for....
And I finally realized I'd have more fun working with
him. Being outside, playing with boats and boat yards,
buying and selling and making deals. Living by our
wits..." Spooning up a section of orange, he offered
it to her deftly. "I like art, Ali, like it a lot, but admiring a Degas doesn't begin to compare with smash-
ing a bottle of champagne on the bow of a boat you've
designed and had built."

That she could believe. "But why did you think
*Alicia* was a fake?"

"Oh...well, what started it was that I was doing
office work for Dad one summer—he despised paper-
work." His eyes distant with memories, Ty stopped to
savor an orange. "And while I was reorganizing his
files, I came across the bill of sale for *Alicia* here,
along with a letter of authentication signed by her last
owner."

"You mean she has a provenance?" It was more
than she and Forrest had expected.

"Oh, yes. She came with a letter from a French
marquis, testifying that she'd been in the family gallery since 1897."

"So what made you suspicious?" She opened her
mouth to intercept another load of cool sweetness.
Feeding her half the spoonful, Ty finished it himself.

"It wasn't the letter. That and the typed translation
that came with it were most impressive. And the little
hole-in-the-wall gallery in Paris where Dad found
*Alicia* had vouched for it, as well, but it was the price
he paid that started me wondering." Ty turned to
study the painting again. "Dad bought it in '47, so of

course prices were lower, but still...for an authentic Minot, it struck me as incredibly low, even for a post-war bargain.''

"Didn't your dad think of that?''

Smiling, Ty shook his head slowly. "He was so shrewd, Ali, about some things, and so incredibly naive about others. Dad just could not accept that a painting—'a scrap of canvas, four boards and some house paint,' as he used to tease Mother—could cost as much or more than a prime piece of waterfront or a new stern trawler.''

He'd forgotten the oranges; so, lifting the can from his fingers, she took over the feeding.

"Anyhow, value them or not himself, Dad went to France bound and determined to find a painting to replace Mother's first Minot —the one she sold to get him started.... I think Dad always felt a little guilty that he'd wooed her away from the Channing millions. He was always trying to make up for that, I'm afraid.''

"She didn't miss it, I bet.'' Alison finished off the oranges and Ty collected the tin.

"No, Mother never missed it at all.... She had what she wanted.'' Eyes gleaming, he studied her for a moment. Then, tipping the can, he drizzled a line of orange syrup across her breasts.

"Hey!''

"Mmm?'' Burying one hand in her hair to tilt her head back, he slid the other around her waist and proceeded to lick her clean, his tongue rough and greedy as a cat's.

Scowling and shivering with delight, eyes closing, she gave herself up to the sensation, senses spiraling inward until she seemed to be falling.

She was. Her back touched the mattress and then Ty settled warmly upon her, his forehead resting against hers. "I...think...we were discussing a painting?" Her voice had a breathlessness that might have been due to the weight she was bearing. Or might not.

"We were? Well...so...Dad found *Alicia*." Ty paused, obviously collecting some sadly scattered thoughts. "Paid what he considered to be a staggering sum...the price of two new fishing boats, as he put it to me, which was all he could afford at that point, and then some. And he brought it triumphantly home to Mother." Shifting restlessly, Ty fitted his hardening contours a little more snugly against her.

"So that was why you thought it was a fake? The price?" she asked quickly.

"Ahh...no...no. That made me wonder, but it wasn't much to go on.... I didn't get back to it till about two years later...was taking an art-history course in college my sophomore year, and I needed a topic for the term paper. So I thought I'd do an in-depth analysis of *Alicia*." His hand found and cupped the end of her shoulder, then, sliding up its curve to her collarbone, traced that shape across with idle, exploratory fingertips. "So I started reading up on Minot, and right away I found out that all nine paintings he made of Alicia were supposedly burned.... So that was curiouser and curiouser, as another Alice said." His fingertip nestled in the hollow at the base of her throat, then swirled to circle first her left breast and then her right. As he outlined the darker, hardening peak, she rippled beneath him, lifting them both.

"You sure you want to talk?" He almost blurted the question, as if an alternative had just that second occurred to him, but laughing breathlessly, she nodded. He sighed, his stomach pressing warmly against hers with the breath. "I was afraid of that. You've got a mean streak, for an angel.... So I had till the end of January to write my paper. Jake and I were off to Switzerland on a grand skiing expedition—for Christmas, and we had a stopover in Paris. I decided to hunt down this marquis who had written the letter and talk with him—or his survivors, if he was dead, since this was twenty years after Dad had bought *Alicia*."

Alison suddenly remembered the conversation in the *Bluebird*'s main cabin— Good Lord, could that have been only last night? "Jake started to say something about that...."

"Uh-huh, till I kicked him under the table."

"The marquis didn't exist?" He fingertipped her again, and she surged up against him in gasping, involuntary response.

"Ohh..." For a moment, as he stared down at her, it appeared he'd forgotten all words, but finally he continued. "Oh, he'd existed all right... But he died in late '46...and that letter was written in '47."

"I *see*..." So the provenance had been faked, probably at the little gallery where Pat had found it; it had been done before. "So what did you do?"

"Came back and wrote a third-rate paper on Utrillo."

He reached for her again, but she caught his wrist. "But why?"

"Why?" For a second he seemed almost annoyed. "Just think a minute, Ali.... And in the meantime, if you don't want to play, I guess we better have a shower and get going. It's nearly two."

"I've had mine already," she told him smugly.

But, bending down, he rubbed his nose slowly across her breasts. "Hate to say it, lady, but you need another. You smell like a mandarin orange." Dipping his head again, he followed her curves with a hot, lazy tongue. "Taste like one, too," he added. "Besides, I need a back scrub. What do you think I'm marrying you for?"

The word was like a blow to the stomach. Owl-eyed, she stared up at him. "You're...marrying me?"

His eyes were suddenly sharp as his brows drew together. "Any objections to that?"

"Let me think a minute...."

"Uh-uh. *Don't* think. Just jump. I'll catch you."

It was one thing to want him—it was getting hard to remember a time when she hadn't wanted him—but marriage? Once upon a time she'd even wanted Don....

But Ty was rolling off her, sliding off the bed. "On second thought, if you're going to look *that* worried, maybe I should take the question back."

But that only worried her more.

TY INSISTED ON DRIVING her back in the BMW. "We'll be up this way again in a day or two. I want to see how the *Ali O* is coming."

"The *Ali O*?"

"The party boat I'm having built in Bristol." His sideways glance held a challenge, but when she didn't speak, he dropped the subject for a few miles.

"How do you learn to trust...once you've lost it?" she asked at last.

His eyes luminous in profile, Ty considered that gravely. "Very simple. You test me." Reaching across the stick shift, he caught her hand. "In this case, you do what I ask. Once you see how well it works out, you'll trust me a little further. And we'll build from there."

"And you're asking?"

His hand tightened. "That you marry me. The sooner the better."

This was the gradual approach? "Ty...I'm scared...." The tension in her throat turned her response to a harsh little whisper.

"I know." His own voice was low and soothing. "But just close your eyes and jump, anyway. It's going to work out fine, Dark Eyes—trust me. You've made the hardest leap already." Lifting her hand to his lips, he kissed it and set it free, then shifted down for the red light ahead. As the car stopped, he turned to inspect her. "I didn't hurt you last night, did I?" His eyes caressed her face and shoulders. "Or this morning?"

Reliving those hot, sweet hours on her bed, she shook her head slowly.

"And I'll be just as careful with your heart, lady." Reaching across, he rubbed the back of his hand slowly across the part of her nearest that thumping organ. "That's a *promise*."

They both started as a car horn blared behind them. After he'd shifted up through the gears, his hand came back to curve in light and restless possession upon her thigh.

Without some distraction, they'd never make sixty miles this way, Alison decided, catching his hand. "But why didn't you tell Harriet or your father once you suspected the painting was a fake?"

He accepted her diversion. "What good would that have done anyone? Mother had a painting she dearly loved. She's always kept it right there on the bedroom wall—only shows it to her most favorite people. You don't know what an honor she was doing you, Ali, when she tried to show it to you last month. I don't think half a dozen people have seen *Alicia* since Mother got her... Not even her own mother." Glancing over his shoulder, Ty changed lanes to let a Volkswagen zoom past like an enraged junebug.

"And to tell Dad..." He shook his head, frowning. "*Alicia* was his wedding gift, as well as payment in full on a debt of honor, and he never stopped being proud of the way Mother loved it. Do you know what he'd have done if he'd found out he'd bought her a fake? He'd have charged off to find a genuine Minot. And then he would have discovered that he couldn't afford the real thing, because as far as he'd come since '47, the price of French Impressionist paintings has risen further." Twisting his captured hand around, he twined his fingers with hers.

"We've got a comfortable little family business, Ali," he continued thoughtfully, not realizing he'd shifted into present tense, as if Patrick still shared it with him, "but most of our assets are tied up in land and boats. And any cash we keep is for use in new speculations—like that boat yard on City Island."

He let go of her hand as they approached a rotary, then collected it again as they curved out the other side. "There's always been enough to keep us comfortably and enough to buy Mother a new painting every year or two...but you'll have noticed she limits her collecting to paintings of undiscovered artists or the cheaper watercolors and sketches of the more famous ones.

"So...to buy a genuine Minot..." Ty shook his head again grimly. "Dad would either have beggared us or broken his heart, trying to finance it somehow."

"And so that's why you didn't want Forrest or me to see the painting." So much for all Forrest's dark suspicions!

"Right," Ty agreed crisply. "Dad was past hurting by then, but *Alicia* means all the more to Mother since he's gone. And she's so fragile right now..." His hand flexed unconsciously, pinching her fingers. "There was no way I was going to let that sneaking little squirt spoil her painting for her." He threw her a glance so ferocious that she would have ducked under her seat, had it been meant for her. And it should have been, she realized with a guilty wince.

"But, you know," she said after an unhappy moment, "at one time your mother must have questioned the painting's authenticity herself." And she went on to tell him of Professor Harrison's mysterious visitor and the uproar that followed.

"Now that's strange..." Ty frowned, thinking. "I know she did meet Dad in New York when he sailed back from France, because family legend has it that I was conceived in the honeymoon suite at the Plaza..." He grinned briefly. "So Mother was certainly in town around that date...but...what did that note in his appointment calendar say again?"

"'Eliza Channing's daughter, bringing a painting for my evaluation.'"

"Daughter... So he didn't say which one? Mother had a sister, you know, also very involved in art. And Aunt Glenda always lived in the city. I wonder if it could have been her? But there was no way of knowing, short of asking Harriet, and *that* was out of the question," Ty declared quietly, his jaw set.

"But what am I going to tell Forrest?" Alison wondered as they joined the stop-and-crawl traffic through Westerly. For, whatever else happened, she intended to finish her dissertation, and that put her at Forrest's mercy. The professor was not going to give up his thirty-five-year quest that easily.

"I suggest you let *me* tell him a thing or two," offered Ty dryly. "I don't think he'd be very thrilled if the president of Brown learned how his head of the Art Department conducts basic research."

Forrest wouldn't be thrilled with *her*, that was certain. "We couldn't...just...show him the painting?" she proposed timidly. "Since it's not a Minot, he won't include it in his catalogue raisonée."

But Ty shook his head. "He can't be trusted. You can't tell me, Ali, that Osgood wouldn't want to mention it, either in the book or in a separate article. It's just too tempting. And Mother reads every major art magazine in the country. No way…"

"But—"

"No way, lady," he repeated, crisply, flashing her an impatient glance. "You're either with me or against me on this one."

*I'm stuck right smack dab in the middle, is where I am,* Alison thought unhappily.

"Anyway, you can leave Osgood to me," he instructed her as they sped out of town.

No, she couldn't, but the image of a bug-eyed Forrest Osgood turned over to Ty's tender mercies kept her smiling for the last few miles.

They took the hill up to Shady Breeze in a rush. Swooping past the turnoff to the front, they glided down to the garage in back and into its sheltering darkness. "And *now*…" Ty announced, swinging around in his seat and reaching for her.

But Alison had no intention of facing Harriet with her lips still throbbing from one of Ty's kisses. "No— later," she countered, half out of the car already. She gave him a sassy grin across the top of the BMW as he stepped out his side and shut the door.

He looked more amused than thwarted. "Don't forget *Alicia*."

"I thought you were waiting for Harriet's birthday?"

Ty shook his head. "There's no use making her wait that long now. I'll find her another birthday gift."

But when Alison shut the back door, the painting in hand, she found Ty looming between her and the sunlight, carefully dusting off the back fender of his car.

"I'll take that." He set the painting on top of the BMW. "And now—" His hands closed around her waist.

Each time he touched her was more arousing than the last. Her body was learning to anticipate what those hands would do to her. Suddenly dizzy with desire, she was not surprised to find her feet no longer on the ground.

He set her down on the back fender. Nudging her knees gently apart, he stood between them and leaned against her, his hands holding her thighs close against his hips. "Well?" he demanded sternly.

"Well?" she parroted, wide-eyed. Well, would he just please, please take her *now*? Now. Not in five minutes, not in three, but now?

But he had a mean streak, as well. Having found the hem of her dress, his hands were now gliding up beneath it and sliding sensuously up the outsides of her thighs. Reaching her panties, his fingers slithered inside them, cupped warmly around her buttocks and pulled her closer against him. "Well?"

"Could you just kiss me?" she suggested, rubbing her breasts against his chest, her blood throbbing in time to his kneading fingers.

"Say 'yuh' first," he commanded.

"Yuh?" A nut, as well as a sadist.

"That's good. Now say *S* as in Saratoga."

Whatever the man said. "S!" Smiling giddily, she rubbed her nose along the V of his shirt. His hands tightened pleasurably.

"Good. Now say them both together, three times, as fast as you can," he ordered.

A nut—why did she love him so? "Yuh—ess, Yuh-ess, Yuh—ess," she gabbled obediently.

"Aha!" Leaning back to see her face, he was grinning triumphantly. "That was the answer, and the *question* was... Will you marry me immediately, if not sooner?"

"Wait a—" she yelped against his lips, and the last word was swallowed whole.

"Mmph!" she protested inside his mouth, then "Mmm?" as his tongue started its sweet persuasion and hers answered instinctively. "Mmm!" she moaned against him finally, hungrily, her arms sliding up around his neck as he bent her slowly backward.

Supporting her upon his forearms, his hands cupping the back of her head, Ty held her just inches off the car's dusty metal while he plundered her mouth with a silken, merciless tongue.

Heart pressed to hammering heart, her legs locked around his, Alison arched up against him. "Ty!" she protested as their lips parted.

"Say yes!" he commanded fiercely, his whisper caressing her lips.

"Yes..." Whatever he wanted...whatever...

"You want me?" he demanded as he brushed her mouth with his own.

"Yes!"

"You'll marry me?" he insisted, tantalizing her lips with just the tip of his tongue.

Thinking or trying to think, she hesitated, and felt his arms tense. "Yes," she agreed softly, staring up into those deep water eyes...out of her depth eyes... Whatever the problems to come, whatever her fears, if he wanted her, *yes*, she wanted him.

"And you love me?" he whispered, as if this were somehow not quite believable.

Eyes glittering with tears, smiling, she nodded. "I love you, Ty."

His eyes suddenly too bright also, Ty buried his face in her hair as he squeezed her tight. He'd been holding his breath, she realized, as he let it out in a long drawn-out sigh that tickled her ear—a sound of relief and satisfaction...and peace. "'Bout time you figured that out," he said finally, his voice suddenly matter-of-fact.

Laughing silently, she smiled up at the rafters overhead and hugged him closer.

"Woof!" With a sound that was part grunt, part bark and all impatience, Milo reared up beside them, his claws scrabbling on the metal. From the reproachful look in those chocolate eyes, she assumed he'd been standing by for some time now.

"Watch the claws, sport!" Ty admonished. "Down!" And the dog disappeared. Turning back to her, Ty sighed, but it turned into a rueful grin as he met her eyes. "So much for romance!" Pulling her gently upright, he wrapped his arms around her, stood holding her, rocking her slowly, his chin resting on top of her head. "If we were married...I'd put you in this

car so fast.... We could be home in fifteen minutes....
And then..."

"Mmm?" she purred, lifting her head to smile up
at him.

"Then bedtime for you, Angel Eyes...if we made it
that far." He kissed the tip of her nose. "There's always the couch." He kissed her chin. "Or the rug...it's
a nice, soft rug..."

"You wouldn't feed me first?" she teased, arching
her back to press closer against him.

"Later!" he murmured roughly.

Best to train him early. Smiling, she shook her head.
"Before."

"Between," he decided, with the authority of a man
who knows a good compromise when he's found
it.

"Woof!" Milo interjected, shoving his nose between their legs.

"All right, all right!" Ty gave her a final hug before backing off, and Milo swarmed upon him instantly; Ty leaned to grab his ears. "Why don't I meet
you up at the house? I'm going to take a quick cool-
down walk."

But she didn't want to face Harriet's knowing eyes
alone. Perched on the top step to the back patio,
Alison waited for him, holding *Alicia* at arm's length.
Clear laughter rang out from the sunset side of the
house, and she turned, listening. Perhaps June had
stayed late? Or could Eliza Channing have remained
after bringing Harriet back from Boston? Please God,
not that. Not today.

"Scared to face the music without me?" Ty collected the painting while sliding his other arm around her waist.

"Will she mind?" she asked quickly, glancing up at him.

"Don't be silly. She'll be thrilled." He eased her toward the back door.

"She's out on the side porch. I just heard her talking...."

"Wonder if Eliza's still here?" he murmured, changing course to find out.

"*She'll* mind." Alison pulled away a step.

Ty let go of her waist, but dropped an arm on her shoulder in a way that suggested he meant to hang on to her, grandmother or no. "She will," he agreed easily, "but don't let her scare you. She's a nice old fossil."

As they turned the corner, Milo leading the way, Harriet laughed again.

Halfway down the porch, they stood together, Harriet half a head taller than the man in tropical whites who was just then refilling her glass of lemonade with a flourish.

Squeezing her shoulder, Ty pulled Alison to a standstill, then dragged her backward a step, but it was too late. The couple turned and saw them.

"Why, here she is!" Harriet cried gleefully. "And Ty, as well." And hooking a slender, proprietary hand inside his elbow, she urged her pale-faced companion forward. "So come meet my son, Forrest!"

## CHAPTER FIFTEEN

WITH THE EYES OF A DEFIANT RABBIT above his tiny, frozen smile, Professor Forrest Osgood allowed himself to be led forward. Alison watched his pastel blue bow tie quiver as he swallowed. Around her shoulders, Ty's arm was too tight and utterly motionless; she felt as if she were standing by a very large cat as it gathered itself for the pounce.

Only Harriet was missing the tension. "I've appropriated your visitor, Alison," she explained gaily as they neared. "He tried to reach you from Stonington several hours ago, and we had such a delightful conversation over the phone that I invited him to come wait for you here." She gestured behind them. "We've been debating all afternoon. He prefers my Cassatt sketches to the Degas!"

Following her gesture, Alison noted several chairs lined up along the porch, facing the late-afternoon sunlight. Each chair held one framed picture from Harriet's collection, propped upright. So they'd been having their own little art lovers' festival out here.... Harriet's face was delicately flushed; never had Alison seen her so carefree or vivacious as she completed the introductions. "Professor Osgood is an old friend of

Alison's from Brown. He's head of the Art Department."

"Indeed," Ty murmured grimly, extending his hand.

Looking as if he'd sooner shake hands with a bear trap, Forrest put forward his own. A small, silly smirk of pure relief skittered across his face when he retrieved it intact.

Ty was not done with him, however. "Professor, since you're an old friend of Alison's, perhaps you could answer a few questions for me—in private." He jerked his chin toward the back porch.

But even as Forrest flinched back a step, beaming in polite terror, Harriet noticed the painting Ty held face-in against his side. "*Ty!* Is that *Alicia*?"

Ty hesitated perhaps one beat too long, as he rocked back on his heels. "Nope...it's something new. Ali and I picked it out in Providence...."

Smiling, she shook her head. "You've always been a dreadful liar, Ty!" Setting one hand lightly on the frame, she caressed the edge of it. "I know the back of that canvas as well as the front." Her brows drew together suddenly. "She...wasn't damaged in the cleaning, was she?"

"*No!* No, she's better than ever. But it's three weeks till your birthday," he reminded her as she put a second hand on the frame. "I've got to gift wrap her."

As her fingers curled gently around the edges of the painting, Harriet's chin lifted slightly, but her voice was still coaxing. "I'm having my birthday early this year, didn't I tell you, Ty?" She glanced sideways at the professor for support, but he was oblivious, his eyes riveted to the back of the painting as if, with a little more effort, he might squint through the canvas to the paint beyond. "Forrest, I have something *very* special to show you, if Tyler will only cooperate." She turned back to her son. "Ty, please...I want her now. Don't be difficult."

"Mother..." He shook his head helplessly.

*"Ty..."* The storm warnings were clear in those widening gray eyes and the delicate pink sweeping across her cheekbones. It was going to be an O'Malley war to end all wars if he refused. "Please..." she repeated with ominous restraint.

He knew when he was beaten. With a tight little shrug, Ty let the painting go.

Taking a swift step backward, as if he might change his mind, Harriet reversed the painting and stood staring down at it. Sucking in her breath, her eyes suddenly radiant with tears, she gave a jerky little nod of satisfaction, then hugged it to her breast. The smile she bestowed on Ty over the top of it more than canceled the tension of the past few minutes; properly harnessed, it could have lit Shady Breeze for a year or two.

She turned back to the professor, who was almost goggle-eyed with impatience. "Stay there, Forrest," she commanded and, with *Alicia* still concealed, walked slowly down the porch to where the other paintings were arranged.

It was all the chance Ty needed. Catching Forrest by the bow tie, he swung him around and hauled him in on tiptoe. "Tell her it's fake and you're *dead*, Osgood. Got that?" he whispered savagely. Dropping him flat-footed, Ty transferred his hold to the back of Forrest's collar, a grip that would be invisible from Harriet's perspective.

Meeting Forrest's eye-rolling, mute appeal with a grimace and a helpless shrug, Alison fell back half a pace. Digging her fingers into Ty's back jeans pocket, she gave a gentle tug. *Down, boy!* But if he felt it at all, Ty gave no notice; all his attention was fixed on Forrest as Harriet propped up the painting and stepped aside.

"Well, Forrest?" she beamed.

"Errrr..." Whether this hesitation was artistic uncertainty or a survival tactic was hard to say. From her vantage point Alison could see Ty's fingers tightening on the professor's collar even as Forrest's bird's nest brows rose toward his hairline.

"Who painted it?" Harriet prompted.

Looking like a small bulldog straining against a choke chain, Forrest tottered forward, pulling Ty at his heels. It was scholastic lust, not terror, that was driving him now, Alison decided; Forrest might just say anything. She gave Ty's pants another warning tug. *No violence, friend. Please!*

"I'll give you one clue," Harriet said softly as the three of them lurched closer. "It's not a Minot."

The words took a moment to sink in.

"Not—" Ty croaked, and then his voice trailed away as his jaw dropped.

"Ahhh..." Forrest intoned, his eyes darting from the canvas to Harriet's face and back to the canvas. One small fat hand crept up to jerk at his bow tie.

"That's the one thing I'm sure of," Harriet continued, turning so she, too, could gaze down at the painting. "But if it's not Minot, who is it? I've been racking my brains for thirty-five years now."

"Uhh…" Forrest hedged, then stole a wild-eyed glance up at his captor.

Still staring speechlessly at his mother, Ty gave a bewildered, absent shrug and let him go.

"Ah…" Forrest took a long, low step forward, out of Ty's reach, and stopped again, transfixed by the painting. "You're absolutely correct, dear lady," he murmured dazedly. "It's not a Minot." A maniacal little titter escaped his lips and then was covered instantly by a fit of coughing.

Shaking his head in disgusted wonder, Ty reached to cover Alison's fingers in his back pocket.

She was going to giggle aloud! Ribs aching with the struggle to contain her laughter, Alison smothered her face between Ty's shoulder blades. But she'd miss the show, so she peeped out again.

"No, but why do you think it's not?" Harriet was challenging Forrest with the eagerness of one seeking vindication of a pet theory.

Squaring his shoulders, Forrest seemed to be rapidly regaining his confidence. He cleared his throat. "Aside from the subtle differences in style, there's the hair color, my dear Harriet…. Alicia's hair was red, but not of this Titian hue, according to Minot's correspondence with his brother Paul."

"*'Cheveux d'un jet de bourgogne,'*" Harriet quoted.

"Ahh, so you speak the language," Forrest agreed instantly, as if he, too, were fluent, and Alison swallowed her smile. Well, as often as she'd translated that passage concerning Alicia's wine-dark tresses for him, the professor *ought* to be able to recognize it.

Harriet nodded. "I was fairly certain from the first moment I laid eyes on her that she was not by Minot, whatever the signature said. I grew up with fourteen Minots in the house, so..." She shook her head as if shaking that thought aside. "Anyway, a few weeks later I discovered that passage, and then I was sure. But I'd give anything to know who *did* paint her. He was fully as good as Minot, I think." She moved to stand shoulder to shoulder with the professor. "So who is he? A talent like this should be known."

"As yet I've simply no idea," the professor confessed, his eyes still devouring the smiling redhead. "By any chance, did you show this painting to Professor Drew Harrison, back in '47?"

"So you've heard of that affair?" She spared a smile for Alison and Ty as they came forward to lean against the porch railing beside her. "Yes, I did, the day after my husband brought her back from France. He had some business to do in town, so I snuck off with *Alicia* while he was out." She shook her head sadly. "Poor man.... My mother had always considered Professor Harrison the highest American authority on French Impressionism. Perhaps I simply met him on an off day, but drunk as he was, I was astounded he could even make out the signature. And I certainly didn't trust his judgment...or his enthusiasm..."

"But why didn't you respond to the appeals in *ARTnews*, once Drew was dead?" There was a note of despairing indignation in Forrest's question. "The whole world was waiting to know the truth!"

"But by then, I'd found Minot's letter to his brother...and *I* knew the truth." Harriet's expression was serene and inward turning. "I had more important considerations, Forrest. *Alicia* was a very special gift from my husband, and I had his pride to protect." She glanced sideways at the professor in quick appeal, smiling as she noted his look of utter incomprehension, and turned back to the painting. "I've spent the past thirty-five years hiding *Alicia* away up in my bedroom. If my mother had ever laid eyes on her, she'd have known instantly, and she'd never, ever have let my husband forget he'd bought a counterfeit." Harriet shrugged gracefully. "There was nothing to do but hide her and wonder.... But who *could* have painted her?"

Forrest shook his head dazedly. "First, dear lady, I think perhaps I'd better have another drink...."

"That makes two of us, Professor!" Ty decided, crossing to the wicker table. "What are you drinking?"

Through the library's open window, the phone trilled, and Alison pushed off the railing. "I'll get it."

Returning a moment later, she found Harriet had followed her inside. "It's for you, Harriet. Long distance." Her daughter Patsy, Alison guessed.

Nodding, Harriet put a light hand on her shoulder to stop her retreat. "Well?" she asked, her eyes mischievous as they searched her face.

"Well, what?" Alison parried. *Let Ty tell her!*

"Well, you have eyes like stars today, Miss Erik-sen, and I couldn't help noticing..." But her own eyes sparkling, she let her observation trail away on a teasing note. "Never mind, I'm being nosy." She turned toward the living room, and then stopped again. "Oh, Alison, would you mind if I invited Forrest to stay for dinner? He's really very amusing."

"No, that's a wonderful idea." With Forrest there to distract Harriet, she would have all the more time to enjoy Ty. "Shall I start organizing?"

"Please. June had to leave early today—a dentist appointment, I believe—but she finished the cooking." Harriet moved away. She was walking quite smoothly these past few days, if still very slowly, Alison noticed proudly. And her Boston trip—or Forrest—had made a difference, as well. Life and people were what she needed now.

When Alison returned to the porch a short while later, Harriet was still on the phone. Ty was returning the paintings to their rightful indoor locations, except for *Alicia*. Sitting face-to-face with the redhead, Forrest sipped a gin and tonic—not his first, or his second, Alison suspected—while his eyes tracked inch by inch across the canvas. "Forrest?"

"Thirty-five years," he marveled without turning.

His collar was twisted up in back and, gently, she turned it down for him. "You're staying for supper."

"Am I?" he murmured absently. "How delight-ful.... Delightful woman, your Harriet."

"What are you doing here, by the way?" she asked, trying unsuccessfully to break that obsessive gaze.

"Ahh... There's an auction in Manhattan on Monday...Sotheby's. I decided I deserved a little junket, and on my way down, I thought I'd see how you'd progressed." Moving slowly, as if hypnotized, he sipped his drink, his eyes never leaving the canvas. "I had intended to meet you for luncheon in Stonington again, but when I reached your employer instead...and she seemed so very hospitable..." His voice faded away.

So he hadn't been able to resist the opportunity to exert his charm, and perhaps to steal a march on her. His visit would have been a triumph of ingratiation if Ty hadn't appeared to spoil it. But that was not what was depressing him now.

By the time the four of them sat down to supper, though, Forrest's disappointment appeared to be on the wane. Returning from the kitchen with the lasagna June had left for them, Alison found that the Jamie Wyeth watercolor had been removed from the dining-room wall; in its place *Alicia, After* gave the professor her dreamy smile by candlelight.

"Just for tonight, to please Forrest," Harriet explained, following her eyes. "After this, it's back upstairs with her."

"I'd say she's more at home in a bedroom," Ty agreed, pouring the Chianti.

Forrest lifted his wineglass. "May I propose a toast?" His eyes swept the table, gathering their attention, then returned to the painting. "To the lady who brings us all together tonight." And he lifted his glass to the redhead.

*"Alicia,"* they echoed with smiling solemnity, and the crystal chimed.

"I have a better toast," Ty announced, after a moment. Turning to face Alison, he raised his glass again. "To the lady I'm going to marry," he pledged softly, his eyes unwavering. "Alison." Dimly she heard the exclamations of the other two, and then her name and the sweet cry of the crystal. The candlelight seemed to be filling her eyes; Ty's tender smile blurred before her.

"Well!" Harriet exclaimed, on a note of teasing satisfaction.

"You don't mind?" she dragged her eyes from his face to ask.

"Mind? I've been wondering how long it would take you two! I am absolutely, utterly, completely, whole-heartedly delighted!"

"And may I be the first to bestow my felicitations?" Forrest inquired, rising to offer Ty his hand. "And you, my dear." He aimed a little bow in Alison's direction. "You are marrying into one of the finest young collections in the country. I'm delighted for you!"

And for himself, Alison suspected with a rueful grin.

"When will the wedding be?" Harriet wanted to know.

"Just as soon as I can get the license," Ty announced firmly.

"Good, because I'm off to California just as soon as you do—that was Patsy who phoned. She's all right," she added quickly as he started to speak, "but the doctor has confined her to bed for the duration of her pregnancy, and with Bill teaching this summer, she's bored to tears already. "I'm commanded to come out and hold her hand till delivery."

Ty's frown was deepening as she talked. "You're sure you're up to that?"

Ignoring him, Harriet turned to Alison. "I suppose I should warn you, Alison—he's a worrywart."

"Ohh...I guess I can stand it." Meeting his eyes with a grin, she nearly jumped as a large, bare foot found her own under the table. "Somehow..." she added softly, as his toes stroked up the side of her calf and down again.

"Now, Professor." Turning tactfully away from them, Harriet drew Forrest into the conversation. "Suppose you tell us who painted my *Alicia*."

More than pleased to regain the spotlight, Forrest brightened immediately. Preening his bow tie, he gazed judiciously up at the painting. "I do have a delicious hypothesis," he admitted, after a dramatic pause. "It may take years of research to validate, although, actually, if you would be so kind as to allow me to have the painting X-rayed..." Ignoring the salad bowl that Harriet was attempting to pass him, he bounced to his feet. "Alison, how would you say 'Alicia, after a painting by Minot'?"

With five warm toes kneading a secret message of desire along her inner thigh, it took a moment to gather her wits. *"Alicia, d'aprés une peinture de Minot,"* she translated finally, striving to keep her voice matter-of-fact, wondering if goose bumps showed by candlelight.

"Exactly," Forrest agreed, as if he'd simply been testing her proficiency with the language. "Now observe this center section of the bedclothes and the size of the gap between 'Alicia' and '*après*,'" he commanded, his fingers outlining these areas without touching them. "The artist grows clumsy here. The brushwork is suddenly fussy...overworked...lifeless." Turning to the table, his eyes gleamed as his voice hushed theatrically. "I propose that these two areas of paint were added *long* after the original work was created! I propose that beneath these crude additions lie a letter *d* and three words, *une peinture de*—'a painting by'—which leaves us with what seemed to be a rather suggestive title, *Alicia, After*—" he touched the words lightly "—and a signature—Minot."

"So you think that the original artist had no intention of creating a counterfeit?" That notion seemed to please Harriet.

"Precisely, my dear lady." Forrest nodded approvingly. "But I do suspect that this artist had seen Minot's *Alicia* series, and that this painting is simply an admiring, frank and very successful attempt to recreate Minot's style. An *homage*, as it were...a pastiche..." He turned back to the redhead. "I further suspect that one of Minot's *Alicia* series *was* nearly identical to this painting, but that the artist simply altered Alicia's hair color out of mischief or to suit his own taste."

The foot between her thighs was growing a bit too bold, and beneath the table, Alison clamped her knees firmly around his ankle. Across the table, Ty's head was half-turned to follow the professor. "Renoir saw the *Alicia* paintings that night before they were burned," she reminded Forrest. "And *he* certainly favored red hair." Putting one hand casually under the table, she traced a teasing spiral down the sole of Ty's captive foot, then clamped her legs tighter as it jerked in attempted escape. Ticklish, by gosh! Now she knew how to handle him.

"Indeed he did, Alison, but consider the opacity of the paint film throughout the canvas, the impasto treatment of the hair…. There's a bit of his translucency about her face, I'll grant you, but…no, I'll eat my favorite fedora if this is a Renoir," Forrest vowed.

"The student Gilbert!" Harriet exclaimed suddenly. "Renoir's disciple saw the paintings that night, as well!"

"Exactly." Forrest nodded, his voice heavy with satisfaction. Clasping his hands behind his back, the professor paced down the table toward her. "How like a young and ardent painter! One can envision him reeling back to his studio that very night, his head awhirl with cheap wine and admiration for this breathtaking new style of painting that Minot has just shown him." Reversing himself, Forrest bobbed away in the opposite direction. "It is a revelation, a whole new way of thinking! Of seeing! Down he sits at his easel, and from memory, Gilbert attempts to recreate one of the paintings that has so astounded him."

Turning again, he swept the table fiercely with his eyes, as if daring them to dispute it. "And, as an *homage*, once it is complete, he signs it 'Alicia, after a painting by Minot.'"

His foot still squirming for freedom, Ty's teeth were clamped on his bottom lip as Alison traced a final torturing caress across his sole. But the glint in his eyes, wide with his effort not to laugh, warned her that she'd pay for this pleasure later. And enjoy the payment, Alison suspected, giving his big toe a mocking tweak as she freed him.

"But then who blocked out the middle words?" Harriet was asking.

"That I suspect we shall never know, dear lady." Forrest had ceased his lecture-room pacing and was rocking slowly from heel to toe and back again as he did when taking questions from the class. "It's an old, honored ruse used by con men—to pick up a painting by an unknown artist and to alter the signature to that of a more valued artist."

Taking his eyes off Alison, Ty turned to the professor. "But why did Gilbert never become famous in his own right?"

"Alas, my friend..." Forrest made a mournful face. "Gilbert did not survive to earn his fame. I shall have to verify my facts, but I know he died at a tender age...perhaps a mere matter of months after the night he saw Minot's work...."

After that, reluctantly, the professor sat down again. Their lasagna was cold by that time, but with the looks she was fielding from across the table, Alison was warm enough.

She wasn't really hungry, after all, she decided—not for food, anyway, and went to the kitchen to brew their coffee. Bending over the coffeepot, she was not really surprised when Ty's arms encircled her waist from behind. Sighing her pleasure, she leaned back against his chest, arching her back as his hands smoothed slowly up her ribs. As he cupped her breasts, she bit back a tiny moan and shuddered.

"Hope you sleep better than I will tonight," he murmured ruefully, nuzzling her ear. "Tell Mother and Forrest good-night for me."

"Don't go..." Her body made the plea, as well, her hips rocking back against him till he surged forward to meet her.

"I've...got to." He laughed breathlessly, as his lips brushed the side of her face. "I'm going *crazy*, just watching you across the room. Might as well go home and watch the clock, and when it's morning, I can get up and find out about that marriage license."

Perhaps it was best. It almost hurt, having him there and not having him. Shivering again, she nodded.

"Going to miss me?" he demanded huskily.

He could still doubt it? Eyes closed, she nodded again, her hair rustling against his cheek.

"Show me how much?"

Smiling, blinded by tears, she turned in his arms. Framing the rough warmth of his cheeks in her hands, she showed him on his eyes, his lips, the end of his funny nose and his lips again. "Good night!" she whispered finally.

Lifting her hands away from his face, he kissed first one and then the other. "'Night, Angel." Touching her nose, he gave her a rueful, lopsided little grin and almost ducked out the back door.

Who would he dream of tonight, she wondered, wandering slowly back to the coffeepot. *"Me..."* she murmured defiantly.

A silky thumping caught her ear, and turning, Alison saw Milo, sprawled by his dog bowl in the corner, his tail knocking the base of the cabinets each time it swung across the floor. Kathy's dog...

Slowly she walked across to him. Well, Kathy had had good taste; they'd loved the same things. If they'd ever met, perhaps they would have been friends....

"Me," she told the dog firmly. Stooping to run her fingers through his glossy coat, she began to smile. "Me..." Each time she said it, it was a little easier to believe.

ALISON SLEPT LATE the next morning and was a long time in getting downstairs. But there was no way to move faster; every few minutes she would return to the present to find herself standing statuelike, toothbrush or sandals or whatever she'd forgotten this time still in hand, with an incredulous grin on her face.

Downstairs, Harriet was nowhere to be found. Having taken her orange juice out to the porch, Alison sat on the front steps while June polished the dolphin door knocker. Letting the cheerful flood of words wash over her, she thought of Ty and mumbled "Oh?" and "Hmm!" at what she trusted were appropriate intervals.

"The problem with door knockers is that people insist on using them. I swear I've always wanted to put a sign by this one that says Look, But Don't Touch, but then, I guess if they didn't use the knocker they'd just put smudges on the door and I'd have to wash that, and I guess when you think of it, I'd rather polish than scrub, so I shouldn't complain." June backed off to study her handiwork. "Anyway it's done now and all that rubbing's made me thirsty, so I think I'll have another cup of coffee. Could I fix you one?"

"Oh?"

The momentary silence that followed brought Alison back to the here and now, to find June squinting down at her. "I believe you could use a cup, sleepyhead," she decided finally, "and there's nothing like a good jolt of caffeine to get you moving. Why—"

"June, where's Harriet?" Alison interrupted hastily.

"I don't know just where she is. She's been out and about all morning, and let me tell you, it took me back to the good old days to see her walk down those stairs in her old gardening coveralls. Why, I haven't—"

"She *walked* down?"

"From the landing, she most certainly did, though I believe she rode the chair down to there. But she handled those stairs as well as you or me, though she hangs on tight to the banister, but then, any sensible person would, so—"

"I think I'll go find her. Maybe she's ready for a cup of coffee, too." Collecting her glass, Alison retreated to the kitchen and then out the back door.

But Harriet was nowhere in the back gardens. In the garage, someone—Harriet?—had recently pulled a couple of boxes down from the storage shelves built into one of the old horse stalls. Several cans of half-used paint and a bundle of old paintbrushes had been laid out along the workbench, but these offered no clue to Harriet's whereabouts.

Mystified, Alison circled back around to the front of Shady Breeze, but Harriet was not out on the hillside. Far out on the sound, a white sail cut the sunlit blue. Someday she would get Ty to teach her how to sail... Ty... Glancing quickly around, she found she was still alone, so, throwing her head back and arms out, she spun around in a pirouette that no doubt showed more jubilation than grace, while the sun and blue sky pinwheeled above her. Collapsing at last in the grass, she hugged her knees and pretended her arms were wrapped around that muscular, springy waist. *Ty...*

But all this wasn't finding Harriet. Either she'd missed her somehow and she was back in the house, or she was down the road. She had not walked down the hill since her accident, but that was all the more reason to suspect that that's where she was. Harriet nowadays reminded her of a young hawk with a broken wing, practicing, ever practicing, eyes on the sky.... But then, wings were easy to mend. Hearts were the problem.

*No problem, no problem,* her own assured her blithely as she turned toward the drive.

Her guess had been correct. Down at the bottom of the tunnel of trees, where he sat like a big, goofy dandelion among the weeds, Alison spotted first the gold of Milo's coat and then Harriet, her back turned as she bent over the mailbox. Coming quietly down hill, Alison saw what she was doing—removing her husband's name with a piece of sandpaper. The *c* and finally the *k* vanished, and then the *and* that preceded Harriet's own name. For a moment, the older woman stood motionless, her eyes on the now-shiny patch of aluminum. Reaching out, she smoothed the metal with a delicate forefinger.

Alison stopped. Would it be possible to retreat up the hill without Harriet's noticing? But Milo had seen her already. Heaving himself to his feet, he ambled up to greet her, tail waving, and Harriet turned.

Those gray eyes were too bright, but glad to see her all the same.

"I wondered where you were hiding," Alison explained, coming reluctantly down to stop beside her.

"I've been so restless all morning. And this needed doing." Turning back to the mailbox, Harriet swiped the square of sandpaper across the block letters of her first name.

"Hey!" Alison protested, staring down at the row of scratches.

"I'll be in California, remember?" Mouth an even line, Harriet scrubbed at the letters, careful not to disturb the "O'Malley" just beyond.

"But you'll be coming back?" Alison's last word ended on a rising note of uncertainty as Harriet met her eyes.

"No, I won't, Alison," she said gently. "At least not to Shady Breeze. She's too big.... Too full of memories." Her eyes filled again. "She wants laughter and love and children. It's time to pass her on."

"You're selling her?" How could it hurt so? She'd lived here less than two months. She'd never even seen her in autumn, or rising dark above a snowy hill, fire-light warming the windows...

"No." Harriet shook her head quickly. "I couldn't ever sell her." She put the sandpaper to the last of her name and rubbed. "I was hoping I could persuade you and Ty to take her," she murmured casually, head bent.

"I—" But her throat closed at the thought.

"Oh, you don't have to decide just yet!" Harriet assured her anxiously. "We could just say you're house-sitting. I don't mean to tell Ty that I'm gone for good yet. He'd only worry, and anyway, you'll need someplace to stay once you're married." Her words ended on an almost pleading note.

*It's not just kindness,* Alison realized slowly. *She really wants us to have her.* Wouldn't she herself feel the same? Would she—someday—be *doing* the same? But that flash of foresight, of her standing old and alone, without Ty, handing on the home they had filled with so much laughter and tenderness, was too vivid, too sweetly painful to acknowledge or own. It was gone as swiftly as it had come, leaving tears in her eyes for no reason she could explain. "I...you know I love her, Harriet, but I don't know what Ty would..."

"Oh, Ty's not a problem!" Harriet answered eagerly. "He's always loved Shady Breeze. Ask him yourself, Alison, but it's only you I worried about. She is big, I know, and rather isolated, but..."

"All right...I'll ask him... About house-sitting? I can't tell him the truth?"

"Not yet. He's worrying too much about my going already. Let's just prepare him one step at a time."

Brushing off the last of the paint dust, Harriet reached into the mailbox and pulled out a ruler and pencil.

"But he'll guess, won't he, with your name off the box?"

"Oh, I doubt it." Harriet scribed a new base line along the aluminum. "If he asks, I'll say I scratched up my name as I was sanding off Pat's, and once I'd done so, I decided to change names to keep the mailman happy; he'll be forwarding my mail, after all."

"Have you thought what you'll do out there?" Alison asked finally, watching that intent and delicate version of the profile she loved.

"I have…" Reaching into the mailbox again, Harriet pulled out a cardboard stencil of block letters, and proceeded to trace an *N* in front of O'Malley. "Patsy and Bill's house is almost on campus. I thought, once the school term begins…I might just take a class or two." She glanced up at Alison almost shyly, then down again as she traced out an *O*. "I married too young to go to college, you know, Alison…and I've always regretted that." Carefully she blocked in an *S* ahead of the *O*. "Talking with your Forrest last night made me think of it again, that and going up to Boston with Mother." An *I* followed the *S*. "Who knows? If I enjoy it, perhaps I'll go on for a degree…if I can handle the work." She outlined the *L*.

"Handle it? You'll be teaching the professors before you know it! Do you know what you might study yet?" Alison asked, but she guessed even as Harriet spoke.

"Ohh…art history, I think." Completing her name with an *A*, Harriet glanced up at her with a twinkle.

"*If* I ever make my peace with Mother, I'm sure she has a place for me on one of her foundations, presuming I get my degree..."

"I think it's a wonderful idea!" Alison decided warmly. New people, new challenges... As Harriet blocked out the word *and* in smaller letters, her face held a vivid purposefulness that had not been there even a week ago.

"What about a companion?" she continued, after a moment. "I feel awful deserting you like this.... Was there anyone else you interviewed—"

But Harriet was shaking her head decisively. "No. I don't need a companion." She shot Alison a laughing glance and began to trace a large *R* above the bottom row of letters. "Don't be hurt, but I would never have hired one in the first place, but for Ty..."

"So he wouldn't worry about you, you mean?" In spite of her words, it did hurt a little.... So Harriet hadn't wanted her....

"Well, yes...there was that..." Harriet paused while she outlined the *E*. "You know how he frets about fires at night, with my being alone. But that wasn't the real reason I gave in..." Smiling to herself, she blocked out the *L*.

"What was it, then?"

Her smile faded gently. "When I was in the hospital, Alison, those first few months...with Ty sitting there beside me day after day...going home when visiting hours were over to his empty apartment...I began to understand how very lonely he was." She stared down at the mailbox sightlessly for a moment, then moved the *Y* template into position. "Of course I'd known how he missed his Kathy all along…but it's one thing to know it here." Meeting her eyes, Harriet touched her own temple lightly. "With Pat gone, I knew it *here*." Her eyes glistened as she touched her heart, and she looked quickly down again. "So…" Her voice took on a note of determined lightness as she fumbled the *T* into place. "I decided I'd do something about that!"

"Do something?" Alison watched as she completed Ty's name. Those penciled letters were like an outline for her future, still too faint to be quite believable, but taking on more reality with each passing moment.

"Yes, do something, but I wasn't quite sure what, till I came home and Ty started bullying me to hire a companion." Backing off to survey their names, Harriet nodded with satisfaction, then turned to her, her face full of mischief. "Then it dawned on me—this was the next best thing to placing a personal ad!"

"You mean—"

"I mean that in spite of Ty's telling me what I needed, I didn't interview one woman over thirty-five. And I've never talked to so many women in my life before. As it was, it was a long shot, and I'd just about despaired when you turned up."

Aghast, Alison stared at her. "You mean you thought I'd…that he'd…"

Laughing softly, Harriet nodded. "He's my son, Alison, and I know him very well. I would have bet on you, anyhow, but as it worked out, Ty was there to see you. All I had to do was look at his face…" Her brows drew together. "Perhaps I shouldn't have told you. You don't really mind, do you?"

"I'm..." Alison shook her head helplessly. "Stunned..." Forrest with his machinations on one side, Harriet scheming on the other... But then, that meant Harriet had wanted her from the start...thought that she'd be right for Ty. The letters on the box before her seemed a little more substantial already.

"You'll get over it," Harriet decided after watching her face for a moment. Collecting her sign-making tools, she shut the mailbox. "I suppose I ought to let you talk with Ty before I paint this. And I'm tired of standing...."

"I'll take those," Alison offered quickly.

"Thank you." As they turned up hill, Alison let Harriet set the pace, while she tried to absorb the revelation.

But Harriet was still feeling guilty. "You know, you smile so much more than you did when you first came here."

"I do?"

She nodded vigorously. "And Ty...it's been years since I've seen him look like he has these past few weeks." Milo bounded up beside them just then, and she leaned down to thump his side. "No, I don't think I'll apologize, after all," she decided.

"You won't, huh?" Alison returned her sassy grin. "In that case, I have a confession, as well...."

"Oh?"

"Why I accepted the position in the first place..."

THE SLOW RAP OF THEIR HEELS on linoleum echoed from the walls of the airport corridor. Overhead, an ascending roar drowned out their footsteps for a moment as another jet split the sky. The two women exchanged silent glances of shared excitement. *She looks like a kid leaving home for the first time,* Alison decided, *off to conquer the world.*

She shifted Harriet's overnight bag from right shoulder to left. Ty had wanted—most urgently—to check it, but Harriet had insisted she could manage it, as well as the rectangular item she carried. "Forrest will never forgive you, taking *Alicia* out of his reach," she warned, nodding at the package.

"Tell him he can come visit her—and me—in California," Harriet said with a twinkle.

"He may just do that!"

The threat amused her. "I've been thinking about it, Alison, and I don't see any reason I should let Forrest do all the research—and take all the credit—for *Alicia*. I may need a topic for a paper before long."

"A paper? She's the best subject for a doctoral dissertation I ever heard of! Or a book, for that matter," Alison assured her. "Perhaps you and Forrest should collaborate."

Laughing, Harriet shook her head in quick modesty.

"It'll take him—" *and me*, Alison added mentally "—another two years to complete the catalogue raisonneé on Minot. By then, I'll bet you'll be ready." Forrest liked to collaborate, especially with academic unknowns who were more than grateful to do most of the research in return for second billing.

Shaking her head again in smiling dismissal, Harriet still looked as if she were considering the idea as they walked on in companionable silence. Heavier footsteps were overtaking them and she glanced over her shoulder, but it wasn't Ty. A much older man, and taller, moved with a gangly authority, his suit bag slung over one shoulder—a white-haired Abe Lincoln without the beard. Retired lawyer, or perhaps a heart surgeon, Alison decided, as sharp blue eyes met her own, softened and then looked courteously beyond her as he loped past. It never failed to amaze her how some men could be attractive without being handsome. *And then some men could be both,* she thought quickly as Ty lifted the bag from her shoulder to his own and stepped between them, shortening his stride to match their own.

"Trust me with *Alicia*?" he asked his mother, nodding at her package.

"No."

They grinned at each other and he slipped one arm through her elbow instead, then reached for Alison with the other. "The plane's late," he informed them. "Forty minutes, they're saying."

"In that case, I want you two to go home. There's nothing more boring than hanging around an airport, waiting to tell someone goodbye," Harriet declared as they joined the line waiting to pass through the metal detector.

"Don't be silly," Ty told her. "Of course we'll wait."

"Not with me you won't. I brought a good book along, and I'd just as soon sit and read as think of forty ways to say 'Goodbye—I'll miss you' in the next forty minutes.''

Just ahead of them, Alison saw the tall man smile to himself and turn his head slightly to inspect from the corner of his eye the owner of this clear voice.

"Well, at least let me carry your bag as far as the gate,'' Ty was petitioning, but Harriet was adamant. Here was the place to say goodbye. And now was the time.

But in spite of the fighting tilt to her chin, she was close to tears as she hugged Ty. Then it was Alison's turn. "*Enjoy* yourself, Alison!'' Harriet whispered fiercely as she embraced her. "And don't let him bully you!'' she added, giving Ty a mischievous sideways grin.

"Hey, now that's subversion!'' Ty protested, clapping his hands over Alison's ears from behind.

Laughing, she shook her head free and his hands fell to her shoulders instead. Easing her gently backward out of the line, he held her, his fingers giving her an absent, cat's-paw kneading as he watched his mother.

Her bag was already on the conveyor belt and passing through the detector. After a moment's hesitation, Harriet entrusted *Alicia* to the belt, then turned and walked through the archway beside the machine, her head high.

She gave them a little grin of self-mocking relief as she collected *Alicia* unharmed on the far side, then turned as the tall man waiting at the end of the belt said something they could not hear.

For just a moment, she stood stock-still, her chin angled as if she were about to shake her head. Instead, an aloof little smile crossed her face and she nodded. The man swung her bag to his shoulder, his eyes crinkling as she spoke, and they moved away down the corridor.

"Well, how do you like that!" Ty marveled. Moving to stand beside her, he took Alison's hand. "Won't let *me* carry her bag, and then she gives it to a perfect stranger!"

"Maybe he asked nicely," she teased him.

Still staring after the pair, Ty gave a little shrug of baffled amusement and searched with his thumb for her ring. Idly, he turned it around her finger. After only three days, the gesture was well on the way to becoming a habit.

They made a handsome couple, Alison decided, watching the attentive bend of the stranger's head as Harriet made some polite remark. Another few minutes and they'd turn the corner and be gone. "I wonder if she'll ever remarry?" she murmured, her finger tingling with the revolving caress.

Without looking down, Ty smiled at this absurdity and shook his head. "You didn't know my father, Ali. He was a pretty hard act to follow."

"Ohh...I know him all right!" Turning, she locked her forearms around his waist and leaned back to smile up at him. "Like father, like son!" She stole a glance over her shoulder at Harriet, who still had not turned to wave. "But she has so much to give, Ty. It's just got to come out. People can love again."

She had all his attention now as his hands slid around her waist and clasped behind her. "Yes," he agreed softly, wholeheartedly, drawing her closer. "Yes, they can." Lost in each other's eyes, they missed Harriet's farewell wave as she reached the corner.

"Good for them!" the man at Harriet's side applauded, glancing back with her. Memories and laughter echoed in that low voice and, this time, Harriet looked up at him with something like recognition.

"Yes," she said simply. And walked on beside him.

# Six exciting series for you every month... from Harlequin

### *Harlequin Romance*
### The series that started it all

Tender, captivating and heartwarming...
love stories that sweep you off to faraway places
and delight you with the magic of love.

◆

### *Harlequin Presents*
### Powerful contemporary love stories...as individual as the women who read them

The No. 1 romance series...
exciting love stories for you, the woman of today...
a rare blend of passion and dramatic realism.

◆

### *Harlequin Superromance*®
### It's more than romance...
### it's Harlequin Superromance

A sophisticated, contemporary romance-fiction
series, providing you with a longer,
more involving read...a richer mix of complex plots,
realism and adventure.

# Harlequin
# American Romance™
## Harlequin celebrates the American woman...

...by offering you romance stories written about American women, by American women for American women. This series offers you contemporary romances uniquely North American in flavor and appeal.

◆

# *Harlequin Temptation*™
## Passionate stories for today's woman

An exciting series of sensual, mature stories of love...dilemmas, choices, resolutions... all contemporary issues dealt with in a true-to-life fashion by some of your favorite authors.

◆

# Harlequin Intrigue™
## Because romance can be quite an adventure

Harlequin Intrigue, an innovative series that blends the romance you expect... with the unexpected. Each story has an added element of intrigue that provides a new twist to the Harlequin tradition of romance excellence.

# Harlequin Books·

# What readers say about Harlequin romance fiction...

"I absolutely adore Harlequin romances!
They are fun and relaxing to read, and
each book provides a wonderful escape."
—N.E.,* Pacific Palisades, California

"Harlequin is the best in romantic reading."
—K.G.,* Philadelphia, Pennsylvania

"Harlequins have been my passport to the
world. I have been many places without
ever leaving my doorstep."
—P.Z.,* Belvedere, Illinois

"My praise for the warmth and adventure
your books bring into my life."
—D.F.,*Hicksville, New York

"A pleasant way to relax after a busy day."
—P.W.,* Rector, Arkansas

*Names available on request.

# Take 4 novels and a surprise gift FREE